Deadly
Descent

Books by Charlotte Hinger

Come Spring

The Lottie Albright Series
Deadly Descent
Lethal Lineage

Deadly Descent

Charlotte Hinger

Poisoned Pen Press

Poisoned
Pen
Press

Poisoned Pen Press
6962 E. First Ave., Ste. 103
Scottsdale, AZ 85251
www.poisonedpenpress.com
info@poisonedpenpress.com

Printed in the United States of America

In memory of my mother, Lottie Josie Smerchek Southerland,
who knew how to keep secrets

Acknowledgments

Deadly Descent is fiction. For that matter, there is no Carlton County, Kansas, or Gateway City. So please don't assume this book is about your county or your family just because I've rummaged through the boxes in your historical society and lurked in your archives while doing research. And yet, and yet, there are deadly secrets hidden there.

What is not fiction is the debt I owe to the hard-working volunteers in local historical societies and the outstanding staff at the Kansas State Historical Society.

I want to thank Dr. John Rand Neuenschwander for medical information, Ron Greninger for crime scene background, and acknowledge the contribution of the late Sheridan County Sheriff Jimmy Johnson for insight into the workings of a small county sheriff's department.

Barbara Peters is an extraordinarily talented editor and I can't thank her enough. I also want to thank Robert Rosenwald for the creation of Poisoned Pen Press, and Annette Rogers and Jessica Tribble for their contributions toward making the company into one of the foremost mystery houses.

My agent, Phyllis Westberg (Harold Ober Associates), surely knows by now how much I appreciate her unwavering support. She's simply the best!

My late husband, Don Hinger, sustained me in all the ups and down of my rather peculiar writing career. I regret that he did not live to see this book published.

Whoever goes about slandering reveals secrets,
but he who is trustworthy in spirit keeps a thing covered.
—Proverbs 11:13 (ESV)

Chapter One

She was coming for me. From the belly of the vault, I could hear
Fiona Hadley making her way down the main hall of the county
courthouse toward my open door. No mistaking those authorita-
tive, high-heeled clicks echoing across the marble floor.

It was a dusty Friday, the first week in September. Heavy,
malevolent, sinus-destroying dust. I already had one headache. I
didn't need another. Outside, fast-moving clouds scuttled across
the sky like dingy cottontail rabbits looking for a hole. This cold
snap was sudden, unsettling and the threat of tornados always
hovered in Western Kansas.

I looked at the hodgepodge of layouts, family photos, bottles
of glue, masking tape, old magazines, and stacks of memorabilia
cluttering the office of the Carlton County Historical Society.
The place was not always a dump. I wished the mother of our
youngest state senator could see us at our shining best. Just once.
Then, perhaps, she would coax her son to squeeze more funds
out of the legislature.

I caught a glimpse of her taut face as she rounded the stairwell.
Countdown time, and I still had not decided how to handle her
sister's submission to the county history book. If Fiona knew
about Zelda's story, all hell was going to break loose.

She paused in the doorway. I rose and made a swipe at my
hair, wishing I had worn it in a chignon instead of a long braid.
At the historical society dress-down Friday is patched Levis, an

old denim work shirt, and cowboy boots. Dressing up is new denim, shirt tucked in. I was quite a contrast to The Lady, who was dressed to kill.

Fiona Hadley wore a forest green cloche pulled over her brassy yellow curls. Her hat was the exact shade of her exquisitely tailored gabardine suit. A face lift? A little tuck here and there? Probably. But it had never been mentioned in the press. She should have been an easy target, but the whimsical deities who manipulate the media gave everything Fiona did or said a benign spin.

Although over-dressed and out-dated, she reminded columnists of an actress from an old thirties movie. Garbo, Harlow, Colbert? Someone. Some fetching beauty.

"Hello, Fiona."

"Lottie Albright. You're just the one I was looking for. You're hard at work, I see." Short, curt pleasantries when it usually took her fifteen minutes to get a proper hello-how-are-you out of the way. Fiona's nose wrinkled as she looked at the crazy tangle of old pipes running the length of the twelve-foot ceiling in our narrow, hot room.

"As usual. Deadline, this week." In addition to being the director of the Carlton County Historical Society, I was Fiona's son's election committee chairman for this area. Perhaps she was here about Brian and not her sister's story.

"What can I do for you, Fiona?"

"I want you to give me Zelda's story. I'm going to burn the damned thing."

Stunned by her presumption, my skin prickled with fury, but I can nearly always choose my words. "How did you know about it? She just turned it in yesterday."

"She called me. She said it would cause Brian trouble. I want it destroyed." Her voice was haughty, commanding, but her mouth trembled.

"Fiona, Zelda's story is now a historical document in her own hand. It's under lock and key. Before I agreed to put together the county history books, I insisted on sole editorial control over every word, picture, drawing, or clipping included in these books. There were good reasons for that."

"Zelda doesn't have the right. You don't have the right."

"I can't let people start tinkering with other folks' stories. There would be no stopping the changes. It would be opening a Pandora's box of misinformation and family quarrels."

"Please." Tears trickled. Runlets of mascara splotched her powder.

"I don't intend to print it as is. I'm going to persuade Zelda to delete certain paragraphs and tone it down overall." I had already made a number of discreet phone calls to ask families to omit embarrassing truths or straighten out inconsistencies.

"She won't," Fiona whispered. "She wants to ruin us. All of us. From what she told me, her story isn't right. Vicious lies, in fact."

"Actually, most of what's in these family histories isn't quite right, but no one is going to change one single word of an original story except the person submitting it. I can't make it any plainer than that. I've not deviated from this policy once. Write your own story. Contradict every single word your sister wrote if you want to, but you can't change what *she* wrote."

I edged closer to the framed degrees hanging on the wall, but my Ph.D. in history from Kansas State University obviously meant no more to her than a certificate in advanced yoga techniques.

"You'll be very, very sorry you did this, Lottie."

"I'll talk to her. These books aren't intended to hurt people."

"I want to see exactly what she turned in." She rummaged in her purse, took out a white linen handkerchief and began dabbing at her eyes.

I'd made a working to-be-edited copy, of course. Normally, I would show her that one. Originals were precious historical narratives and kept pristine. Handwriting, choice of paper, even the ink told a story. Many archives have researchers wear white gloves while handling material. I don't go that far. However, after I made a copy, there should be no need to handle the original again.

I eyed the weeping woman. What the hell. It wouldn't hurt to let Fiona see the primary document, with me standing right there protecting it.

I went to the locked master file where all the original pictures and stories were in alphabetical order, retrieved Zelda St. John's story and handed it to her sister. I moved back about five feet, and observed Fiona like a cop looking through a one-way mirror. Her enormous blue eyes, framed by thick black lashes, weren't made for concealing feelings. I followed their movement as she quickly read the story, then looked up at me. Perhaps I make too much of body language, but her relief was evident.

The blood rose in my cheeks and I drew a deep breath. She was relieved! How dare she be relieved? When I'd first read it yesterday, I had burst into tears and closed the office for the rest of the day.

"I thought," she began. "I…this doesn't…I thought perhaps…I'm sorry, Lottie."

She read it again, glanced at the back of the sheets, and then gasped. She closed her blue-veined lids, and the color drained from her face. The skin around her mouth whitened, leaving her lips thin. Ugly.

The pages fluttered to the floor.

Chapter Two

Fiona ran from the room before I could stop her. I started after her, following until she rounded the bottom of the staircase.

Clusters of county personnel gathered at windows and eyed the approaching storm. Three women hovered around the front door tracking the clouds: Inez Wilson, the county health nurse, Minerva Lovesey, the register of deeds, and Priscilla Ramsey, the home economist. One look at Fiona's face and they fell silent, parting to let her pass through the heavy glass doors.

"What was that all about?"

Priscilla Ramsey *would* ask. She was fifty-something with short blond curls topping a powdered, kindly face and built like a pickle. I would bet she wore a girdle under her collection of navy and white rayon print dresses.

"Oh you know," I said lamely, "nothing really. People get sentimental when they start thinking about their families."

"Didn't look like sentiment to me," said Inez Wilson as we watched Fiona drive off.

It wasn't a smooth exit. Her tires squealed and she narrowly missed backing into a car parked across the street.

"Goodness gracious." Inez turned to me, her dark eyes glittering with curiosity. "Now what…?"

Minerva Lovesey cut her off. "Well, ladies. I'm sure we all have work to do." Not a gossip, she pointedly left the group.

I sighed. Inez wasn't a discreet person, even if she was a member of the medical profession. Skinny as a crane, she flapped around spreading hysteria like a mental health Typhoid Mary. This would be all over town by nightfall.

"My God, I wish it would rain," I said, hoping to take their minds' off Fiona. Priscilla and Inez nodded, and we looked up at the sky. In an instant I was one of them again. An insider. Included. Despite being married to Keith Fiene only seven years.

It hadn't taken me long to figure out after coming to the Great Plains that the great unifying element among Kansans was a willingness to talk about the weather. All the time, every day, forevermore.

Lightning ripped, followed by ear-splitting thunder. Sulfurous clouds boiled. Lights flickered, then went out. Inez and Priscilla joined the blind courthouse grope to shut down computers. We are on daylight savings time, so it wasn't totally dark.

I lingered. I have an offsite backup system that triggers automatically, switches to batteries, exits programs, and neatly shuts off the computer. Then with a start, I realized I'd left my office unlocked and the master file open. I fumbled toward the staircase. The lights flickered once, twice, then stayed on. I hurried down the hallway.

I glanced around. Relieved, I picked up Zelda's story from the floor. Furious to see this original treated so carelessly, I checked to make sure all the pages were there, then locked Zelda's story back in the master file. I had an hour to kill before closing time, but there was no point in booting up again as I was too upset to concentrate.

I reached for a folder of black construction paper and began making letters for a display. Calming work akin to knitting, it gave my hands something to do while I thought about Fiona and her twin. Their maiden name was Rubidoux, and they never let anyone forget their aristocratic Southern background for an instant.

An identical twin myself, I've always been intrigued by The Ladies, as Fiona and Zelda are called. I like to think my sister

Josie and I are both normal. Different styles, but normal. The difference between Zelda and Fiona had everything to do with sanity. I'd always looked upon Fiona as the sane one, but after today's encounter, I was beginning to wonder.

Zelda, like Fiona, wore clothes that were out of step with the times and preened like a peacock, but unlike her twin, Zelda always managed to look a little crazy. With overly permed bright blond hair, and outrageously red lipstick no matter what the color of her costumes, she ghosted about in the past. Her wounded blue eyes recorded every slight.

A decade or two earlier she would have fit in as the quintessential club woman, if she had been a bit more reliable. But she had a habit of starting projects, then losing interest after a few teary clashes with people.

My twin, Josie Albright, is a psychologist in Manhattan, Kansas. She also teaches part-time at Kansas State University. Sometimes, when the dust blows in Western Kansas, I envy her clean, elegant, childless existence. The path I had not taken. She deals with plain vanilla crazies, not Fiona Hadley's brand of arrogance that passes for normal in our community.

Too distracted to continue with the lettering, I went to the bank of file cabinets where I kept all the working copies of the family history stories and removed Zelda's. All these drawers were unlocked so volunteers could have access. Even though the originals were kept pristine, these versions that would make their way into the family history books bore my many red-pen edits. As I had tried to tell Fiona, I'd persuaded a number of authors to correct dates, rethink fuzzy details, and delete mean-spirited truths.

Once in a while I get a submission centered on one topic. One old bachelor's story was about money and only money. His narrative began with the first dollar he'd ever earned. He lived in a shack. Handwritten, there were no margins on the paper and no space between the lines.

Zelda's one-topic wonder was all about the family's relationship with African Americans. Although I encourage people to write what they want, this was a blatantly racist piece and it stated that Brian shared those views. He absolutely, positively did not. Did the family honestly think I would continue to organize his campaign in Carlton County if he did? For that matter, until I read Zelda's submission I had no idea the twins were *that* backward and Old South.

I seethed whenever I even thought about Zelda's senseless diatribe, and was even angrier that Fiona had read right through those pages and never raised an eyebrow. I was sure of that. It wasn't until she'd looked at it a second time that she'd become upset.

Bewildered, I decided to read it again. Obviously Fiona hadn't objected to her sister's view of blacks, but perhaps there was something else there I'd overlooked because I'd been madder than hell.

The Rubidoux Family History

by
Zelda St. John

Our beloved and courageous ancestors, Clarissa and Jonathan Rubidoux, came to Carlton County in 1880. They filed on 160 acres of prime homestead land, they bought another 320 acres through pre-emption, and another 160 acres through a tree claim. Previously they lived in Arkansas, having fled there from Georgia following the Late Rebellion. Eternally grateful for the kindness and generosity with which they had been treated during the time they lived on my great-grandparent's magnificent plantation, five household slaves went with them to Arkansas and continued to serve the family until they moved to Kansas. Then these five were lured away by treacherous and errone-ous propaganda from blacks living in the county next door. Biting the hand that had previously fed them, they threw in their lot with other land-hungry ex-slaves and filed for their own homesteads.

Naturally, Jonathan was devastated. He had not healed from the deep wounds caused by those who exploited the failure of the noble Southern Cause. The Rubidouxes suffered greatly, having lost all of their property, not only their magnificent plantation but their investment in a goodly number of slaves they had purchased for a pretty sum. Now even these last five were leaving them.

Jonathan had planned to forge a life for his family in the new land but he simply could not manage that amount of land after his blacks deserted. To add insult to injury, his children Jacob and Melissa would be forced to attend school with a Negro teacher or do without.

I smiled. The lofty Rubidoux had obviously settled close to Nicodemus, Kansas, and blacks there had formed the first school district in Graham County. This colony had preceded the great migration of African Americans who left the South for Kansas in 1879.

Due to the strain of the war, the hardships of the new life, and her sense of grief over her abandonment by the Negroes upon whom she had lavished nothing but kindness all her life, Great Great Grandmother Clarissa was plagued by melancholy and a mere shadow of the woman she was in the South.

When the Negroes tried to organize the county, Jonathan fought these greedy politicians tooth and toenail. In fact, his very own slaves popped up in all kinds of county offices, and one even was county clerk. Naturally, having personal knowledge of their treachery he considered it his duty to warn other deserving white folks in the county that the man was a fool and illiterate and none of their transactions would be kept private. Until he died, Jonathan protested against blacks holding office where they would be privy to white folks' business and made his children swear they would take up the cause.

The cause. Keeping blacks out of politics? Negating the whole civil rights movement? Tears started again. I specialize in African American history. Were the early Rubidoux Klansmen?

> I'm proud to say that the children and their descendents have carried on this tradition and we even had a Rubidoux doing his best to block the disastrous outcome in Brown v. Board of Education. We believe the races should be segregated, and now, I'm proud to say, we have another Rubidoux descendent, senatorial candidate, Brian Hadley, who understands the importance of genetic purity.

I sat with my hands folded in my lap for a moment. How could Fiona *not* have been upset the first time she read the story? Even if reading about her family's racial history hadn't thrown her into a tizzy, how could she have tolerated the implication that Brian went along with this attitude? Was the woman so stupid she couldn't see what it would do to his campaign?

I went to the coffee pot, tossed the old filter, walked to the restroom to rinse out the old sludge, then headed back to complete the rest of my closing ritual. But the routine couldn't lift my mood.

Sometimes the room seemed to fill with the spirits of the people who had lived in this county. On top of the Rubidoux fiasco, a number of the stories I'd edited this week dealt with accidental deaths.

Since the county was founded, children drowned in ponds or died from infections that went untreated. They were run over by wagons or gored by bulls. Women got scalded or cut during butchering or burned during canning. Men were gassed digging wells or caught fire or had limbs sheared off by equipment. The list was endless and we still had our share of accidents in the twenty-first century.

Western Kansas was a hard row to hoe. I recalled the horrified expression on Josie's face when she visited Gateway City
for the first time.

"You'll die," she'd snapped. "Your soul will shrink into a little
rock. You've never liked the wind. You're an educated woman,
Lottie. What will you do for entertainment?"

"It's not that bleak. Besides, there's always Denver. We do
have cars out here, you know."

"Denver is three hundred miles away."

"That's nothing. A morning's drive."

"Lottie, are you sure? You're marrying a man with grown
children older than you are."

"I'm sure of the man, Josie. That's all that matters to me
right now."

Seven years later, I was still sure of the man. Josie had been
right about the soul-shrinking incessant wind, but as far as my
work as a historian was concerned, I'd hit the mother lode.
Originally seen as part of the Great American Desert, academics
tended to ignore Western Kansas. There were enough unwrit-
ten stories here to keep me publishing for the rest of my life.

I adore this county. For over a century, its families had become
tangled in little webs of intrigue. Known and unknown.

As I neatened my desk, my thoughts kept returning to Fiona.
The woman's sobs seemed to remain in the room. Even given
Fiona's capacity for theatrics, her distress did not seem staged.

It had been a long day, ending an absolute bitch of a week.
I loaded my briefcase with Zelda's working copy, and other
family stories that needed editing, turned out all the lights, and
left the courthouse.

I would call Zelda when I got home and set up a meeting.
Even though I'd retain the story now on file, together we could
come up with another one for the book. I would urge her to
write about the family's achievements. Or something.

Lightning flashed again, but the clouds were moving further
west. Irritated at being cheated out of rain, and having to drag
work home, I hurried toward my Tahoe. Josie was coming this

weekend along with two of Keith's daughters and our grand-children. My sister drove out twice a year for long weekends. The visits were to convince herself that she had forgiven me for choosing to live here.

During these bi-yearly treks, she had met Tom, Keith's son, and Angie, his middle daughter, but by some quirk of fate she had never met Elizabeth and Bettina. Career women, they couldn't get away when Josie chose to come. They said.

I wanted all the children to make a special trip home to honor our seventh anniversary. But two days ago, Angie called. She absolutely, positively had to work. Tom called last night. He had a special assignment. Keith assured him it was no big deal. We would see him in a couple of months for the opening day of pheasant season. Our seventh anniversary was a big deal only to me.

As if I weren't wired enough already, my sister would be hearing our family's music for the first time and it wouldn't be the same without Tom and Angie. Josie had sweetly consented to bring her own violin.

"It's the land that's flat, not my life," I kept telling her.

I drove steadily toward our home on a hill eight miles north of town. On a clear day you can see its white three-story exterior from miles away. It was huge and wonderful, with enough turrets and hiding places to drive children crazy with delight.

When Josie saw the colossal sprawl of Fiene's Folly the first time her eyes sparked with surprise. She was fun to watch. She imagined she always maintained a psychologist's inscrutability, but she was not quite quick enough for me. I knew her too well.

"But we're already rich," she said in verbal shorthand, relying on this to fill in all the gaps. That we had trust funds. That a house wouldn't compensate for a life.

"I didn't marry him for his money."

"He's still a dirt farmer, Lottie."

"He's an educated man. A veterinarian."

"So? Why doesn't he practice? Contribute something."

I'd had enough sense to shut up. Keith's main income was from wheat and cattle. He wrote occasional medical and economic pieces for veterinary trade magazines and he *did* have a very informal practice, along the lines of helping thy neighbor.

Truth was Keith couldn't stand high-strung women with yapping little dogs.

Josie owned a miniature shih tzu. On our farmstead we had two real dogs. Totally non-neurotic border collies.

Josie would have been surprised at the net worth of my dirt farmer.

Chapter Three

I passed through the mud room into our kitchen/family room. I had designed the light golden oak cabinets. A number of the doors bore stained glass insets. In winter, the floor-to-ceiling fireplace dominating the north wall warmed the facing tan leather sofa and flanking chairs. Ample reading lamps invited curling up with a book.

The woodwork gleamed. It would even pass Elizabeth's inspection, though the credit went to hired help. Keith's oldest daughter doesn't hold with women who don't do all their own work.

There was a note from Keith on the island saying he had been called over to the Arley farm to look at a cow. I threw myself into a final orgy of housewifely fussing.

Then I called Zelda St. John. The second quick scan of her story had sent Fiona into a tailspin, not the first read. Perhaps she knew the reason, and would tell me during our rewrite session.

There was no answer.

I had hoped Elizabeth would not be the first to arrive, but her little yellow Volkswagen came buzzing up the drive. Single, one year older, and five inches taller than I, she could whip me verbally with one tongue tied behind her back.

I pulled myself together and flung open the front door.

"Hello," I called cheerily. "Did you have a good trip? Can I help you carry things in?"

I felt a step-mother's awkwardness in extending the hospitality of a home that had always been hers. I wished she could understand it was still. Keeping my maiden name was my only move that met with her approval.

Elizabeth is a "poverty lawyer" in Denver. She works out of a wretched little storefront with like-minded zealots. She dresses like Cinderella before the fairy godmother hit. I think she's affected as hell.

"I can manage. Where's Dad?"

"Out doctoring. He's on his way home by now I hope."

"Good." She breezed past me carrying two suitcases. Fierce, Junoesque, she is a dazzling beauty with short wheat-colored hair. She returned from her room, flipped her cell open and scowled at me. I shrugged. Our spotty service is not my fault.

"So. What have you been up to?" Elizabeth is quite decent to me as long I keep the focus on her work.

We were catching up when Bettina, Keith's youngest, came through the door with a diaper bag flung over her shoulder. She was followed by her husband, Jimmy, and their two sons. She is a hospital administrator in Denver and Jimmy Silverthorne owns a construction company.

I knelt and held out my arms, which were instantly filled with puppy warm little boys. No tip-toeing around or feeling my way with our grandsons. They were mine. I was their Grandma Lottie. I had been right here in this house before and since they were born. Four-year-old Joshua's and two-year-old Kent's thatches of black hair and light brown eyes echoed their father's American Indian ancestry. No one would connect their petite mother's fine-boned features and wide hazel eyes with this sturdy pair.

"Can I have a cookie, Grandma Lottie?" asked Josh.

"Yes," I said. "Lots and lots." Happily, I hugged them tightly until they squirmed in protest.

"Hello, hello, greetings and all that. Hi, Mom." I laughed as always at the "Mom," as little Bettina wrapped me in a warm hug. She whisked her youngest son off to the bathroom. She's the only one of Keith's children who is real time, real world. The others are more theoretical. While we're having grand discussions, Bettina is cleaning up messes and turning down the flames under smoldering pans on the stove.

Keith came through the door.

"Grandpa's here," called Josh.

Josh and Kent ran at their grandfather like linemen. I looked into Keith's eyes, which glinted with tears. I heard the horn, and my stomache tightened.

Keith opened the door. Josie's black Mercedes sparkled like the devil's horns under the yard light. She came up the walk, carrying Tosca, her little shih-tzu, and her violin case.

I saw Elizabeth's disbelieving face as she looked at the pampered little dog. I groaned and closed my eyes for an instant, knowing the price of Tosca's haircuts. But Josie was my sister, my twin, my best friend. I hugged her inside and made introductions. Elizabeth could just go to hell.

Josie had not, would not, come to the wedding.

My step-daughters looked at her, then at me, eyes narrowing in feminine evaluation. Josie's hair is blue-black, as mine had once been. We both touch up, but I frost a bit to supplement my premature tinsel-silver and she goes the other direction. But then, I'm always trying to look like I'm old enough to be married to my husband.

Josh and Kent rushed over to pet Tosca. Josie tensed. Tosca shrank even further in her arms.

"Boys, stop!" Jimmy called sharply.

"You should ask Josie's permission," Bettina said.

"No, they should ask the dog's permission," Jimmy said. He folded his tall lean body down to Tosca's level and peered at her. "Don't like strangers, do you girl? Me neither. My kind of dog."

Josie laughed, but there was no mistaking her appreciation for his diplomacy.

"I *am* sorry," she said to the boys. "Perhaps later, when we've been here awhile."

I took Josie's fine woolen cape and whisked it off to the clothes closet. I wished I'd told her to wear jeans. Her black cherry turtleneck and exquisitely tailored grey pants were just too perfect. Like Tosca.

Relationships change among a group the instant another person walks into the room. There's usually an accommodation as subtle as water enfolding a rock thrown into a pond. *After* the ripples settle down. But after Josie came in, we could not get back to normal. I did not think it was her fault. She was on her best behavior. She swore she didn't mind the drive across Kansas. She was properly cheery, bearing gifts. It's just that Keith's family was tight knit. They did not open up easily to outsiders.

My meal was too heavy for Josie. By Western Kansas meat-eating standards, she hardly touched a thing. Keith's dark home brew brought tears to her eyes. We did dishes and started to tune up our instruments. We always tuned to the piano. Elizabeth played a wicked rag-time and it's the one instrument that can't be re-adjusted. Bettina's dobro was off key and it took a number of tries before she got it right. Josie settled on the sofa, Tosca on her lap.

It was eight o'clock. I went to the kitchen and tried to call Zelda St. John again, but there was still no answer. I left another message on her answering machine.

"Must you keep popping in and out?" Elizabeth snapped.

"Yes, I do. I have to make a call. It's important." I kept my voice polite, but pointedly looked at her holstered phone. She flushed. "On our landline. Cell service is spotty at best out here. Not enough towers, and then they are vulnerable to storms."

Josie frowned, looked at Elizabeth hard, then turned her attention toward my husband.

Keith was too tall, too wide, and took up more than his rightful share of space. Territorial and watchful, he had the alertness of an old range bull. His neck looked like a guillotine would bounce right off it, but his nails were buffed to a gentleman's sheen. I hoped Josie would notice.

He looked at her in his troubling, sharp-eyed way.

"Do you like bluegrass, Josie?"

Trapped, wanting to please, she looked at me expectantly, but I would not help her. This was a chance for Keith and his children to see my Josie as I knew her. Vulnerable, in the raw. She never lied about music. It was the way she had survived our childhood. She never allowed anything to touch her music. Her first husband had tried.

"No, I've never liked Country/Western."

"It's not the same," Keith said.

Suddenly overwhelmed with the anxiety of wanting all these people to just love each other, I fled to call Zelda again.

Josie had given the right answer, I thought, as I redialed. People who fake affection for Country/Western or Bluegrass are painfully obvious to those of us who love it.

No answer. Again I left a message and went back into the living room. Jimmy, who did not play an instrument, sprawled on the floor watching his sons struggle with Lincoln Logs.

Keith launched into June Apple. Josie raised her eyebrows as I picked up my guitar. We played for a half hour.

"Bedtime, boys," Jimmy said. "Pick up your toys and say your goodnights."

Bettina rose to help with their bedtime routine, but Jimmy smiled and waved her back.

"Go ahead and enjoy yourself."

Exhausted from the trip, Josh and Kent sniggered through a volley of hugs and goodnights, then cheerfully followed their father up the stairs.

"Would you like to join in, Josie?" Keith asked.

"I don't know any of your songs."

"Then play what you like. We'll listen."

"Lottie? Will you help?"

"My piano is a little rusty since I've switched to guitar, but I'll try to keep up."

Josie smiled and went to her case, and lovingly pulled her violin from the red velvet. We played a haunting old Hungarian rhapsody. We Czechs are good at this kind of music. We have a natural affinity for tragedy.

Then whisper soft behind us came the eerie overtones of a second violin. Josie looked at Keith, amused, then was clearly annoyed at his intrusion.

"Your choice, lady," Keith said.

"Mozart's violin concerto number four in D major," she said sweetly.

I winced at her ploy. The song is very difficult. If he did not know the music he couldn't possibly play by intuition, but I was too out of practice to accompany her decently.

"I can't Josie. It's been too long." I lowered the lid over the keys.

"It doesn't sound right, played alone," she said.

"No it doesn't," Keith said. "I'll help you out. I need to make a little switch here. Need a gut-strung. Can't play that with steel strings. It's been a while," he said quietly. "Too long maybe."

He walked over to one of the long ceiling-to-floor cabinets built into the wall of the room, opened one of the tiers of double doors. Josie gasped when she saw that it housed a whole collection of musical instruments. He carefully withdrew another violin, began to tune it to hers.

"So what it this? Dueling banjos?" muttered Elizabeth.

Keith shrugged. "Maybe." His eyes glittered.

Josie played the first movement, Keith filling in when he could.

"Beautiful," said Keith softly when she had finished.

"Your turn," she said.

"Same piece, second movement. *Andante cantabile.*"

Josie sat motionless as she listened to him play. Her face reflected the humiliation of having deeply underestimated another human being. I had tried to tell her. Who this man was. What he was like. He stopped abruptly and began to play a heartbreaking rhapsody.

After he had played several lines, he stopped. "I'm Volga German, Miss Albright. A German from Russia."

Her cheeks flamed, and she looked at him with bewilderment. Not knowing what he meant. What he was trying to tell her.

He began his music again. I knew it was a song Josie had never heard before. By the time he had finished, she should have known everything about this man's soul. His people.

Even though we were identical twins and I was considered slender by Western Kansas standards, Josie was ten pounds lighter, sometimes making her black/brown eyes look as hugely vulnerable as those of a deer. Her wonderful eyes were now focused on my husband.

I could feel the charge of energy between them, and suddenly goose bumps rose on my arm.

The phone rang. Already on edge, I jumped as though it were a siren.

Bettina answered. "It's for you, Lottie."

I took the call on the kitchen landline, then went back to the living room, and looked down at my trembling hands.

Keith stopped playing in the middle of a run. They all turned toward me.

"That was the sheriff. Zelda St. John has been murdered."

Chapter Four

"I don't understand. Why would the sheriff call you?" Josie put her violin in its case and reached for Tosca.

"I've left several messages on Zelda's answering machine tonight, and he wanted to know what they were about."

"How did it happen?" Bettina asked. "Who did it?"

"She was beaten to death." My voice shook. "Bludgeoned."

"My God. Poor Max," Keith said.

"Max is her husband," I told Josie. "He's much older."

"Do they have any idea who did it?"

"No, but Sheriff Sam Abbott is coming here right away to ask me some questions. He'd heard about an incident with her sister today at the historical society." I filled them in on the riff with Fiona, and twenty minutes later Sam rang our doorbell.

Bettina let him in.

"You've got to be kidding," Josie said, seeing him start down the hallway. "Where did they find him? Central casting?"

Sheriff Sam Abbott had had the same effect on me the first time I saw him. His white mustache drooped like his sad old eyes and a fringe of long white hair brushed the top of his collar. Although his liver spotted hands betrayed his age, he carried his tall body with military bearing.

His office needed more personnel and he needed more rest.

My stomach was sour, my eyes wet.

"Hello, Lottie. Keith. Sorry to be disturbing you folks this time of night."

"It's all right, Sam." I stepped forward. "I don't know what help I can be, but I'll be glad to talk with you."

"You know my two daughters, Elizabeth and Bettina," Keith said, "and this is Lottie's sister, Josie."

Sam bobbed his head in acknowledgment. "This is a bad deal, I'll tell you."

He glanced sharply at Elizabeth. I followed his gaze. Her eyes did not swerve. Neither did his. Elizabeth is the only person I know with turquoise eyes. Right now, they were hot and hostile.

I could not imagine what Sam Abbott had ever done to her.

"Do you have a place where we can talk privately, Lottie? I won't keep you long."

"Sure. Let's go into Keith's office."

He nodded and followed me into the book-lined room.

"I'm still shocked."

"We all are. Not a single other murder in this county since I've been in office. Just doesn't happen here."

"Thank God."

"Why all the messages on her machine, Lottie? They sounded urgent. The Kansas Bureau of Investigation will be looking everywhere. At everything and everybody."

"The KBI? So soon?"

"We're a small county and piss poor to boot. We don't have the talent and the resources to investigate a murder. They do. I had the right to call them in. The show-downs between the local sheriff and the big bad feds are an invention of TV. *Most* of the time."

He did not blink, but there was a tell-tale bob in his Adam's apple. "There's a guy, Jim Gilderhaus, assigned to this region. Lives just fifty miles from here. He's a fine fellow. Know him well. He's over at the Hadleys now. I'm trying to clear up a few things for him because I know all the people in this county. Keeps it quieter if I handle a few of these details myself."

"Well my messages were hardly urgent." I shoved my hands into my jeans pockets, crossed the room and stared into the black night. Embarrassed, I turned and faced him.

"It's been an upsetting evening. Josie meeting Bettina and Elizabeth for the first time. And my sister's a bit of a snob. Equates bluegrass with barefoot and ignorant. And Elizabeth is..."

"Elizabeth is Elizabeth," he said flatly.

"Exactly. If I hadn't been so edgy, I wouldn't have called Zelda so many times. I just couldn't stand the tension in that room, so I kept ducking out. But back to Fiona. She caused quite a scene when she came into the office today."

"I know that. So does everyone else in town."

"Surely you're not thinking Fiona had anything to do with Zelda's murder?"

"Of course not. A tiff between The Ladies is hardly news. If one of them was going to kill the other, she'd of done it a long time ago. I'm just tracing time. But just for the record, what was Mrs. Hadley so fired up about?"

"Fiona wanted me to destroy her sister's story. I couldn't do that, but I could ask Zelda to write a different one for our book."

He leaned forward.

"So that's all. Your messages said you wanted to talk to her, but you didn't say why. The St. Johns have an old machine that doesn't track time and date. Your calls could help us establish the time of death. Exactly when did you call the first time?"

"About five-thirty, when I got home from work. Then everyone started arriving. I didn't call again until seven-thirty or so. It was after supper. I remember that."

"So you would have called the first time before Max got home from the hardware store and the second time after he had left for the Lion's Club meeting at seven o'clock."

"I called again around eight, again at eight-thirty, and finally a little after nine. Then you called me. As I said, it really wasn't urgent. I'm a wee bit compulsive."

He grinned. "Since you're not a suspect, I don't really care why you called. No one is under suspicion right now. But the times when she didn't answer the phone could be very important."

"Any idea of motive?"

He patted his breast pocket wistfully like a scolded smoker. "Gilderhaus thinks robbery. Bank cards gone, purse missing."

"But you don't," I said, noting the politeness of "Gilderhaus thinks."

"No. There was no forced entry. Jim was raised in Kansas City. Believes a lot of guff about rural people that just ain't so."

"That we all keep our doors unlocked?"

"And that we would all open our doors to rank strangers."

At Fiene's Folly we don't have a yard light that burns automatically all night. We don't want one acting as a beacon, advertising our isolation.

"What was in that story?"

It was a smooth ploy. Asked abruptly that way, I responded in kind.

"Frankly, an exposure of their family's vicious prejudice. If the press ever got hold of it, there's no way Brian could convince voters he didn't share those attitudes."

Sam thoughtfully rubbed the side of his large Roman nose. "Knowing Fiona, if she thought it could hurt Brian, she'd be livid."

"Actually, I think Fiona shared her sister's attitude toward blacks and was blind to the damage it would cause Brian. Something else set her off."

"No idea what?"

"None whatsoever. I'm sorry I can't be of more help. How's Max taking it?"

"Hard. Already had enough on his plate with health problems, then his old hardware store got Wal-Marted."

"And Fiona? She okay?"

"Don't know." His mouth tightened. "I had to work the scene. I sent Betty Central over to break the news to the Hadleys. She hasn't called me yet. You know how short-handed we are,

Lottie," he said, seeing the look on my face. "I have to work with what I've got."

Betty Central's mean, loud mouth could turn a missing pencil into a four-star crisis. It was hard to imagine anyone less sensitive, less appropriate, to break this kind of news to a family.

Sam flushed. "I've put ads in the paper, Lottie. Asking for part-time help. Not many people are dying to be in law enforcement, and this county operates on a shoestring. People go to work for us, they have to buy their own guns."

He slapped his hands on his knees and stood.

"At least we have a clearer picture of time, thanks to you."

I walked him to the foyer.

When I went back into the family room, Elizabeth was seated at the piano, raging through a complicated piece. Her hands faltered. She rose, ran to Keith, and sobbed on his shoulder.

"What's wrong, Elizabeth?" I asked. I looked over at Josie, who was sitting very still, cuddling Tosca. Her eyes grave, professionally alert.

"The last time I saw that meddling old fool was when Mom died."

Josie rose and walked toward father and daughter. She patted Elizabeth on the shoulder.

"Can I help? Lottie's told me your mother died tragically. When you were just thirteen?"

Elizabeth spun around, dislodging Josie's hand.

"Tragically? Like in an accident? A car or something? No, Ms. Albright, we're the suicide's kids. Didn't you know that?"

Josie blanched. "No. I didn't know. I'm sorry, Elizabeth. Still, I *am* here this weekend. Perhaps it would help you to talk about it."

"It won't, and even if talking would help, I doubt I would have much in common with a shrink driving a Mercedes."

"I want you to apologize to my sister at once, Elizabeth."

Then she turned on me.

"Or for that matter, a lady whose idea of real life is working with dusty old manuscripts analyzing the lives of people who lived a hundred years ago."

"Elizabeth! That's enough," Keith thundered.

Then this thirty-nine-year-old woman who Wonder-Womaned around Denver, unbattering women and tying up gang members in Byzantine legal procedures, ran from the room like a heart-broken adolescent.

I couldn't breathe. The muscles in Keith's jaws jerked. He watched Elizabeth's flight up the stairs like he wanted to call her back. Make her say the right words. His great hands dangled at his sides as if they were on the end of clay clubs.

Tears welled in Bettina's eyes.

"So sorry," she said. "I'll see what I can do." She hurried after Elizabeth.

Josie sat back down on the sofa, terrier tense, ready to spring.

Keith walked over to his violin, carefully loosened the tension on the strings, put it back into the case. He placed it in the storage cupboard. When he had calmed himself, he turned to face her. He suddenly looked every bit twenty years senior to me.

"Josie, you have my sincere apology for this miserable evening. I'm very sorry."

She nodded at him. Smiled gently.

"I'll see you ladies in the morning," he said, heading for the stairs. He left us alone.

Chapter Five

Josie rose and pulled a hassock closer to the sofa. She sat down, took a Virginia Slim from an elegant gold case, and lit it. She put up her feet, laid her head back, and took a deep drag. She looked at me silently, as though I were a specimen under a microscope.

"I suppose I should have told you," I looked at the floor, drew circles with my foot. "All the details. About the suicide, I mean."

She blew a perfectly formed smoke ring, watched it dissipate toward the ceiling.

"I really, really wish you didn't smoke," I said finally.

"And I really, really wish you'd never married the dirt farmer."

"How can you say that? Think that?"

"Are you crazy, Lottie? I don't care how great you think he is. I'll admit that he's a different man than I thought he was, but there's enough baggage in this family to fell an ox. Which you are not. You have a much frailer personality than you would like to believe."

"That simply is not true. You're the one who's hung back, protected yourself. Fiddled while Rome burned."

She quietly shook her head. "Your insistence on jumping into the middle of everything is because you cannot, *cannot,* bear not fixing things. Making them right. Think a minute, Lottie. You kept calling this woman over and over to get her to change her story. Couldn't let it go. Couldn't stand the friction between the sisters."

"Oh, must we fight? I wanted everything to be perfect when you met Elizabeth and Bettina."

I laughed ruefully, hearing my own words in the light of her lecture.

"Do you have some decent scotch, Lottie? I don't intend to drink your husband's vile home brew ever again."

"That's the only sensible idea I've heard all night."

I went into the kitchen and mixed us both drinks.

Keith and I had met when I was working in the library at Fort Hays State University. Forsyth Library has priceless holdings of material about Germans from Russia, known as Volga Germans. Persons using this room always had to be under the scrutiny of university personnel. I had done my dissertation on ethnic groups, and eagerly volunteered for the monitoring job as it gave me access to the collections. Keith came in one day, asking for material on his family.

Before then, I would have scoffed at the notion of love at first sight. But it happened. Happened to me. An old maid of thirty-one. I loved his grave sense of honor. *Gravitas*, the Romans called it. He was not a light man.

I carried the drinks back into the living room.

"How did it happen?"

"She hanged herself. Elizabeth found her."

She took a long drag, closed her eyes for a moment.

"Do any of them know about Mummy," she asked. "Our own Lady Macbeth? I should think our own sunny childhood would be enlightening to your resident Queen Elizabeth. She who holds the patent on hard times."

"Keith knows Mom was an alcoholic, but I don't think he realizes how much it affected us, or how well I understand how living with Regina's instability scarred his kids. And him. But Keith's a rock. Like Daddy was."

"Bingo."

I scowled. "Oh, go to hell."

"Be forewarned, Lottie. Queen Elizabeth is the kind of person who doesn't like to be at a disadvantage. She may resent your seeing this side of her."

Tosca yipped, like she was in agreement. I started, spilled my drink, and hustled off for towels. "Back to the Ladies," I said when I returned. "The Rubidoux girls. I'll show you the story."

She smiled at my quick change of subject. I went to my briefcase and pulled out the working copy of Zelda's story. She read it quickly. Her eyes widened. "My god, Lottie. I can't believe anyone still thinks like this. It's despicable."

"Confederate thinking," I agreed. "Old South."

"May I take this back with me? I have a friend who does a lot of work with handwriting. There's some shapes here that intrigue me."

"Of course."

"Bludgeoned." Stroking Tosca, Josie speculated on the night's events. "Sounds like an unreliable way to kill someone. I would just bet the person didn't go in intending to kill her. There're smarter ways. I don't know anything about profiling, but there are some things here that are very obvious. This murder was impulsive and the murderer had to be a strong person."

"Not necessarily. Zelda was frail. If the first blow landed just right and managed to crush her skull, it wouldn't have taken much strength at all."

"Did the St. Johns keep money around? Jewelry? Antiques? Any chance they would be singled out by a thief?"

"No. Rumor has it they were very hard up."

I jumped when a stick snapped in the fireplace. It did not seem possible we were sitting in my living room calmly discussing macabre details as if Zelda St. John were some anonymous distant person.

"Sam Abbott. You seem to be bosom buddies."

"We are. We did our horses together."

She quirked an eyebrow.

I laughed. "Carlton County has its own carnival. When we got our carousel, volunteers painted all the horses. Sam and I just happened to be working at the same time. We talked a lot."

"No Mrs. Sam?"

"Nope. He's a widower. He lost his only son in Vietnam."

We talked for hours. About her work. About my work. But we kept coming back to Zelda St. John over and over again until we were exhausted. We finally gave it up and headed for bed.

She turned on the staircase. "I have one more question."

"Yes?"

"The horses. What was his, what was yours?"

Miffed by her playing psychologist, I sulled up.

"Come on, come on, come on," she teased. "Pretty please?"

"Mine was Princess Di. Jewel colors and feathers. Sam's was a patriotic Desert Storm horse."

Her laughter pealed through the house.

◇◇◇

Bettina volunteered to go with me to the St. Johns for my traditional death-in-the-family call the following afternoon. I placed my usual food offerings in a wicker basket in the back of my Tahoe. A meat loaf for those who needed something solid and real to stomach death, and a custard pie for those who had a hard time getting food past the lump in their throat.

The radio was tuned to our local station, and I listened to the account of Zelda's death for the second time that day.

> "Zelda St. John, wife of local businessman Maxwell St. John, was murdered last night. St. John was the aunt of state senator, Brian Hadley, who is campaigning for the United States senate seat now held by Pat Roberts. Her body was discovered at approximately nine o' clock by her husband, Maxwell St. John, who had returned from a meeting at the local Lions Club.
>
> "Although the actual cause of death has yet to be officially established, pending an autopsy being conducted by County Coroner, Dr. William K. Kasper,

she appears to have died from blows to her head with a blunt instrument.

"Brian Hadley is expected to arrive from Wichita later today to be with the family. Details of the funeral service have not been announced."

There were several cars parked in front of the St. John's. The sprawling white farm-house has multipane windows framed by peeling dark green shutters. Overgrown pfitzers blotched with dead branches sagged at both sides of the doorway. Elephant skin blisters marred the lapped siding.

I rang the doorbell, stilled by the solemnity of death. It's always sudden, even when it's not murder. As shocking as a bolt of lightning. Even if a family has been keeping a cancer vigil for a year.

Zelda's and Maxwell's only child, Judy, opened the door. A waif with spiked orange hair, her huge blue eyes were red and swollen.

I knew her well through helping with the Carlton County Neighborhood Entertainment Company. She had perched beside me between scenes when we produced *The King and I* and told me her time-old teenage story. A little problem with drugs, a little problem with sex, a little problem with a juvenile record. All past now, but recorded forever in the collective memory of a small town.

"Judy, honey, I'm so sorry."

I hugged her and patted her on the back. She tried to speak between spasmodic sobs.

"Mom always tried so hard. She was a wonderful mother."

"I know, honey. She was devoted to you."

"Folks made fun of her all the time. But she was my mother and I loved her. Still love her. Death isn't going to change that."

She eased off my shoulder, nodded hello to Bettina, and dabbed at her eyes.

"Dad's not doing well. We'd better go inside. He's in the living room." She pointed down the hallway to an open door where Maxwell St. John sat with his head buried in his hands.

Bettina headed for the kitchen, carrying our basket of food. I went directly to the living room to pay my respects to Max.

Their living room looked like an old-fashioned parlor set in a museum. White doilies crocheted in the pineapple motif protected the maroon cut-velvet sofa and matching chair. Umber and green marbleized tiles framed the gas-log fireplace. A glass-shaded, brass-footed lamp was centered on an imitation Duncan Fife table in the bay window. Heavy walnut framed portraits of generations of Rubidoux hung on plastered walls.

Maxwell rose unsteadily to his feet. He extended his arthritic hand, and my heart ached at the misery in his bleak face. Although he was eighteen years older than Zelda, Maxwell had doted on his crazy younger wife.

"Maxwell, I'm so sorry. Our deepest sympathy."

All he could do at first was nod.

"I can't believe she's gone," he said, when he could summon his voice. He tugged at slipping frayed suspenders fastened to stained chinos. Tiny singes from pipe embers pocked the front of his rumpled pin-striped shirt.

The doorbell jarred the room. Judy's quick steps echoed down the hallway. Then I heard her shouting.

"Get out," she yelled. "All of you. None of you are welcome."

Chapter Six

I dropped Maxwell's hand and turned. Edgar and Fiona Hadley stood framed in the entrance. Behind them, high-lighted by the sun was Brian. *Son of the Morning Star.* Crown Prince of Carlton County. His razor-cut gold hair gleamed like bullion.

Across from the road turning into the farmyard, TV crews circled like buzzards, cameras in place, wanting to record every minute of Brian Hadley's visit to the grieving family.

"Murderer. Murderer." Judy looked straight at Fiona. "You killed her. Just leave us alone."

"Judy!" Nervously eyeing the cameras, I quickly pulled the Hadleys inside. The media teams were not close enough to pick up sound. "Please go on into the living room." The Hadleys were mute with shock. "Max needs you."

"So sorry," I mouthed silently to an ashen-faced Brian as I steered Judy toward the stairs. He nodded and guided his parents down the hall.

His political success was a testimony to his steely will to overcome his inherent liabilities. Only in America would looking like a young Brad Pitt be an obstacle to having his ideas heard. The press maneuvered constantly to get him to say or do something naughty. Senior citizens just fell all over him.

Brian Hadley is a fine man. Moreover, he is not a fool, even if he is a Republican. I voted for him last time when he ran for state senate. Although I'm a Yellow Dog Democrat, when he decided to run for the national seat, I didn't mind crossing party lines to organize his campaign in this county. I *like* politicians. I respect persons who are willing to make honorable and reasonable compromises. It's what makes the world work. Over my dead body would I allow Judy St. John to slander this man who might have a shot at the presidency some day.

I led her into her bedroom.

"Please try to get yourself under control. I just can't stand by and let you say things you'll regret later."

"She hated my mother. Enough to kill her."

"You can't believe that! Now is not the time and place for this, Judy. Don't disgrace your mother's memory by turning this into a family brawl. Zelda would just hate it. You know how much she cared about appearances."

"Aunt Fiona killed her or hired someone else to kill her."

"Judy, I'll be right back. Please lie down. I know you're exhausted."

I had to shut her up. I ran down the stairs and opened the door to the kitchen. I stopped cold when I saw our county health nurse, Inez Wilson. Her back was turned toward me. She stood next to Minerva Lovesey. I didn't want Inez near Judy St. John. Clearly, none of them had heard Judy's carrying on as Inez was warning Bettina and Minerva of the dangers of the coming flu epidemic.

Bettina saw me at once, and before the others could turn to follow her glance, I put a finger to my lips and gestured her to step into the hallway.

"Excuse me, please," she said brightly to the assembled women. The heavy swinging kitchen door whooshed shut behind her.

"Get these people out of here, Bettina. All of them. I don't care how. Turn away anyone who comes to the outside door, too. Judy's raising six kinds of hell."

Bettina's a quick study. She nodded and hurried back into the kitchen. I listened.

"Judy is not well," she said to Inez and Minerva. "She's overwhelmed and wants to be alone with her father. It would be best for all of us to leave and not take it personally. I'm going home right now and Brian will drive Lottie home later."

"Well, if *she's* going to stay, I know the family would want me around," said Inez. "They could certainly use a nurse more than a historian."

"Max and Judy have asked Lottie to assist with funeral arrangements. They really do want all the rest of us out of here."

"I was just trying to help," Inez said sullenly.

I could just imagine her dramatic account of the prostrate grief-stricken daughter that would be making the rounds by morning. I listened a moment longer, just to be sure Bettina wouldn't need reinforcement, before I returned to Judy.

"Some people *do* just want to be by themselves," said Minerva.

I smiled. Good old Minerva. Chief secret keeper of Carlton County. Gatekeeper of thousands of records, she was the soul of discretion. Intensely private about her own affairs, she even doctored in Denver and mail-ordered prescriptions because she didn't want medical personnel gossiping about her health. Or so it was said.

She must have mail ordered all her clothes from L.L. Bean and Eddie Bauer because they had that look and she never shopped in town. She wore her graying red hair in a neat bun. Her only nod to femininity was maroon polish on her short nails. It seemed out-of-character, since she shunned all other makeup.

We would have been better friends if I could have seen her eyes. I can't tell what people are thinking if I can't see their eyes. Minerva wore dark amber Varilux lenses that did not change color with the light. Inez had told me that Minerva had very light sensitive eyes that need protection, but I'd wondered if they didn't reflect her intense sense of privacy.

Satisfied Bettina had everything under control, I turned away and tried to think of something I could say to the Hadleys.

Brian was waiting for me in the hallway. He ignored my outstretched hand and hugged me instead.

"So sorry, Brian. For everything. Save some time for me this weekend. We must talk and I want to know how you've been. Not that the papers don't report your every little move."

"You've got that right. Thanks for your quick thinking, Lottie. I hate to think what the media would have made of this. Do you know what set Judy off?"

"Maybe. I'll talk to you about it later. Right now I think it's best we play like nothing's happened."

I stepped into the living room. Knowing how hard hit in-laws are sometimes, I cupped Edgar's hands in my own, patted them. "So sorry. Terribly sorry."

Edgar Hadley nodded, grief deepening the lines on his coarse heavy face. When I first met Edgar, I took one look at the jutting jaw, the gun rack in back of his pick-up, his anti-government bumper sticker, and decided he was a Neanderthal. I was partially right.

He didn't hold with free school lunches, Jane Fonda, working wives, Democrats, farm programs, Wall street, communists, foreign cars, gold-threaded cowboy shirts, high-heeled boots, golf, the lottery, coffee beans, or chickens.

Luckily for Brian, the press had decided his father was an American primitive. In a class by himself. Just like his wife.

I turned from Edgar to Fiona.

"It must be devastating to lose a sister, let alone a twin." She nodded and clung to my hand.

"I can't believe this," she said. "It can't be true."

Then her mood changed abruptly and visibly. "How did you manage to shut up that sullen little delinquent? Judy belongs in an institution."

I glanced at Max. He'd heard, all right. His face crumbled with confusion. His mouth worked helplessly.

"Brian," I said, "may I please have a word with you?"

We went into the foyer and shut the door, closing off the hallway.

"Please take your folks and go home until a little more of this plays out. Talk to your mother or chloroform her. I don't care which. We need to keep this from turning into a three ring circus."

"Right," he said tersely.

Chapter Seven

Three days after Zelda's funeral I gave myself permission to take a Dumb Day at the historical society. What I really wanted was a day off. But I had a whole assortment of piddling tasks I did when my head wasn't clear enough to edit. I typed file folder labels, entered data on the computer, organized photographs.

I was paid a token wage for professional and political reasons having to do with the county's mill levy. Everyone else who worked here volunteered, and at the Carlton County Historical Society we prided ourselves on being open when we were supposed to be, by god.

Nevertheless, it was gorgeous outside, and I wanted to be home doing fall gardening, not working in a stuffy old courthouse surrounded by one hundred years of yellowing newspaper clippings and old pictures.

I had been too restless to work well all week. I could not put the question out of my mind. Who *had* murdered Zelda? Despite the theft of Zelda's purse, Sam was not convinced the motive was burglary. Josie was sure bludgeoning was an unplanned crime of passion. Passion would indicate someone who knew her. Like her sister.

There are ghosts in this vault. Men and women clutching at my sleeves, murmuring, "I want to tell you my story. Please let them know my life counted for something. Please tell them. Who I was. What I did."

Zelda was the newest haunt.

The funeral had gone well. Heavily sedated, Judy had behaved. Brian had made a sweet, earnest speech about his happy memories of his beloved aunt. And Max. The poor, pitiful, lost, weepy-eyed old man was enough to break your heart.

Judy St. John blew into the vault like a wisp of fog. One moment I was thinking of Zelda, the next I looked up and her daughter was standing in front of me.

Warily, I waited for Judy to speak. When she did, the words seemed strange and hollow. Like they were put there by a ventriloquist.

"Lottie, I know Aunt Fiona murdered my mother. I just know it. How can I convince you? If you won't believe me, no one in this town will believe me."

My fingers tightened around the pencil I was holding. I couldn't think fast enough. I had thought this nonsense was over, a passing hysterical notion of an unstable woman. She was right that no one around here would believe her. But outside the county? The press would have a field day with Brian's campaign.

"Judy, if there's trouble in a family, a funeral brings it out. People are inclined to think terrible things." I picked around for words. "Thoughts they never would have had otherwise."

"It's not my imagination." Tears welled in her enormous blue eyes. "Somehow, someway, Aunt Fiona is behind all this." She reached for a Kleenex and pressed it against her trembling mouth.

"Judy," I said carefully, "I wish you would…"

"Wish I would what? Shut my mouth? Not make waves?" She quivered like a little Chihuahua.

"I wish you would be a little more sensitive to what's at stake for Brian if you make accusations. The press will tear him to shreds if you even hint at anything amiss."

"I know what's at stake. His whole career. I don't care." But her body language said she did. She sat with her legs rigidly thrust in front of her, white knuckled hands clutching the edge of the chair, as though she would fly up and hit the ceiling if she relaxed her grip for a second.

Josie has an uncanny ability to tell when people are lying or merely have a skewed sense of the truth. She would know everything about Judy St. John in two hours time. I didn't. However, I was certain she believed everything she was saying.

"What is it you want from me, Judy?"

"I want you to go with me to the police."

Stunned, I could only think of the impact this would have on Brian Hadley's career.

"I'll go to the press if you won't go with me to the police."

"Judy, I know you must trust me, or you wouldn't be here. You would find someone else. But you have to know Brian won't be elected dogcatcher, let alone senator if you go through with this."

It was the right tone. Her car keys slipped out of her clenched fist and clattered to the floor. She leaned forward in her chair and picked them up.

"I trust you more than anyone I've ever met," she said. "You listened to me once before. Believed me. Everyone else saw me as dingy and a little crazy, like my mother. Everyone else just remembers the drugs, the drinking, the freaky boyfriends."

"Okay, then. I'm going to make a deal with you. Please, please keep quiet about your suspicions. I have ways of finding things out. I work right here in the courthouse. Let me look into this. I'll put everything else aside for two weeks. If I find something to connect Fiona Hadley or anyone else to this murder, I'll go to the police. If there's nothing there, you've got to promise me you'll drop it."

"Oh, you'll find something all right. Start by finding out why my mother was so mad at Aunt Fiona. They had a huge fight the night Mom died."

Startled, I bit back a flow of questions. Sam Abbott had not mentioned this fight. I was positive he didn't know about it. Was she making it up?

"How do you know that?"

"Mom called me that evening. She said she would never speak to her sister again."

"Your mother called you the night she died? Had Fiona been to see her? Didn't the police talk to you?"

"I wasn't here of course, but Betty Central called me right after Dad phoned."

She didn't have to say another word. Betty would have had her mind made up. She wouldn't have asked a single intelligent question or followed up on a single lead. "Betty asked me if my mom and I got along and where I was that night. That's all."

"Did your mother say when Fiona was there?"

"Early. About five-thirty or so."

I nodded. Fiona must have driven there right after she left the historical society.

"Mom said she would tell me all about it the first time I came home. She said it was high time I knew a few things about the family."

"Was she frightened?"

"No, Mom was mad. Furious, in fact. And that same night she was murdered."

I picked up a pile of papers and whacked the edges against the desk to bring them in line.

"Did your mother mention her story? Have you seen it?"

"No."

"I want you to read it." I started to get the working copy, then remembered Josie had taken it back to Manhattan for handwriting analysis. Judy would have to see the original, and I hated having it handled again. Nevertheless, I unlocked the master file, gave the pages to Judy, and positioned myself where I could see every nuance on her face as I watched her read.

She paled, laid it down and pressed her hand against her forehead before she picked it up and continued reading.

There was a catch in her throat. "Lottie, please believe me. I'm not like this. Brian isn't either."

"I thought you didn't care about Brian."

"I care about justice. I care about seeing my aunt pay for my mother's murder. If putting her away ruins Brian's career it can't be helped. I'm just saying that Brian isn't a racist. I don't know what Mom was thinking. As to the ancient Rubidouxs, I hate to admit it, but that part is true. But I know my cousin. He's fair play all the way."

"Did you notice anything else? You'd be surprised at the amount of controversial material that's camouflaged. Just last week I had another pair of sisters in the middle of a family quarrel. They were devout Catholics. One of them wanted to delete a line saying there had been a divorce in the family, saying it wasn't a true marriage to begin with."

"You're kidding." Distracted by the story, she started to relax.

"It was just a simple line saying that Kenneth and Roberta were divorced in 1929, but it unleashed a storm within the family. Then there are the widows who don't want their husbands first wives mentioned. Or the kids who don't want their father's late-in-life wife in the history. The stories *read* just fine, but there's something hidden or omitted. A date that's a red flag. Something."

"You're not going to get a Paul Harvey ending from me. You know—'and now for the rest of the story,'" Judy said. She looked away then dug around in her purse for a Kleenex and blew her nose. "Is this *exactly* what you showed her?"

"Yes. The very pages your mother turned in."

Good historians know the importance of actually seeing primary documents. It's part of our training, but her attention to detail surprised me. It had to be part of her personality. Came from being whacked by life, I decided. She only trusted her own five senses.

She fanned the pages, then turned them over and glanced at the back. "There's a shadow on all of them. A rose."

Startled, I moved to her side and studied the faint imprint. How had I missed that? I held the pages up to the light. Perhaps the faint watermark had not been pronounced enough to show up on the working copy.

"Nice, Judy. Very observant. You noticed a detail I overlooked."

She shrugged, but blushed at the praise. I put Zelda's story back in the master file, and locked the cabinet. "Where can I get in touch with you? In case I find something."

"I'm taking a leave of absence from my job, Lottie. Dad needs me. I'm going to stay home with him for the next couple of weeks. And I intend to help *you*. Thanks for everything." She gave me a tremulous smile as she walked out the door.

Chapter Eight

I snapped my pencil in half. The last thing I wanted was Judy's help. The muscles leading from my neck to the tops of my shoulders became as hard as tree trunks, signaling the on-set of a tension headache.

I reached for my notebook containing a sequence of research procedures I follow. I don't follow the money here in Western Kansas. I start with the land. Follow the land.

I reached for the telephone and called Minerva.

"Would you have time to trace the holdings of the Rubidoux family?"

"Not today, but I can do it tomorrow morning."

"Tomorrow is fine. Just the bare facts." It would do little good to say this. Everything she did was detailed and concise. She even typed sticky notes. "In fact, if I can get William Webster to take over here, I think I'll take the rest of the afternoon off,"

I groped at the muscles in the base of my neck. Gone to petrified wood. I needed to transplant my mums, and there was nothing like a little physical labor to break up muscle tension.

William said it would be another hour before he could get around and he would like a little more notice next time.

I said if he didn't want to do it I could find someone else.

He said there was no need to get snippy.

It was the usual pattern of what passed for conversations between us. We all have a cross to bear. William Webster was mine.

Just as I was hanging up the phone, I heard footsteps in the corridor. I rose when Fiona Hadley and Brian walked through the door.

"We came to thank you, Lottie, for everything you've done these last three days," Fiona said.

"I don't have to tell you how disastrous this would have been if you hadn't taken charge," Brian added.

"The vicious little misfit has always been jealous of our Brian. She's just like her mother. She and Zelda both just hated him."

Brian's face was white. I stood stone still, my heart aching, realizing the enormous handicap his mother was going to be to his campaign.

"You know I don't agree with anything you're saying, Mother." Brian forced calmness, but there was a tremor in his hand as he reached to touch Fiona's arm. "It's history now anyway. No need to speak ill of the dead. That's another reason I'm here, Lottie. She was my aunt. She contributed a lot to this town. I'd like to write a tribute to her for the book."

"I'd love to include it."

"Good. I'll turn it in before I leave town. And of course we want the family story she turned in for our family scrap book."

"I can make you a copy, but the original stays here." I glared at Fiona. "Your mother and I have already had this discussion."

She stopped breathing for a full ten seconds. When she started again, her nostrils were pinched and white, and there were twin spots of color on her cheeks.

"You aren't actually considering printing that silly piece of work, are you?" she asked. "Her dying changes everything. She can't be reasoned with now. Surely you aren't going to keep a story that reflects so badly on my poor deceased sister."

"I'm not considering it. I'm doing it," I said, wondering when Zelda had suddenly become the poor deceased sister instead of the jealous monster.

"Why?" asked Fiona.

"Because it's a vivid example of how people used to think. And some obviously still do." I looked pointedly at Fiona. "But the main reason is that it's her story. Her view of the world, and she turned it in before she died."

"Even if it ruins my son's career?"

"I don't intend to print it now. But it's still a historical document. Material for scholars."

"No big deal, Lottie." Brian smiled winningly. "Just so my tribute gets in."

"It will."

"Excellent," said Brian. "May I have a copy for my personal records?"

"Sure," I said. William Webster came into the office just as I was heading toward the master file to copy the original as Josie had my working copy.

"Brian. Fiona. My deepest sympathy."

"Thank you, William," Brian said. "It's been a blow."

William Webster, retired railroad engineer, carried a small canvas bag containing carving tools and a block of cedar. On idle days, the women volunteers quilted or sorted or filed when they answered the phones. William carved. He was the only person I knew over eighty years of age who didn't require glasses for reading. I loved the odor of cedar shavings that permeated the vault after he left.

I had had a hard time passing William's subtle character tests when I was hired. He asked the toughest questions of any of the board members and had been very reluctant to let an "outsider" be in charge of the books. He had grilled me like F. Lee Bailey over my insistence on editorial control. In fact, it had been a battle royal.

"The buck has to stop somewhere," I'd insisted. "You can't have a committee making editorial decisions."

I won. Not only the battle, but William's respect. He'd been a tough sell. Even now, he had a habit of stopping in unannounced, as though he expected to find me eating bon-bons and reading novels on the county's nickel. His blue chambray work shirts were patched over and over. His sharp eyes saw everything, but after a while I could feel him switch to an occasional ally. If you could call a porcupine an ally.

"B'God, boy. You look like you haven't slept for days," William said, glancing at Brian. "If I didn't know you, I'd figure you were coming off a three-day drunk. Your eyes look like a dried-out chamois cloth."

Brian flushed. Press-jittery like most politicians, he was usually able to mask any signs of irritation. Not this time. His jaw muscle jumped like a shocked rabbit.

"It's been very trying, and I'll admit that I haven't been able to sleep."

I, too, had noticed his muddied eyes and his sallow complexion today, but a weekend with Edgar and Fiona would be a strain on anyone, even without a death in the family.

Flustered by William's comments, Fiona and Brian said their goodbyes, and left without a copy of Zelda's story. Even my empathy for Brian was overshadowed by my annoyance with his mother. She was bringing out what my husband called my Mammy Yokum streak. All I lacked was a corn cob pipe and sawed off shotgun as I defended the Historical Society from foreigners. Guarding the gold in them thar hills.

I reached for my jacket. "I guess I don't have to tell you not to let anything out of this room, William."

Chapter Nine

The next morning, when I opened the office, Margaret Atkinson, my favorite volunteer came in right behind me.

"Good morning, Lottie."

A tiny woman with a tightly permed cap of Hereford red hair and skin like a withered marshmallow, she could have stayed out in the sun for the rest of her life and never tanned a whit. Her family has been in this county since it was formed and she knew everything about everybody.

She was our conscience.

About five persons in a county, any county, are the key to projects being successful. The board would never have hired me without Margaret's approval.

Her clout came from her integrity and the contribution she and her family had made to the community. She created the first library in the county, manned it herself, and persuaded people to donate books. She wrote the grant for our hospice organization. She started our county museum.

She liked me. What a wonder. Even though her function in the historical society was something between that of a spy and a guardian angel and I was her boss, we both knew she could ruin me anytime she wanted.

Margaret had been out of town for a week and missed out on the worst tragedy our community had faced in years.

"You've heard everything?" I headed toward my desk.

"Heard nothing but," she said tiredly. "From everybody. My phone started ringing the moment I got back."

"Something's wrong." The hair on my neck prickled. "Someone's been in here." My paper clip holder was on the wrong side of my desk pad. My family photos were grouped differently.

"Were you the last to leave yesterday?"

I shook my head. "William Webster was. He got here about two."

"Well then, maybe he moved something."

"Maybe, but it's not like him to touch anything of mine. He sits over there." I waved at a corner. My desk drawer was locked, as it should have been, so I clamped down on my uneasiness. "No big deal, Margaret. If someone came in needing something, William had a perfect right to rummage around." I had too much to do to be fretting over trivia.

"First off, I want you to read the Rubidoux Family Story. Maybe you can see something I've missed. Then I'm going to finish laying out pages."

If I had been going to tell anyone Judy had accused Fiona of murder, it would have been Margaret. So far, the only ones in the loop were the Hadleys and Keith and Bettina.

"I'll run off a working copy," I said, not mentioning the one I'd already made was now in Manhattan Kansas. That wouldn't set well with Margaret. I unlocked the master file cabinet and fingered through the R folders.

The Rubidoux story wasn't there.

Thinking I had misfiled the original under St. John, I went to the Ss. My jaw tightened so hard my teeth ached. It wasn't there. I looked again, willing it to materialize. I opened the last drawer, hoping I had witlessly put it under Z for Zelda. It wasn't there either.

"Margaret."

"What?"

"It's not here."

"Let me look," she said. "I'm sure it's slipped down behind a folder or something."

From the beginning we'd agreed that neither was to be insulted if the other insisted on double-checking material. There's something about fresh eyes looking. At least, I *think* that's what it is. Sometimes I could swear Margaret *made* things appear. As though she were a conjurer.

"It has to be here," she said. Her wrinkles quivered.

I sank into a chair and watched anxiously. She finished checking all the obvious files, walked to the supply cabinet and put on rubber fingertips. Beginning with the As she carefully opened each individual folder and stroked through the pages, making sure Zelda's story hadn't slipped inside another. She laid each file in neat staggered rows on the desk, so she could tell if there were papers at the bottom of the drawer. Finally she removed the entire drawer, making sure papers had not become flattened against the back wall of the cabinet. She went through all the other drawers, using the same method.

It took her hours to go through every scrap of paper in that file cabinet. My heart beat like a trip hammer as I watched.

"It's not here, Lottie," she said finally. "It's not in this cabinet."

"Okay," I said. I blinked back tears and tried to look professional. It was no use. Margaret knew me too well. I had never lost a story. Now an original hand-written story by a dead woman had vanished.

I splayed my hands across my face and tried to think while Margaret sorted through miscellaneous piles of paper on desks.

"It's not here, either, Lottie. I've looked everywhere." Her face was a shade whiter, her gaze reproachful, dull red circles burned on her cheeks.

"Are there others missing? We need to check."

"I don't know. Please, no. Oh please, please don't let it be true." I jumped up and hurried to the master file cabinet and riffled a special folder containing old letters. There were five missing.

One had been signed by George Armstrong Custer.

Kansas was rich with original documentation. The Kansas State Historical Society in Topeka housed one of the largest collections of newspapers in the world and the state's county courthouses were full of hidden treasures.

Documents signed by Wyatt Earp and Matt Dillion had disappeared from Dodge City and been sold for a small fortune to unscrupulous collectors. Fossils disappeared from museums. In Carlton County, we were just beginning to identify and catalogue everything that came into the vault. I was the guardian of these documents.

Someone had just trashed my reputation for reliability. Anger throbbed so deeply, my whole body was suffused with heat. I had forgotten what it felt like to be this furious. Beneath the heat was the beginning of a cold rage. Cold and calculating.

"We have to call the sheriff, Lottie. The Custer letter was very valuable. It will be in all the papers," Margaret said sadly. "And people were just starting to trust us with their old photos."

Chapter Ten

I drove home that evening oblivious to the onset of autumn. Although I still missed the glorious Eastern Kansas panorama of fall leaves, out here air quickened. Geese flew overhead and shadows sharpened. I'd come to appreciate the year-round dark green of sheltering cedar windbreaks.

On a farm, winter is a time of rest and deep healing. Years ago work animals needed slack time. Now families whacked by the zaniness of farm programs and the perversity of Mother Nature needed the lull. In winter we pull ourselves together, organize our so-called finances, and plan spring crops.

At home, still seething, I sipped chamomile tea while I talked to Josie. I told her about the theft and asked her to keep her mouth shut about the copy of Zelda's story she had taken with her for handwriting analysis. It didn't eliminate my despair over the Custer letter, however.

Relaxing a little, I lighted the fire, collapsed into my over-stuffed tan leather chair, put my feet up on the matching hassock, and huddled under an afghan Bettina had made for me. Surrounded by creature comforts, I began to unwind and tried to make sense of what was going on. Finally I reached for the pad lying on the table next to my chair and turned on the lamp.

I listed the sequence of events: Zelda had turned in a story. Fiona had tried to get it back. Zelda died. Judy had accused Fiona of murder and later asked me to investigate. I had agreed for Brian's sake, then the story disappeared along with old letters. One of which was very valuable.

I listed what everyone knew and what only certain people knew. A number of people now knew Zelda had turned in a story accusing Brian of bigotry.

Judy and I were the only ones who knew Fiona had been at the St. John's house the night Zelda died.

Outside of the Hadleys and my own family, I was the only one who knew Judy had accused Fiona of murder.

Only Margaret and I had keys to the office and master file. No one else had access to our room. In theory. But what about the janitor? Were his always in a safe place? For that matter, when I was there, Margaret usually left her keys in her desk when she went to the bathroom or during short breaks. Did she leave her keys when I wasn't there? And the office had been unlocked for about ten minutes last Friday while I watched the storm.

Keith came through the back door in a gust of fresh air.

"You aren't going to believe this," I began.

He hung his jean jacket on the peg, turned, and listened.

"Any idea who it could have been?"

"None. Until this happened I would have thought it impossible." Dizzy with gratitude for his easy acceptance of my account, I walked over and hugged him. He hadn't said, "Are you sure you didn't put it someplace?"

"Thanks," I whispered against his chest.

"For what?" Then he pressed for more details.

Responding to his loyal matter-of-fact questions, knowing he respected my judgment, helped assuage the guilt I had felt under Margaret's disapproving looks.

The phone rang. Keith answered.

"Hi, Elizabeth."

I walked to the pantry, grabbed a box of Hamburger Helper, flashed the label in front of him and mouthed, "okay?" He nodded and as I browned the beef, I listened absently until his tone changed. Then I was all ears. He had been telling her about the theft.

"No, I'm sure she didn't, Elizabeth. She doesn't do that kind of thing."

Abruptly, I turned off the stove, went to the living room, picked up the extension.

"I'm on now too, Elizabeth," I said.

"Well, *hi*. Dad just told me about your terrible day and I was telling him about this wonderful subliminal tape that improves memory and it's full of techniques…"

"Elizabeth, a valuable letter was stolen from our courthouse. Got that? Stolen. I did not misplace it."

Silence on her end. I had never spoken sharply to any of Keith's children before. I was overdue.

Then she came back with sweet reason. Handling me. Voice low and pleasant. "I just thought, Lottie, with all your work focusing on the past, not requiring a high degree of alertness, it would be easy for you to slip into abstracted ways without realizing it. We've all heard the cliché about the absent-minded professor."

"That's what it is, Elizabeth. A cliché."

I hung up, leaving Keith to finish the conversation with his darling daughter. Furiously, I stormed past him and concentrated on the hamburger.

"Talk to you later, Elizabeth," said Keith, glancing at me sharply.

I slapped the plates onto the table, nuked some vegetables, and slid a loaf of bread, still in the sack, by Keith's place.

"Supper's on," I said coldly.

"Lottie!"

Angry that he would address me like a parent trying to reprimand a child, I stood with my arms crossed and glared.

"There's something you two women need to know. I don't do cat fights."

"You could have stuck up for me."

"I did," he said solemnly. "If you'll think back to before you got on the phone, I told her you didn't lose that letter."

"Why did you bring it up at all?"

"You know it'll be all over town by tomorrow. And in the paper Thursday, since you reported it to the sheriff. So I thought she should hear it from us. Me. Besides, she had just lost a custody case and was feeling rotten. Inadequate."

"So knowing I had been knocked flat too was going to make her feel better somehow?"

He looked stricken. "You're right, I was wrong. I know Elizabeth never misses a chance to give you a hard time. And I give you the credit for not fanning the flames. I hate this kind of thing, but you're my *wife*, Lottie. I'm going to stick up for you. Unless you're dead wrong. Don't you know that by now?"

"Oh, Keith, I'm sorry." I ran over to him and he kissed my trembling mouth. "I'm sorry I took this out on you."

He hugged me hard. "It was weird to see you lose control. Maturity doesn't have much to do with age, sweetheart. You're old beyond your years," he said. "Hate to put the burden on you, but if you can find it in your heart to cut Elizabeth a little slack, I'd appreciate it. She's under more stress than usual right now because a number of her cases have involved abused children."

I didn't lose control, I thought. *The lady needed to be told off. I did it on purpose.* "I'll make every effort to keep the peace with Elizabeth."

◇◇◇

That night when I curled up against his broad back, I could not sleep. I stiffened whenever I recalled Elizabeth's jab that my work didn't require a high degree of alertness. What utter nonsense! I felt like grabbing her by the hair and forcing her to watch me for a day.

When I did manage to put her words from my mind and was about to doze off, I jerked awake, still tormented by the theft and burdened by my promise to Judy to look into her mother's death.

I had to be in a position to ask better questions. And fast. The way came to me after two restless hours. A way about as real-time, real-life as it gets. It would show Elizabeth, too. I knew at once it would be better not to inform Keith until after it was a done deal.

I smiled before I drifted into the deep soundless sleep of the innocent and the ignorant. The sleep of a woman who thinks God's in his heaven and all's right with the world. The sleep of a woman who in her heart of hearts doesn't really believe bad things happen to good people.

Chapter Eleven

"Can I help you, Lottie?"

"I'm here about the ad."

Sam Abbott looked at me blankly.

"Ad?"

"In the paper. The one asking for volunteers to become deputies?"

"Yes?"

Sam was not a stupid person, but he really did not understand.

"I want to become a deputy."

He blinked slowly. He reached toward an ash tray for his pipe. He opened his desk drawer, took out a little zippered pouch, got up, walked over to a roll of paper towels, and ripped one off the holder.

I could feel my cheeks growing hot and red. If he thought a little bit of silence was enough to scare me off, he had another thing coming.

He came back to the desk. He smoothed the paper towel, steadied the pipe on the paper, shook tobacco into the bowl, and tamped it down firmly. He creased the paper and shook the leftover tobacco back into the pouch. He took his time putting it back into the drawer. He puffed patiently and steadily on the stem.

He blew a series of rings into the air. I out-waited him.

"Keith know you're here?"

"No," I said, keeping my voice neutral, stung by his faint, patient smile.

"I think you should talk this over with him first."

"No need, Sam. He understands women making their own decisions."

There was a flash of quick amusement in his eyes. He was plenty smart enough to pick up on the implied rebuke.

"Okay," he said mildly. "Why?"

"Why what?"

"Why would you want such a miserable stinking job?"

"You need me, I know you do. If I may speak frankly?"

He nodded, waved his pipe.

"I heard about some of questions Betty Central asked the night Zelda was killed. It's not going to do you any good to have an officer of the law talk to anyone like that."

He gave me a look. There was more than acknowledgment in his eyes. Something closer to despair. I had hit upon a sore point indeed, but he did not give me the satisfaction of agreeing with me.

"There's got to be things that come up. Crimes against women. Rape, incest, where you need all the good help you can get."

With a bitter glance, his head bobbed in curt agreement. His pipe had gone out: he reached for his supply of matches, patiently coaxed it back to life.

"You didn't answer my question," he said again. "Why you would want to do this? It's a dirty little job, and you'll know more about the people in this town than you've ever wanted to know, far more than what's good for you."

He waited.

"No, the question is, do you want to hire me? That's the question I'm interested in."

He paused and looked at me hard. "Got a hidden agenda, Lottie?"

I swallowed hard. "All right. Maybe I do have a special reason. It has to do with Zelda St. John's death."

"What about it?"

Sam would have to know. I told him about Judy asking me to look into it.

"And you know you need decent help with this, Sam. Why not me? I know more about research than anyone else you could hope to find. I'm an historian. Dead people are my specialty. That's what you've got here. A dead person. I need the authority to ask questions I would have a hard time asking as the director of the historical society."

He let out a long sigh, touched his hand to his forehead.

"You'll get excellent reports," I coaxed.

He almost smiled.

"Now it's your turn, Sam."

He quirked an eyebrow.

"I answered a question for you, now you answer a question for me. Why would you not want to hire me? As you've pointed out, people aren't exactly beating down the door for this job."

"No, they're not," he said flatly. "The truth, Lottie?"

"What else?"

"You're too elite. You don't belong out here. You belong in an ivory tower. You don't fit in. You're an outsider. Law enforcement is a dirty business, and you're not the kind to get your hands dirty."

So that was how they saw me, the people in this town. I looked at him wide-eyed. Stoic. If he expected tears, he would be disappointed. Then it dawned on me I had just passed my first test with flying colors.

He was a cunning old bastard. I wouldn't underestimate him again.

"I do belong out here. I'm quite capable of getting my hands dirty. Sometimes people will talk more to an outsider than they will to someone they've known all their lives. The stranger on the bus thing. I'm not asking for a full-time job, Sam. I'm asking for a part-time deputy job so I can help find out who murdered Zelda St. John."

"Do you plan to just pop in and out?"

"Yes, of course. Why not? Part-time. That's all I want. I come with skills. You would have to train someone else in report writing, interview techniques. Stuff I already know how to do."

There was an interested glint in his eyes.

"The county has no money, right?"

He nodded wearily. I was clearly wearing him down.

"This investigation is going to put a terrible strain on the county's resources. You need all the cheap help you can get."

"You still have to have training, Lottie, and we're broke. Police departments are being sued over inadequate training."

"No problem. I'll pay my own way to seminars and teach other people when I get back."

There was a glint of interest in his eyes.

"I'm physically fit," I said quickly. "I work out. I'll take classes in self-defense."

He drew a deep breath, leaned back in his rickety swivel chair, put his locked arms behind his head.

I waited.

Abruptly he swung into a full upright position and fixed me with his sad, old eyes.

"Can you kill someone, Lottie?"

"Kill?"

"Yes, kill someone, woman. You've thought everything through but that, haven't you? It would be your duty, your obligation, to use deadly force if necessary."

"I think so," I stammered.

"Can't be *think so*. Gotta be *know so.*"

I gave him a look and left.

Chapter Twelve

I managed to get out the door without crying. But then I've always been good at saving face. I was ashamed of my little venture into the big bad world. My stomach tightened as I drove home.

We have photos of jack rabbit hunts at the society. Men stood proudly behind a mesa of rabbits neatly stacked as high as the roof of a porch. Clubbed to death. Years ago, it was a form of recreation second only to wolf hunts in general popularity. The children watched, and the womenfolk served pie afterward.

I have pictures of children watching public hangings. They, too, were family affairs. Occasions for picnics.

"Can you kill someone, Lottie?"

I was free to cry now.

"Not even a rabbit," I whispered softly. There was no one to see my shame.

Our farmstead is chock full of guns. We have shotguns and rifles. Hunting is a way of life. Two of Keith's daughters, Angie and Bettina, hunt game. Surprisingly, Elizabeth does not and I never do. Don't know how, don't want to learn.

I turned on the radio and was assaulted with information about the newest murder in Western Kansas. It had taken place in a rural farmhouse. A young couple shot. Just a little over a week ago, in our own pristine little town, a fine lady had been bludgeoned to death.

"Can you kill someone, Lottie?"

Who was I to expect other people to kill on my behalf? I wanted to keep my own hands clean. Yet I expected a peace officer to kill for me in a heartbeat. Wanted him to have the sin on his head. His hands bloody.

Ironically, I knew all about hand guns. They had been my version of teenage rebellion. Josie and I had attended a private Eastern boarding school. When our father insisted we adopt a sport, I took up archery and target pistols, and Josie fencing. Loner activities, despite the fact we competed against teams from other schools. It was not what Daddy had in mind.

I had a whole collection of purple ribbons. Handguns were a sport to me.

By the time I turned up our lane, I had made myself profoundly miserable and could hardly stand my own double-minded company. Once inside, I sought refuge in front of the TV. I flipped over to PBS and stared stupidly at Jim Lehrer.

Elizabeth's nasty words kept echoing in my mind. "A lady whose idea of real life is working with dusty old manuscripts."

Keith came through the back door, and I jumped at the sound.

"Nothing ready for supper," I mumbled.

"That's okay," he said with a quick glance. "You all right, hon? Can I fix you something? Headache coming on?"

"No," I said coldly, taking umbrage. I felt like there was a sign on my forehead. "Neurotic, pampered, high-strung bitch. Beware of the headache."

"Okie, dokie," he said carefully.

I closed my eyes, heard him start down the hallway.

◇◇◇

That night I snuggled up against him, making myself small against his bulk.

"Keith, do you think it's wrong to kill people?"

"What?" He shot up, clicked on the lamp on his night stand, and turned to me, his head braced in the palm of his hand. "Do you have anyone in particular in mind?"

"You're safe," I laughed. I propped my pillow up against the headboard and sat up.

"What's bothering you, Lottie?" he asked, gently stroking my hair.

"Nothing. Nothing, really. Well Zelda's murder, I guess. Do you think it's right to kill someone? I really want to know."

"Not murder. But self defense? Of course. Why would you ask? You have to know how I feel about that, from my service in Vietnam. I trained for it, even though I was in the medics."

"If someone came to this house and you thought he was going to kill us, you wouldn't think twice?"

"I'd do it in a heartbeat," he said flatly.

He turned out the light and reached for me, pulled me closer, closer. I clung to his warmth. His sure sense of right and wrong. Hearing him talk like this, there was no other possible conclusion. It was my own personal hurdle. There could be no room for hesitation. That much I did know. If I did carry a gun, I would have to be ready to use it.

Western Kansas was an arsenal already, I reasoned. Morally, what was the difference between owning a handgun or a shotgun or rifle, if you really would never be called on to use it anyway? I realized the same rationale could be used to justify a nuclear bomb.

By morning, at some tortured level between dreams and nightmares, I had decided. I was capable of killing another human being.

I couldn't, wouldn't kill a rabbit. But I could kill a person to protect someone's life. Besides, how often would I ever have to draw a gun? Some peace officers went their whole career and never did.

We had a gun dealer in town. I selected a Smith and Wesson Ladysmith. I walked into Sam's office with it two days later.

"Now, about my firearm training," I said.

◇◇◇

I pushed through the kitchen door lugging a storage box containing my new uniforms, booklets, files, nightstick, badge, and gun.

Keith sat at the island shuffling a deck of cards. He lifted his head, looked at me, looked away, rapidly shot the cards into a horizontal solitaire layout. When he flipped over the third card in the row, he turned up a joker.

"Figures," he said bleakly. He scooped up the cards, scanned the deck, removed the other joker and re-dealt.

I had expected temper, prepared myself. Keith's one bad habit. Farmers don't bother to control it. Who's to hear when they let 'er rip under acres of sky? Keeps them happy and ulcerless. However, gentlemen cuss things, not ladies, and Keith never used cruel words. Nevertheless, I expected him to tell me how he felt, loud and clear. Thrown by his gloom, I set my box on the floor.

"How did you hear?"

"Coffee shop."

"Oh Keith, I'm so sorry." I closed my eyes. "I wanted you to hear it from me."

"That's big of you," he snapped. "Did it ever occur to you to talk it over with me first?"

"Yes," I stammered. "But I thought…"

"You didn't think, you knew, knew it was an ignorant, short-sighted move. You knew I would hit the ceiling."

"I knew you'd try to stop me and this was my decision. It's about *my* life."

"No it isn't. This has to do with *our* marriage, not just your life."

The veins in his neck throbbed. He unclenched his fists, rubbed his palms together, studied his fingers.

"I feel by-passed, Lottie. Scuttled. Like you don't trust me."

Stricken with guilt, I could not think of one word to say in my defense.

He rose and started toward me. I expected him to enfold me and reassure me that we could work it out. Instead, he walked past me and didn't speak again until he was half-way up the stairs.

Turning, looking like an old man, his gaze was unwavering. "My life with Regina was miserable, you know that. You're a gift from God. A surprise, after I'd reconciled myself to living alone the rest of my life. I've lost one wife. I'm telling you, woman, I can't stand to lose another one."

It was the word "woman" that did it, though I knew it was an ancient country usage, for emphasis, not a slur.

"I'll be just fine. We'll be just fine," I yelled.

"Like shit," he said, and went up to bed.

Chapter Thirteen

"Sam, are these old cases still open?"

I had been eyeing the dusty, old file cabinet in the corner for the past three days but stuck to studying material on police procedures, knowing he wouldn't trust a woman who headed for the fun stuff right off. Volunteers were manning the historical society this week while I learned the ropes for my new job.

It was going well because I had sense enough to smile when he smoked. The material he had given me on interview techniques seemed familiar, as I used some of the same methods in recording oral history.

"Depends," he said. "No statute of limitations on murder. They're open but hopeless. About five of those in the last seventy-five years have never been solved. Some have had murky outcomes. Like the old Swenson murders."

"Swenson murders?"

"Swenson was the name of the family. Hideous thing. Old case. Happened when I was just a kid."

"Mind if I take a look?"

"Nope. In fact, you really should look at all those files. It will give you a good idea of some of the procedures we use in this county. Or don't use," he added gloomily.

"Can I work on them?"

"There's nothing to work on, Lottie. We're talking ancient history here."

Immediately, the wheels started turning. I wanted to have an active role in investigating Zelda's murder. So far, Sam was treating me like an intelligent, pampered, well-mannered guest. He clearly expected me to go away in a very short time. If I could find new information about an old, unsolved murder, my status would change.

I went to the drawer and found the Swenson folder. I poured a cup of coffee, carried it back to the rickety desk Sam scrounged up for me, and began to read.

Triple Murder in Gateway City

by
Valeria Comstock

OCTOBER 29, 1949. Last Thursday, the Herman Swenson residence was the scene of a bizarre tragedy that is still under investigation by Sheriff Andrew Morrow. His office released the following account of the crime:

Herman Swenson allegedly found his wife, Emily Swenson, murdered in her bed when he returned from a trip to Gateway City. He claims he was a day late getting home and spent Wednesday night by the side of the road after their Model A stalled in the dust storm ten miles from their house. He walked on in to his farmstead Thursday morning.

Swenson claims that upon discovering his wife's body, he rushed outside and began looking for his seven-year-old son, Johnny. When his son did not reply, Swenson went back inside the house and phoned Sheriff Morrow. According to Swenson, the earpiece to the phone was dangling when he got home, indicating that Mrs. Swenson had tried to call out at some time. Sheriff Morrow reports that no one on their party line could call out Wednesday due to downed lines. The line had been repaired early that morning. Sheriff

Morrow went to the farm at once, accompanied by the county coroner, John Babbitt.

Coroner Babbitt reported that although Mrs. Swenson died of strangulation, she was in childbirth.

Sheriff Morrow found Johnny Swenson dead in a well in back of the house. The whereabouts of the baby's body is unknown.

Herman Swenson has been charged with the murder of all three. Dr. Henry McVey has said that Swenson has been in a state of deep shock from the time his son's body was located by the authorities.

"How could it have happened?" I blurted the words, not caring about sounding unprofessional. I looked at Sam.

"We don't know," he said. "No one ever knew, and no one understood it, either. He had always seemed as normal as apple pie. But it was after the war. He was losing his farm, taking it hard, because all around him folks were doing better."

"You said this was one of the murky ones. Why?"

"Herman never owned up to it. Said he didn't do it. Then he was crazy out of his mind for so long no one would have believed him anyway. But it's always bothered me that he never owned up to it. I was a kid at the time, but when I was elected sheriff and got to looking at it, there were some things that didn't seem right. Never have."

"Such as?"

"Can't see where they looked for much of anyone else. 'No need,' they said. Herman was already half-crazy with worry over the farm. In fact, that's why he had gone to town so close to Emily's time. He had talked to the banker, trying to keep them from foreclosing. Didn't work. They were coming Monday morning, anyway. Going to take everything he had. Common knowledge at the time. They figured he snapped. Tried to keep Emily and Johnny and the baby from an even harder life than they already had."

"But you weren't satisfied with this account?"

"Nope. Wasn't then, and I'm not now. Read on."

I opened the manila envelope containing the official police report and pulled up the photos. The hair on my arms rose. I ran for the bathroom and threw up. I marched back out. Not looking Sam in the eye, I grabbed my purse, went back to the laboratory, pulled out my cosmetic bag, gargled Listerine, squared my shoulders. Then I went back to the table and picked up the photos. I risked a quick look at Sam who was disguising a bleak smile with a pull on his pipe.

"Her belly was slit open," I said. "The paper just says 'in childbirth.'"

"Yes. Like a hog being butchered. It was different back then," he said. "We figured the press didn't need to know everything. The *Gateway Gazette* just called Sheriff Morrow for information and he sort of cleaned things up. According to the coroner she was strangled first."

"The mutilation wasn't in the paper," I said.

"No. A lot of folks knew about it. But they didn't print every gory little detail like they do now. They had some respect for families and for cops trying to do their job."

"What would drive a man to do this?" I stared at the yellowed hand-written report.

"Everything I've heard about Herman tells me that he couldn't have, wouldn't have done this," Sam said flatly.

"Where is Herman Swenson buried?"

He smiled. "In the nursing home."

"He's still alive?"

Sam snorted. "If you can call it that. He had a stroke ten years ago. Been at Sunny Rest ever since."

"Can I see him?" I asked eagerly. "Do you mind?"

"Won't do no good. He can't talk. Can't think. And no, I don't mind."

"But before I see him, since we don't have a microfilm reader here, I'm going back to the historical society and look at old newspapers."

"Everything that's ever been written about it is in that file."

"That's not the kind of thing I'm looking for."

◇◇◇

Back at the office, I dug out microfilm of early Carlton County newspapers and located birth announcements for Herman Swenson and Emily Champlin.

There's an art to reading newspapers. It's dependent on intuition and open-mindedness. The scholarly analysis comes later, but in the beginning, I Zen it, making connections I wouldn't notice if I began with preconceived ideas.

This initial research is a mystical process. Some mornings when there is a certain slant of light and if I'm not interrupted, it's as though I step into the past. I'm there, living the time, wearing the clothes, eating the food, breathing the air.

Herman was three years older than Emily, born in 1921. Just to be on the safe side, I started reading back issues of the *Gateway Gazette* well before his birth.

There was nothing that caught my eyes about Herman's parents. Back then, local news columns reported everything. No detail of anyone's life was sacred. A couple of months after Herman's birth, another name caught my eye. A Rebecca Champlin had been born September 24, 1921, to the same parents as Emily Champlin.

So. Emily had had an older sister.

Chapter Fourteen

I started a new file, printed off Herman and Emily's birth announcements, copied the story written by Valeria Comstock, and the police report, which I had assured Sam would be for my eyes only as I'd wanted one for cross-checking.

I reread Comstock's account, then I pulled the earlier reel of microfilm off the machine and rethreaded it with the film from 1949.

Swenson Murder

November 2, 1949. Citizens of Gateway City gathered Wednesday for the funeral services of Emily Champlin Swenson and her son, John Sinclair Swenson. Although heavily attended by friends and neighbors in the community, the husband and father, Herman Swenson, was absent as he is still under psychiatric observation in the Osawatomie Mental Institution.

The only family in attendance was Rebecca Champlin, Mrs. Swenson's sister, who had been out of town during this grim ordeal and, alas, had returned to find her only sibling and her adored nephew murdered by her own brother-in-law.

When interviewed by this reporter, Miss Rebecca stated that she could not bear to live in this county a second longer. Heavily veiled and faint from the strain of burying her beloved sister, Miss Champlin requested that her neighbors grant her a measure of privacy while she put her affairs in order.

"I'm leaving," she declared. "I do not have the heart to live here where I will constantly be reminded of my sister's death."

Miss Champlin put her farm and land up for sale the day after the service. The auction will be combined with the sheriff's sale of the Swenson land and property on September 12, as the two properties are side by side. The Swenson auction will be held in the morning and the Champlin Auction in the afternoon. Miss Champlin's land is located just down the road from the Swenson homestead.

As of this writing, the police have not been able to break Herman Swenson's refusal to disclose the whereabouts of the baby's body.

There would have been no laws to protect this man back then. No Miranda rights read. Damn sure no CSI teams. I checked the police report. As Sam said, they never looked for anyone else.

My mind buzzed with unanswered questions. Had Rebecca Champlin ever married? Been courted? Loved? If not, why not? Why were there no parents mentioned at the funeral in Comstock's story? Were both sets of parents dead?

I forwarded two weeks to the sale bills. Rebecca's notice featured a prosperous homestead. Herman's displayed the devastating cruelty of sheriff sales from a time when every county had a Poor Commissioner and a literal Poor Farm. A time when every last penny paid to each person from the Poor Fund was listed in the paper with their name and dollar amount: Such staggering sums as $1.30 or $1.52 per month.

A sheriff's sale listed and described every single item a family owned. He counted each fence post, pot or pan, dish towel, toy, wash tub, harness, tool, canning jar, knife, and spoon. The Swenson's contained an entire separate column for needlework: embroidered and crocheted linens and towels, tablecloths, and bedspreads.

Rebecca's billing listed prime cattle, sleek horses, mahogany furniture. All the trappings of a flourishing and well-appointed farmstead.

In fair weather, the dual sale would have been well attended. I made a note to check historic weather records although I knew the intrepid and gossipy Valeria Comstock would surely comment. I forwarded to the day following the sale. Valeria gushed over the amounts paid for Rebecca's possessions, but she stated Miss Champlin had declined an interview.

She had managed to get a photo, however. Like most of the women in the background, Rebecca wore club-heeled, laced shoes. The neighboring women were in rayon prints; she was in full formal mourning, heavy veil and all.

A week later, there was another article, which answered one of my questions. Herman's parents were alive.

"My boy didn't do it," swears Albert Swenson. "He's a good boy. He loved his wife and son."

According to Comstock, Sheriff Morrow had telegraphed Swenson's family in California, immediately following the murders. They had moved there in 1930 after the stock market crash.

My eyes burned. Why had they moved? Why was Herman Swenson still living in Carlton County after his parents moved to California? One account of the Swenson murder referred to the Old Champlin estate. Emily's parents. Had Herman married into money? Did his parents lose money in the crash? Why was he farming Emily's parents' land?

I stopped and rubbed the muscles in my neck. They ached miserably and it would be impossible to read all the papers from 1920 on in one day. But the questions kept buzzing. Deciding I wasn't starting early enough yet, I stopped, put a sign on the door that I would be back in twenty minutes, and ran up the stairs to see Minerva.

She glanced up from her computer.

"Can you wait a minute, Lottie? I'm just a couple of minutes away from finishing this spreadsheet."

"Sure." I glanced around her Spartan office. Women held most of the courthouse positions. Family photos and sunny little mottos plastered their walls and bulletin boards, forming an odd collage with the obligatory government posters.

Minerva's office was strictly utilitarian, the domicile of a lady who knew how to work efficiently. The county commissioners were crazy about her because she ran a cheap office. High level computer skills, one permanent part-time assistant and a couple of ladies who pitched in during busy times. The whole county teems with computer nerds as bankers love to see farmers adopt management software.

Due to Minerva's expertise and the sheer volume of her specialized entries, I often depended on her to do a search. Margaret Atkinson said Minerva managed to wheedle the latest and greatest technology out of the county budget because of her willingness to act as a kind of mini-trainer for other departments.

I owned my office computer personally, of course, as well as the Nikon camera I used and all of the other electronic equipment. What the county commissioners furnished me was light and heat and a hard time.

"Done," Minerva said.

"I need to know the marriage dates of two couples," I said. "Old, old marriages. Does your information go back to year 1890?"

Clogs clattered on the marble stairs before she had a chance to answer. Judy St. John came through the door. "Hi, Lottie. Inez said she saw you heading up here. She told me all about your moonlighting too."

"Moonlighting?" Minerva asked.

"You mean you haven't heard? I thought everyone in town knew. Lottie's our newest deputy sheriff. Our own Annie Oakley."

My mouth quirked into a self-conscious smile. Somehow, seeing myself through their eyes, it couldn't have seemed more bizarre than if someone had announced my intention to become a rock star. Half the town would die laughing.

"So whatcha up to?" Judy tried to peer at the papers I was holding, but I shielded them with my hand.

"The old Swenson murder, actually," I mumbled.

"So this information you're after now, is it official business? As a deputy?" Minerva asked, her voice suddenly stiff.

"Of course not," I said. "Well, maybe in a way. I wanted to see if I can find some new information for Sam Abbott."

"Doesn't make any difference why you want it, I guess," Minerva said. "It's all public record, and you're entitled to see it. Your reasons are really nobody's business. Just give me a minute."

She typed in the maiden name of Herman's mother and his father's name, retrieved the date of that couple's marriage and then did the same for Emily and Rebecca Champlin's parents. Both marriages were scandal-free, taking place well before the birth of children.

Minerva handed me my printout and I walked downstairs with Judy. My problem child. Obviously, she had meant it literally when she'd said she was going to help me.

"I've been going through some of Mom's things, and I came across a note written less than six weeks ago."

"How do you know that?"

"It was written on the back on an envelope. I'm going by the postmark. It's a list of things that don't make sense, but Fiona's name is on it."

"Okay, Judy, but things have changed now. Changed a lot."

"Changed how?"

"I'm a deputy now," I said sternly. "An officer of the law. New rules." I inhaled deeply. "What I mean to say is, you can't help, can't ask questions. Can't nothing."

She stopped midway down the stairs. "But I took off work, Lottie. For two whole weeks. And it didn't set well with my boss."

"Judy, this is not my rule. Not my call. I'm under strict standards for confidentiality, and until the new wears off of me being a deputy, half the town is going to be watching every move I make."

I'm embarrassed by persons who can't hide their feelings just a little. Tears quivered in her sensitive blue eyes. "I want to help, Lottie. Help find the person who murdered my mother."

Chapter Fifteen

We rounded the corner of the staircase and I stopped dead. The door to my office was open. I knew I had locked up. My key was in my pocket. I peered through the door. There sat William. His hands rested on his bony knees, and he skewered me with his eyes.

"Knocked. No answer. Knew no one was manning the fort," he said sharply. "Called Margaret. She came down and let me in. She called around for you. We couldn't imagine where you'd gone. Then we heard about your new job, and we figured you was gallavanting around sheriffing. She like to had a fit, of course, because you weren't here working on the books. Sam Abbott said you was looking into old murders. Doesn't take a rocket scientist to figure out which one. Sounds important. Murder. Got a nice ring to it. Old murders. But your job is here. You had this one first. Looks bad to have this place closed in the middle of the day. Looks bad. Is bad. No doubt about it."

"Well, I'm back now, and I *intend* to put this job first. You needn't trouble yourself with 'manning the fort' any longer."

I looked pointedly at the growing pile of cedar shavings at his feet. He stood, and I marched over to the whisk broom and dust pan I had hanging on a nail on the back wall. He tugged at the front of his old fedora.

"No trouble," he said. "Part of my duties as a member of the board of directors. Old word, duty. Don't hear it much nowadays."

"I've heard the word before, William. I know what it means. For your information, this is only the third time I can remember when this place has been closed in the middle of the day. Three times! We're open year in, year out. If I'm not here, I always have a volunteer here. I wasn't gone over twenty minutes." I stopped myself before I added that for this faithfulness I was paid a paltry, laughable eight dollars an hour and that was only so the county could have matching funds from the state.

"Three times is three times. Old word, duty. Like I said, not many even know what it means." He walked away then paused in the doorway. "You had a call. From the Hadleys. Said you'd probably call back. If you ever showed back up, that is."

Josie, sometimes. My mother, often. William, always. The only people who could turn me into a snarling wolverine. But William was the only one who did it on purpose, and he had to work at it, as I prided myself on self-control. Surely, he studied ways to get me. Stayed up nights dreaming up the right words.

"I can help, Lottie," Judy said eagerly. "Let me be here. Why not? You're going to be…"

"Gallavanting around sheriffing?"

"Whatever." She blinked rapidly. "There will be things here I can do, and it would help me. Right now, I'm just a reception-ist. Think what it would mean to me to be able to show a few research skills on my resumé. Like it would move me clear up to a whole new level. Please?"

She was wearing me down. I had to have reliable help at the historical society whenever I worked for Sam. But would Judy be the right person?

"I'll be out of your hair and back at my real job in a couple of weeks. With me helping, you could really concentrate on finding Mom's murderer. Please?"

I recalled her insistence on seeing the original story her mother had written, her noticing the shadow of a rose on back of the page. She paid attention to detail.

"Okay. I can't ask William or Margaret or any of the other volunteers to be here every day. But there are going to be ground rules, Judy. You break a single one, and you're outta here. Got that?"

She nodded eagerly.

"First off, just because you see it, just because you know it, doesn't mean you have to say it. In fact, I could tell people things about their families they don't know and don't need to know."

"You think I don't understand *that*?" Her eyes clouded. "You don't think I wouldn't have given my left breast if this town had shown me a little compassion when I needed it? Do you know what I would have given not to be torn down, gossiped about. Ripped to shreds?"

I knew then how good she would be. Hard times can work both ways.

"Deal." I stuck out my hand, changing her from pest to employee. "I want you here every day. On time."

"No problem," she said, her face transformed with joy.

"You know the importance of keeping your mouth shut. The old Swenson murder is a good example. It's all over town now that I'm working on it for Sam Abbott. The walls have ears in this courthouse. This is the last time that people will know about anything connected with the Sheriff's office through the historical society office, unless it really overlaps. I've got to keep the two jobs separate."

"You can trust me, I swear."

"Can you type?"

"Sure."

"Use a computer? Do you know Microsoft Office?"

"You bet."

"Okay. Then you can enter information on Access. Mainly you'll answer the phone. As to the mail, just sort it. Don't open it. I'll take care of that when I'm in. Don't retrieve phone messages either. Once in a while there's things intended for only my eyes and ears." I glanced at my watch. "Eleven o'clock, and I haven't even started on my column for the county paper yet. If you don't mind a tight fit I'll set my laptop on a card table and you can enter old school records."

For the next few minutes we were busy arranging the room.

"This is going to be a good deal for both of us, Judy." *Perfect, in fact.* What better way to keep her under control than having her right beside me every day? "Now, I'd better return the Hadleys' call."

"Brian? I didn't know you were home. I was expecting Fiona or Edgar to answer. I thought you were back in Wichita."

"We have a favor to ask, Lottie. Mom has a story, a submission, ready for your book and we wondered if you could come to the house and pick it up?"

"Well…" I stammered.

"My fault, Lottie. Not Mom's. I just don't want to be seen in town. I can't stand the thought of one more reporter asking me a question. There's got to be somewhere, *somewhere* on this planet, where I can have a moment's peace."

"Of course, Brian. I do understand." *As long as Fiona isn't planning an attack.*

"Can you come over today?"

"Uh, yes."

I looked wistfully at my microfilm machine. Now that I had all the copies of the Swenson/Champlin birth announcements, marriage licenses, and death certificates I wanted to research from 1920 forward. I sighed. It would wait.

I looked gratefully at my new assistant. "In fact, I can come right away."

◇◇◇

On the drive over, I tried to zero in on a topic for my column. I loved doing it. Kept short and peppy, with short quiz's about Carlton County history, the column informed people about the book's progress and coaxed them to write stories. My readers didn't hesitate to set me straight from time to time.

Once I had a column entitled "Tiny Babies," challenging the notion of premature babies born in dug-outs or soddies who lived before the days of incubators. I was flooded with accounts of babies kept in shoe boxes on top of the stove or strapped next to their mother's bodies. After I received proof of a baby born in a soddy whose arm could be slipped through her mother's wedding ring, I changed my mind. In fact, I was preparing a journal article based on just this subject.

I caught sight of the Hadley's massive Tudor house. Edgar owned seven sections of land, which was a God's plenty by anyone's standards.

A white, three-board fence ran along the road on either side of the lane leading to the house. In Western Kansas this is a strikingly silly arrangement if you don't have horses. Unless, of course, you are trying to impress folks, which the Hadleys usually were. Such fences weren't nearly as good as barbed wire for containing cattle, and electrical fences did a better job of keeping out people.

When Brian got serious about politics, the barbed wire came down and the white boards went up.

No amount of finagling on Fiona's part, however, could concoct a tree in proportion to their house, although she had given it her best shot. The massive balled oaks trucked in and planted by the most skilled nursery people in Denver, died, defeated by our unpredictable weather. Mostly, they froze out before they took root.

Our house is bordered on three sides by our cedar windbreak, and our trees are cottonwoods, which can't be fooled by Mother Nature. Uncannily wise, they lay dormant through false springs. They bloom heartily and late and shed leaves early in the fall. They break easily and grow at crazy angles. Landscape artists hate them. I like them because they live.

I turned up the lane. The Hadley house sprawled. Ideal for Fiona's elaborate parties, with broken, steeply sloped roof lines and an array of dormers, it fit in quite well with the larger farm houses in the area. The foyer was set in a round, two-story brick turret.

I was now close enough to see Brian's wife in the backyard playing catch with their two sons. Jenny Hadley was miserably unhappy with political life. We decided early on to keep her in the background.

Fiona had ruined Jenny's chances of being an asset to her husband at the beginning of his career. Because Fiona didn't think the real Jenny was good enough, she had "helped" the poor woman come up with a public image and settled on Jackie O. Inspired, no doubt, by Jenny's wide-set eyes and dark hair. The press jeered at her fake whisper and avowed love of fine arts. Fiona backed off. The only part of Jacqueline Kennedy's persona that actually modeled Jenny was her daughter-in-law's genuine love of home and children.

She waved when she saw me but stayed outside with little Troy and Eric. Brian answered the door at the first ring.

"Lottie, good to see you. Mom, Lottie's here."

She ushered me in with a dazzling smile. "Good to see you, Lottie. Let's go into the living room where we can be comfortable."

No one would be very comfortable in Fiona's living room, but I went along with the charade.

"Tea? Coffee?" she asked, the epitome of Miss Manners.

"Coffee. Black, please."

She returned with a handsome silver Georgian tea set and placed it on the coffee table. Although everyone knew her living room had been "done" by a decorator from Denver, Fiona could have done as well on her own. She had that kind of eye. The room was formal, lovely in elegant brocades and velvet, accented with fine antiques. Hard to imagine kicking back with a good book in that room.

I waited. Something was coming.

Chapter Sixteen

"I must confess, Lottie. I asked Brian to lure you out here on a pretext." With a winning smile, she leaned forward, her hands earnestly clasped on her lap.

"I want to apologize for my disgraceful conduct this last couple of weeks. I'm ashamed of the things I've said and done."

"Of course, I accept your apology."

"In fact, when I was trying to put my thoughts down on paper I realized how hard it is to relate memories properly. But I'm done now." She reached for a folder on the end table and handed it to me.

"Here. I do hope you approve."

"I'm sure whatever you've written will be just fine."

I opened it, scanned the first page, and knew at once it had been pulled together by Brian's main speech writer. "I'll read it thoroughly when I get back to the office and let you know if I have any questions."

"Now that Brian has had this little chat with me, I just wish you still had Zelda's story for your archives."

My stomach soured immediately. The whole town knew about the missing documents. Persons I barely knew stopped me on the street to ask about their disappearance.

"Of course, I hold more enlightened views, but I could just weep when I think there's not a trace of the last thing my darling Zelda ever wrote."

I looked at her steadily, but she didn't blink. She had the unflappable calmness of the practiced liar. There was a copy of Zelda's story, of course. The one Josie had taken for the handwriting analysis.

I glanced at my watch. "Nearly noon. I should be getting back."

"Won't you stay for lunch, Lottie? Such a beautiful day. We could eat on the patio. I've got a nice chef's salad and good bread. Edgar should be getting in soon. You usually close over lunch, anyway, don't you?"

"Yes, I usually do. I'll call Judy and tell her to lock up so she can go eat. But she doesn't have a key to the padlock, so I need to be back at one to open again."

"Judy?"

"Your niece. Judy St. John. She's my new assistant."

"Oh, I wish you wouldn't do that." Fiona's voice dropped a full octave, taking on a strange, harsh tone. "Not because of the things, the terrible things, she's accused me of with Zelda's death. That's over now, though the shock of it nearly killed me. But because she's not well, Lottie. She's half crazy most of the time. I can't imagine what you could possibly be thinking of."

Brian rose from his chair and moved toward Fiona.

"She didn't see Zelda's story did she? She's a vicious little snoop, just like her mother. Her mother, who dared to sneak into my house while I was gone and go through my things, my precious things."

"That's enough, Fiona."

We all turned. Edgar carried the authority of a hen-pecked man who finally speaks out. It is always startling. "Zelda didn't sneak. I let her in myself. She wanted to check some facts for Lottie's book and look at the old miniature of your grandmother. I told her the stuff was probably in a trunk in the attic. Couldn't see no harm in it. She's a Rubidoux, too. She had a right to see it."

"So that's how she got in," Fiona gasped. "She just walked right in the front door, bigger than life. No sneak to it. And you were probably so busy pecking away at your blasted computer the whole Russian Army could have marched right past your door. So it was you, Edgar. You who started this whole thing."

"I don't know what you're talking about."

"You fool, you stupid fool." The skin around Fiona's lips was tight and white, her lips the color of old liver. "Why don't you think? Why don't you ever think? I keep everything that's sacred in that trunk. Why do I always have to do the thinking for us both?"

He glared, jutted his jaw, then started, as though a deeper meaning had just struck him. His face contorted, and he clenched his fists.

"It's gone far enough. Far enough, I tell you."

He slammed out the back door. We heard his junky old pickup start, the steady unmuffled pop of the ancient engine, and minutes later, he roared out of the driveway.

Brian and I looked at one another helplessly. There is no formula for redeeming this kind of situation. No way to make people feel comfortable. I did know it would be a good idea to make a hasty retreat.

"I'm so sorry. We all have times we wish we could keep strictly within our family. Let's have lunch another time, Fiona, when conditions are a bit different." I couldn't have sounded grander.

"I want her gone," said Fiona.

She was looking far off, and the hair rose on my arms. Her eyes were blank, and she didn't seem to see me. Didn't seem to have heard my exquisitely tactful speech.

"You have no business bringing a jailbird in where she can see some of the most sensitive records in this county."

"Judy will be just fine, Mother," Brian said. "I think she cares a lot about people's privacy. I don't know what's behind this crazy vendetta. I don't know what's gotten into you. Judy's lost her mother, and she needs a little kindness."

The words were strong, and what Fiona would not have taken from me she took quite well from her son. She shook her head as though she were coming out of a trance, her mouth quivering with humiliation.

"Lottie, I don't mean to sound like a shrew. It's just that it's been such a shock, such an incredible shock. I've lost Zelda. Then Judy turning on me like she did. I just can't believe it all happened."

"I think it will be good for Judy to be back in this county a while," I said. "Max needs her."

"She's a very fragile person, Lottie. That's what I'm trying to tell you. Very fragile and very unstable. I think you're making a big mistake. A very big mistake."

"I don't think so," I said easily. "Now that I'm trying to cover two jobs, I need someone at the office who really wants to be there."

They both looked at me blankly.

"Now don't tell me you two are the only ones in town who haven't heard about my new job?"

"Another one?" Brian laughed. "Trying to set a record for the number of hats you can wear?"

I laughed. "I'm Sam Abbott's newest deputy."

"Why would a smart woman like you want to do a stupid goddamn thing like that?" All traces of the Southern belle had vanished from Fiona's voice.

"Mom!" Brian reached for her arm, but Fiona twisted away angrily. "That's enough."

"I didn't come here to be insulted, Fiona." Deciding quickly I didn't owe her or anyone else in town an explanation for hiring Judy St. John or working with Sam Abbott, I turned and started toward the door.

She followed. "I'll not have a rank amateur, an outsider who never should have come to this town to begin with, investigating my only sister's murder and agitating my darling niece."

Suddenly, I lost all trace of anger. I think it was the "darling niece" that did it. Profoundly aware that Fiona had been through three, maybe four, complete mood swings in fifteen minutes, I knew something was very wrong.

"Mother." Brian's voice was as sharp as a slap. I turned to face them both, my mind racing. "I want to talk to Lottie in private. Will you come into the den with me?"

I nodded. Fiona left. I heard her click through the kitchen and out the back door.

Chapter Seventeen

Brian led me through the house to a combination den-library dominated by an enormous mahogany desk.

"Drink, Lottie?"

"No, thank you."

"Mind if I do?" He went to a hinged panel in a bookcase that opened to a fine collection of liquors in cut glass bottles. His hands trembled as he reached for a decanter of bourbon. He poured a stiff shot, tossed it back.

"I've got to decide what to do about my mother."

I nodded, and glanced at my watch. "I've got to call Judy." I reached for my cell, then remembered it was on the car charger. "Whoops. Do you mind?" I gestured toward the phone on his desk.

"Go right ahead." He paced back and forth like a jungle cat in a zoo.

I asked Judy to stay in the office until I got back and said I would bring her a sandwich from Bertha's Deli. I watched Brian as I talked. He looked terrible, incredibly weary with dull eyes and that still sallow skin.

"She's crazy," he said, the moment I hung up.

I sat down in one of the leather arm chairs. "The problem with your mother is that she's not crazy *enough,* or there would be plenty of things we could do."

He smiled ruefully. "She's about to do me in."

"After seeing her, hearing her today, I'm seeing Fiona in a different light."

"I don't want to hurt her. Most of what's good about me, most of what's put me ahead of the pack, has come from my mother. Not that I don't love and admire my father. But he's a…"

"Plodder?" I suggested gently.

"Yes, a plodder. Feet on the ground. It's Mom's side of the family, the Rubidoux, who have meant everything to me. I've always loved those people. The stories, the sacrifices. I'm prouder to be a Rubidoux than words can express. They're my blood, and to have Mom show all their worst traits is about to kill me. Not that there's *not* plenty of skeletons in our family closet. But we're heroic people. There's been a Rubidoux in every single war this country has ever fought."

"Brian, I've been dreading this moment, but I've got to ask. Is there any way Fiona could have been involved in Zelda's murder? I'm asking you as your friend and as your county campaign manager."

"No," he said flatly. Coldly. He looked at me steadily. "Absolutely not. I was here that evening. Here with Mother."

"And I didn't know? My God, Brian, I'm your campaign manager out here. Why didn't someone tell me? I thought you were in Wichita."

"I wasn't. The press reported that we arrived the next day, but I had been home for three days. It was just Jenny and the kids who drove up from Wichita the morning when we all went to the St. Johns and Judy threw her famous hissy fit."

"Your parents alibied for each other in the very beginning, of course, but I wish you had told Sam you were here, too. It lends credibility if it's not just husband and wife vouching for each other's whereabouts."

"You can ask me what you just asked as a friend, Lottie." His eyes studied me as he mouthed an ice cube. "But you can't ask me as an officer of the court. You left out the Miranda warning."

"You honestly think I should have gone into the 'you have a right to remain silent' bit?"

He didn't smile. "If this is official."

"It's not official. You called *me* to come out here, remember? Brian, are you all right? Is something else wrong?"

He rose, poured another shot of bourbon, slowly turned the cut glass tumbler in the sunlight as it flashed rainbow prisms of light.

"No," he said finally. "Actually, I'm not. I'm under so much strain right now I'm about to lose it. I know this, Jenny knows this." He downed the whiskey, set the glass on the end table beside him, and ran his hands through his hair.

"Health problems? Marriage problems? Family problems besides Fiona? What, Brian? I have to know if we are going to get you elected. Better me, now, than the press later."

"I know that." He spoke so softly I strained to hear the words. "I'm terrified that what is wrong with my mother is the early onset of Alzheimer's. It would ruin me, I can promise you."

"But that's so common! That shouldn't..."

"Shouldn't? You can't be that naïve! The reality is that every single statistic any quack has ever produced on its hereditary aspects is going to be dragged out, printed, talked about. You know what my opponent is like. The press circles like buzzards. Thanks to the murder, I can't even get decent treatment for my own mother without them video-taping every visit to every doctor."

I was stunned, but it made sense. It would account for Fiona's erratic behavior, the unpredictability of her moods. My heart sank. Brian was right. Senators stayed in office a long time. If the disease were present in the mother in her sixties, the media would look for the same tendency in the son. He had to look ahead.

"Brian, my twin sister, Josie, is a psychologist. We could count on her complete discretion in arranging total medical testing. She would understand everything."

He looked at me with mute gratitude.

"That would be wonderful. Not doing right by Mom is killing me. What kind of son am I, putting my career before my mother's health?"

"It's not you, Brian. It's the media. How many good men aren't running for office because of this kind of scrutiny? You've worked so hard. So terribly hard."

"And my wife. People don't realize the toll this campaign has taken on Jenny. She's shy. She hates the whole charade. It's ironic that Mom just loves politics and she might be the one who brings us all down."

◇◇◇

When I walked into the office, Judy pointed proudly to a new stack of Rolodex cards.

"You've done all that?"

I had left her with a whole stack of early school records. We make hard copies of everything, and these cross-indexed cards were the delight of the growing number of genealogy sleuths who found their way into our office. I picked up the first one. It was correctly formatted and printed.

"This is super, Judy. Flawless, in fact."

Her huge blue eyes shone before she lowered them and studied the ties on her shoes as though they were of intense interest.

Then I, who normally weighed words and actions as carefully as blind justice, surprised myself and made a very impulsive decision. One I would come to regret so profoundly it would haunt me the rest of my life.

"Would you like to work here, Judy? For me, I mean? Full-time, as my assistant?"

It was my right. I could hire anyone I wanted to, pay her anything I liked out of my own pocket. I needed her. Needed someone I could trust to run the office when I worked for Sam.

I turned away, burdened by her vulnerability, unable to stand her sudden bright joy. Her trust. Trust, that most fragile of all emotions, which seems to rise pitifully, again and again, in some persons. Never mind what's said about the strength of love and hope. It is the constant emergence of trust, with its accompanying cycle of betrayal, that breaks our hearts.

"The same rules apply in triplicate," I said, turning to face her again. "Keep your mouth shut and remember I'm running the show, not you. All mail, all stories are to be opened by me. And don't listen to messages."

She nodded, but she clearly had not heard a word since I asked her to work for me.

"I want to call Dad," she sniffed. Then she grinned. "And my boss. My former boss."

She placed her hands together between her knees and squeezed as though she had to keep herself from shooting off the chair.

"I'll get to be with Dad from now on," she said. "We'll have each other. We won't have Mom, but we'll have each other."

I smiled, and she flew over to the phone. I left the room to give her some privacy. When I came back, she had resumed work on the school records.

"It's going to be crowded in here. Until I have time to come up with a permanent place for you, I'll set up a spot where you can plop down with my lap-top. But, I don't have time to reorganize today. I have to get cracking on my column."

I hadn't settled on a subject and although I wanted to get back to reading microfilm, the column for the *Gateway Gazette* had to come first. Our county newspaper had started in the 1880s, survived the depression years, and was still going in the twenty-first century. One thing that never changed was its dependency on local organizations for news.

"Any mail?"

"I put it on your desk."

I sorted it quickly. There were two requests for family information. I rose and went to the Rolodex, then realized this was a job my new assistant could handle. It was a good feeling.

I opened a letter with an Iowa postmark. It was printed on plain white copy paper with no date, no heading.

> What if you don't have fancy family records? What if your family isn't important enough to be in the book?

Two sentences. That was all. No date, no signature, no closing. How did the sender expect me to reply? I date-stamped it
and put it and the envelope in the correspondence file. Inspired,
I knew what this week's column would be about.

Who's Who?

You don't have to <u>be</u> somebody to submit a family
story to the Carlton County History Book. All that
"counts" as a qualification is that Carlton County affected
you or your family's life in some way. We don't care if
you're living on welfare or have lived here only six weeks.
Write about your experiences in Carlton County.

I went on in that vein for another two pages and made an
appeal for articles in addition to family stories. I was certain
that whoever had sent the letter read the *Gateway Gazette*. We
receive many out-of-state submissions from persons who moved
away years ago and still subscribe to the local paper. I sent Judy
to the newspaper office with the finished column.

It was three o' clock before I got back to my microfilm. It's
often difficult to get a handle on a family's finances. Even so, I
found clear evidence that both the Champlins and the Swensons
were quite prosperous. Emily's and Rebecca's parents farmed and
the Swensons were bankers.

I knew Emily's father had been a good farmer because of the
social notices. He had been to this or that sale, bought a horse,
sold a cow, picked up a load of lumber.

The Champlins had attended a wedding, and at that time, every
single gift was printed in the paper. They had given the bride and
groom a complete set of sad irons, including the one for ironing
ruffles. They were made of cast iron, heated on coal-fired kitchen
stoves, and lugged back to the ironing board. The largest iron
weighed five pounds. A whole set was considered extravagant.

The Swensons were equally busy. Mr. Swenson attended
banking meetings, and Herman's mother was president of the
Ladies Tuesday Study Club. I watched for any references to

illness, as the social column always reported trips to doctors or specialists. No quarrels with neighbors or merchants were mentioned.

The clock chimed. Reluctantly, I stopped working. The commissioners didn't like anyone in the courthouse after hours. It was a good policy, but I looked longingly at the film.

◇◇◇

At home, there were two messages waiting for me on my answering machine; one from the library informing me a book was in through interlibrary loan, and one from Bettina.

"Lottie, Dad called this morning and told me about your new job. He doubted you would be home for Opening Day this year. He said you would probably be on duty for the sheriff's department that weekend. Call me. We need to know."

The opening day of pheasant season was our high holy day. A family ritual. All of Keith's children came home and a number of their old friends. Nothing interfered with this ingathering. It had evolved into more of a mini blue grass festival than a dedicated hunt. Managing meals, housing the hordes of people, involved hours of work. Hours I'd had available, before I acquired my badge.

Chagrined, I realized what Keith had meant when he said my decision to become a deputy affected our marriage, our family, not just me. Of course, Sam would expect me to work that weekend. Hunters descended on our little town like a swarm of locust. I had associated law enforcement with sleuthing and high crimes. Exciting work, not parking a bunch of cars at a pancake feed.

I will work this out, I thought grimly. I didn't know how, but I would. Nevertheless, my stomach tightened.

Sam would see me as a dabbler if I refused to do routine chores. Keith would be heartbroken if we didn't honor Opening Day.

I deliberately called Bettina at home, knowing I would get her answering machine. "Of course I'll be here for Opening Day. Nothing has changed."

Chapter Eighteen

Judy was waiting outside the door the next morning.

"Aren't you the early bird?"

"I do have a few virtues."

"More than a few," I said, slipping the key into the padlock. "I'm going to read microfilm all day and turn nearly everything else over to you."

She grinned.

I hung up my jacket and started reading where I had left off the day before.

Finally I came across something new. The Champlins had lost an infant son when he was three months old. There were just two sisters. No male heir to the land.

After a period of years, the *Gateway City Gazette* started mentioning Rebecca and Emily and Herman as individuals:

> "Miss Emily Champlin gave a recitation at the last day of school exercise, 'Oh Captain, My Captain.'"

> "Herman Swenson received a five year pin for Sunday School attendance at the Presbyterian Church."

Five years indicated excellent health and parents who cared about his moral development. The Presbyterian Church was mainstream. Herman wouldn't have been burdened with defending its doctrine.

"Miss Rebecca Champlin played a piano solo at Miss Emma Lou Bascombe's recital."

Normal, happy, included children. There was a handkerchief shower for Rebecca on her twelfth birthday. I made a note to look up their school records and grade cards later.

I found all their names on grade school commencement lists. Then Herman began to emerge as a splendid athlete. There were pictures of him on the football team in high school. He cut a dashing figure. The girls' regularly won prizes at the county fair. Both were expert needlewomen. One year, Rebecca would have an exhibit labeled best of show, and the next year Emily would take the grand prize. They were clearly neck and neck in a number of categories.

Then I spotted a surprising item. Miss Rebecca Champlin and Mr. Herman Swenson were dinner guests at the Laurence Adams residence one summer evening.

Rebecca and Herman.

Not Emily and Herman.

No parents were mentioned at the dinner, so it would have been a date. I found one more reference to Herman and Rebecca as a couple, stopped scanning, and began to read very carefully.

Miss Emily Champlin proceeded to Normal School where she would acquire a teaching certificate. Thinking I had missed something, I searched for information about Rebecca's plans, but I couldn't find anything. I zeroed in on the list of fair prizes again and was glad I had gone back. Instead of the girls sharing all the prizes, I found only Emily's name listed as winning award after award.

What had happened to Rebecca? Why was she not entering her needlework? Had she finished high school? I made a note to check the high school attendance records.

Something was missing. Josie and I used to play *I Spy*. "If it was a snake it would bite you," we'd call gleefully when the seeker came close to the hidden object. *Doubly true now*, I thought. *Some connection as plain as the nose on my face, but I just can't see it.*

The phone rang. Judy answered and shook her head when I mouthed, "for me?" Then I was jarred from microfilm to real time at her words.

"The answer is an unequivocal no." Judy said. "Tell her if she sets foot on the place I'll sic the dogs on her." Her face tightened, and her lips quivered, belying the braveness of her words. "Tell her that." She hung up.

"Trouble, Judy?"

She sat down, fished for a Kleenex and blew her nose. "Fiona had the nerve to call Dad and tell him she was going to go through Mom's things. Stuff in our attic. *Told* Daddy. Didn't ask. *Told* him."

"You're kidding, Judy. Of all the nerve."

"That's my aunt."

"Sounds like you took care of it."

"Maybe. Dad can't cope with her."

"Who can? I'm young and healthy and have all my faculties, and Fiona Hadley is the most difficult person I've ever dealt with."

Knowing this was not the right time to mention Brian's fears about Alzheimer's, I turned back to my microfilm.

"May I go home, Lottie? I need to be there just in case she tries it."

"Sure. I'll be here the rest of the day."

◇◇◇

I looked at the death certificates again, then at Herman's and Emily's marriage license. Emily's parents had died two months after she and Herman were married.

I forwarded to the column reporting on the wedding and searched through the guest list. Both sets of parents were in attendance, but not Rebecca. It clearly had been a prime social occasion, and the list of gifts was long and elaborate. The writer said the gift from Herman's parents was a lovely house on Maple Street and that the industrious and talented groom would join the staff in his father's bank.

So Herman had started as a banker, not a farmer.

Then two months later there was the account of a tragic farm accident. One of the Champlins' cows had gotten out and wandered onto thin ice at the edge of a small pond close to the house. The ice didn't hold. Mr. Champlin tried to save it. Mrs. Champlin heard his cries and went after him. They both drowned. Miss Rebecca, who had been recovering from a lengthy illness, saw the whole thing from the parlor window and called the sheriff, but he was too late. The sheriff said they froze up right away.

Rebecca had been sick for a long time! That explained the lack of needlework in the fair, and perhaps even Herman's dropping her for Emily. Back then, no one could afford to take on the burden of a sick wife. Strong backs in women were prized. It took a lot of physical strength to run a household.

The two sisters were now orphans. Who provided for Miss Rebecca? I rose and poured a cup of coffee, returned and located a photo of the old Champlin homestead. It was a two-story white frame farmhouse, the same house featured in Rebecca's sale bill after the murder. So she had kept on living on the home place, even after her parents' deaths.

Then I saw an announcement that the entire Champlin estate was up for sale. Land and all. What had Miss Rebecca planned to do? What was her illness? That was the key to a number of things. Had she wanted to live with Herman and Emily? It couldn't be too comfortable a situation to be living with your sister and ex-boyfriend. Was she bitter? On the other hand, perhaps I was jumping to conclusions. Perhaps she was the one who had broken everything off with Herman.

I read on through the stock market crash and its accompanying impact on the county. The Swenson bank appeared to weather the collapse, but went under right before the United States entered the war. A run on the bank changed everything for Herman and Emily in a heartbeat. A scant month after this, the senior Swensons left town for their new home in California.

The sale of the Champlin land and homestead was canceled. Herman's and Emily's house in town was for sale, and the social items reported that Herman would be taking over the Champlin land and trying his hand at farming.

There were accounts of his buying lumber to build a house on the acreage. Remembering the sale bill, I knew this was a very modest house indeed, but would have been easy to expand. The house of a young couple who had high expectations.

I stopped to stretch my aching back. *Why did they do that?* It would have made more sense for them to have taken over the big house and build a smaller one for Rebecca.

Then Rebecca Champlin popped up all over. She began raising hogs. Buying and selling them, too. A businesswoman. She couldn't have been very sick. I needed to check with Minerva, but I suspected Rebecca had fought for the house and farmstead and a very small portion of the land, possibly no more than forty acres. Herman and Emily had settled for the land itself. Normally this would have been a good decision. But I knew what had happened directly afterward. The dust storms.

Herman and Emily had gone into farming at the worst possible time, and he wouldn't have known a thing. This was a common mistake on the Great Plains. People came here thinking just anyone could farm. It would be a snap. Just throw a few seeds at the ground.

No one would have helped Herman. I was sure of that. He was the banker's son. *Son of the serpent.* No one would have encouraged him or coached him. He had lost everything the Champlins had spent one hundred years building.

From the two sale bills, it was easy to see Rebecca had been a shrewd buyer and seller. A fine steward. And Herman? Either through bumbling or bad luck, he had ended up with even his wife's pots and pans and tea towels mortgaged.

"Would you like me to get the mail?"

"Sure, thanks, Margaret," I jumped, sending a half cup of coffee to the floor, and with an embarrassed smile, ran for paper towels.

"I hear you have a new assistant."

I stiffened at the disapproval in her voice. "Yes, I do."

She nodded at the "wanna make somethin' of it" tone in my voice and left. She returned in fifteen minutes with a stack of mail, dumped it onto my desk.

"Call me if you need anything."

"Okay. Thanks, Margaret."

She sighed, left. I regretted the awkwardness developing between us, but not enough to fire a perfectly competent person just because of her blotted past.

I opened a letter from Illinois.

> What if you're ashamed of your family? What if your family has been nothing but trouble all your life?

The letter would have fit perfectly with yesterday's column and I could have dealt with both questions at once. The book was not about achievement or prestige. It was about reality. Life.

I date-stamped the page, reached for the daily correspondence folder, then stopped and stared at the letter. Although it had come from Illinois and yesterday's letter had come from Iowa, the two letters were virtually identical in all other respects. I was sure they had been sent by the same person. They were both on plain white paper with no return address, no date, no closing, sent in a dime store business envelope and no doubt printed with a laser printer. Again, I thought wistfully of the column that had already gone to the printers. Then I put the letter back in the envelope and filed it.

I was uneasy that this person would take the trouble to use two separate towns. It was a rather sophisticated thing to do and involved addressing a letter to the postmaster in each town, enclosing a stamped, pre-addressed inner envelope and a note asking the postmaster to forward it.

I decided to address the questions, head on, in next week's column. It would take just a simple paragraph at the end to put this person at ease.

Chapter Nineteen

I found Sam Abbott wrestling with a report, which he willingly set aside the moment I walked through the door.

"Made any progress with the Swenson murder, Lottie?" There was a twinkle in his eyes. He had clearly expected me to bomb out.

"As a matter of fact, I have." He reached for his pipe. I watched serenely as he went through his little ritual and waited, knowing he would be the first to break.

"Well, are you going to tell me about it?"

"So glad you asked," I grinned. "I found out all kinds of things that aren't in that report of yours."

"Not mine," he protested. "The sheriff's report at the time. I just inherited all this stuff. I didn't create it, but I have studied it. Over and over again."

"Well, I learned Herman and Emily came from well-to-do families and Herman was an only child who should have inherited a fine bank. He would have, too, if it hadn't been for the number of loan defaults after farmers volunteered for service. A number of our men eligible for exemption declined. When Emily's parents were killed, Herman took over the farm. He shouldn't have. Everything he touched died. There is some mystery about Rebecca, and the two sisters hated each other's guts. All the other farmers in the county were out to get Herman because he was old man Swenson's son, and everything blew up over passing down the farm.

Startled, Old Stone Face inhaled sharply, then coughed. "Well, well, well. A real Nancy Drew. What makes you so sure the sisters were at odds?"

"The social columns told me Rebecca had dated Herman, and she didn't go to their wedding. The sequence of legal notices after the death of their parents told me there was a lot of trouble over dividing the homestead."

"That's good work, Lottie."

I smiled at the approving look in his eyes.

"It's real leg work, too. It builds a picture. One that's important. There's only one thing wrong."

"What's that?"

"You haven't uncovered one single thing that changes anything. The evidence still points to Herman."

Chagrined, I realized he was right. "I'm not through yet. I have a whole list of to-dos connected with this."

"I'm sure you do."

"I want to see the old mortgage for one thing, and I want to see Herman Swenson."

"Won't do you no good. He can't talk. Can't think. Poor miserable son-of-a-bitch."

"I know, but you can't tell, there might be something there. He may still be able to hear."

◇◇◇

The Sunny Rest Nursing Home is a low single-story brick building with an assisted living center. It's an unusually large complex for our tiny county and even has an Alzheimer's Unit and a secured wing.

Bettina had convinced me that some of the residents were happy. Especially older women who had done grueling labor all their lives. They were grateful to the point of giddiness at the chance to rest, to be warm, to be fed good food they didn't have to prepare, to be kept clean and tidy, and most of all to be around a network of women who cared. They had friends and made few demands. Their arthritic old hands welcomed the peace of jigsaw puzzles and crocheting.

I could stand the women. But the men's faces broke my heart. They looked betrayed.

I did not want this life for Keith. Not ever. But when I imagined Josie and me in adjoining wheelchairs, it didn't seem so bad.

Through Bettina, I knew the whole health management field was unbelievably savage. My favorite doctors were the doctors right here in Carlton County. They were the last of a dying breed.

An teenage aide looked at me curiously when I asked to see Herman Swenson. She was irritatingly peppy as she led me down the hallway to the secured unit. Mr. Swenson sat in a wheelchair facing the window.

"He can't talk to you, you know."

"I've heard he's been totally mute since the stroke."

"Not totally. He doesn't say any real words, but he cries out when he can't help himself. Sometimes it's in his sleep, and once to warn another resident when an aide lost control of a stack of books she was carrying and nearly dumped them into the old man's wheelchair. He made a sound. Several people heard him."

Crying out in his sleep would have been involuntary, but to warn someone of danger demonstrated a high degree of function.

"Thank you," I moved toward the man.

Not wanting to startle him, I tapped first on the door frame, then walked around to face the front of the wheelchair. I pushed it back from the wall, mindful of the fact this was his room, his chair, his life. He was entitled to his privacy. He didn't know me from Adam's off-ox and certainly didn't owe me a thing. I wheeled him around and sat in a straight-backed chair opposite him.

Herman Swenson was thin, big-boned, and even though he was eighty-six years old, I was aware of the muscles he must have had in his youth. Flabby now and covered by a denim shirt and old chinos, he had the aura of a caged old eagle.

Several of the old men I had seen sitting in the TV room off the corridor had a farmer's tan: a white brow where it had been shaded from the sun by a straw hat since they were children, walnut-brown baked cheeks and necks. Herman had not farmed long enough to acquire this marking.

I was not prepared for his eyes. They were old age blue, watery and circled with white, but they were also piercing. Alert and bitter, they held a grief so profound Heaven would not have been able to wash away his pain.

I closed my eyes for an instant, ashamed of my desire to pump this tortured old man for information. He who so clearly wanted to be left in peace. His room was as bare as a monk's. His bedspread was a brown ribbed cotton. There were no pictures, no afghans, no personal possessions other than an extremely worn Bible on his simple pine dresser. On the night stand next to his bed there was a copy of Jack London's stories. I glanced over at his Bible and noted the location of the ribbon, the worn edges. I yearned to know what section he had been reading over and over. I suspected his marker was in Psalms. The dark ones.

"Mr. Swenson, I'm Lottie Albright. I'm compiling the Carlton County history books and I've come to ask you..." Before I could finish speaking, I saw a flicker of rage. It told me what I had wanted to know most of all. He could hear and understand. No doubt, for the last fifty years, people had only wanted to discuss the murders. I cast about in my mind for a safe topic that wouldn't conjure up painful memories. There were few subjects to pick from.

"I want to ask you a few questions about the Carlton High School football team."

There was an answering quickness in his eyes, a touch of self-mockery, a nearly imperceptible expulsion of breath. I was stunned by the intelligence he had conveyed with his body language, aware of his momentary relaxation of wariness. He clearly did not trust a soul.

"Sir, was your school able to field an eleven-man squad or did you play with fewer men?"

A hero. He had been a real football hero. His mouth quirked into an ancient imitation of a smile, but he stared down at his lap.

Disappointed, I prattled on about the game. I told him about an article I had read in an issue of *Kansas History* about early athletics.

Clearly agitated, he looked at me fiercely, then down at his lap again. The fingers on one hand were extended, the other curled into a claw with only the index finger pointing outward.

"I must be running along," I said cheerfully. "I do appreciate the visit."

Impulsively, I reached for one of his old hands and squeezed it. "Mr. Swenson, I know what a splendid athlete you once were."

I could feel his eyes following me. A feeling swept over me as I walked away, the same feeling that came to me when I read old newspapers, when I was about to make a connection others had overlooked. I didn't feel this was an evil man. I couldn't imagine he would be capable of killing his wife and son.

On the way out I stopped at the desk and spoke to the work-weary nurse, who was trying to catch up her charts.

"I just finished calling on Herman Swenson. Does he ever have any visitors?"

"None for the last five years except reporters from time to time who want to dig up all the old dirt about those murders."

"He's never confessed? Never given any details?"

"Nope. All the gory details will go to his grave. He spent ten years in Larned for the criminally insane, another twenty years in Leavenworth. He had a stroke and was transferred here ten years ago. To tell you the truth, I don't think he gives a hoot whether he's here or in prison or in the loony bin. He doesn't mix and doesn't care. We've never been able to get him to take part in any activities. He doesn't even watch T.V."

"Can he read?" I asked. "I saw a book on his dresser. Why would he have a book on his dresser if he can't read?"

"His Bible and that Jack London? They've been there forever. Don't know how he came by them. Maybe one of the volunteers who reads to the residents gave them to him. I do know he watches us like a hawk when we clean. Not many of us have the heart to rip off an old man's Bible, no matter what you read in the papers about nursing homes."

I grinned. Even more savage than the health care industry was the press about the health care industry.

"But whatever Herman does, it's by himself, you can bet on that."

"Church services? Does he attend any of the church services you have here?"

"Never."

"His Bible looked well used."

"So go figure. We have every denomination and he won't do any of the religious stuff either. You just can't please some people."

"Do the residents have to check out books they read?"

"No, they just take what they want off the shelves. It's not like we don't have a way of getting them back." She grinned.

I smiled weakly, shuddered, and left quickly.

I would have given anything to see a list of the books the old man had read in the last fifteen years. It would have told me a great deal about his tastes and interests, his abilities and his state of mind. Josie could have done wonders with it.

◇◇◇

Strangely ill at ease over the visit, I woke up several times in the night. There had been something important about that old man's body. Something I was supposed to notice.

Chapter Twenty

The next morning, still haunted by the visit, I dabbed a bit of concealer under my eyes and headed to the office. Herman Swenson was not nearly as out of it as people thought he was. He could hear, react. He had been angry with me. What could I have said or done that set him off? For once, my preoccupation with body language was invaluable. It was the only way the miserable old man had of communicating.

I closed my eyes, pictured him in that wheelchair again, remembered his pleasure when I had talked about football. He wasn't angry over my choice of subject, I was sure of that. He had been frustrated because he couldn't make me understand. But understand what? He responded immediately to my simple question. Were they able to field an eleven-man team. I thought about his hands again. The one extended. The other curled into a claw with a finger extended. Suddenly, I knew what he had been trying to tell me.

I hurried to the shelves containing back issues of *Kansas History*. I located an article I had read years earlier. In 1934, in Kansas, an alternative to eleven-man football had been developed. Six-man football. Six. The number of fingers Herman had extended. No wonder he had been upset. I was the first person in fifty years wanting to talk about something other than the most painful episode of his life, and he couldn't make me understand.

I quickly read through the article, memorized all the main points, and breezed back to Sunny Rest. The old man was still stationed by his window.

"Mr. Swenson, I owe you an apology. I realized after our visit yesterday that you were trying to tell me that Carlton County switched to six-man football."

He sat perfectly still but his rheumy old eyes brimmed with tears.

"The switch was made because schools lost so many students during the depression. It cut down expenses, too. I understand it was a marvelous game for spectators."

He nodded. I chatted, stifling all the questions that would dredge up painful memories. Questions like: Did you go to these games after you graduated? Could you afford to go? Did you take your darling wife? Your son? Did you meet old friends there? Did you have to sacrifice even this small pleasure while you were losing the farm? I knew I would ruin our rapport if I asked any of these questions.

He was tied into his wheel chair. Lop-sided, now. Through Bettina I knew restraints were better than tumbling out of the chair and spending years in pain. Hands trembling, because I did not want to offend him, I reached under his shoulders, pulled him up. Made him right.

I patted his hand. With enormous effort, he moved his left hand over mine, let it rest there for a moment. I looked away.

He closed his eyes, opened them and looked at me. He opened his mouth and made a strangled perverted sound. Like an half-formed N. It made no sense whatsoever. But the shape of the mouth, the placement of the tongue was unmistakable. He was trying to say something.

"Mr. Swenson, I can't understand you yet, but I will. Give me a little time. Let me look at some videos used by speech pathologists. So I'll understand your lips, your mouth, even if you can't use your voice."

There was a sound at the doorway and I turned and looked at the aide.

"Well, I'll swan," she said. "Looks like you've hit pay dirt, honey. First time I've ever seen Old Herman the German open his murdering mouth."

Furious, I wanted to deck her. Bettina, who's big on dignity, would have fired her on the spot. There's no place for mean people in a nursing home, and no amount of training will change a mean soul. I turned to look at Herman. Wanted to see his reaction. Grief, not anger. I barely trusted myself to speak to the aide, but I wanted Herman to know I was on his side.

"Please leave. Mr. Swenson and I would like our privacy."

"She's history," I said to Herman after she clomped off down the hall. "Count on it. I'll have her job."

I was rewarded by his triumphant smile. Suddenly we both were laughing. Me outright, he with a gruff little heave of breath and the shaking of his chest.

"I'll be back," I said. "You can count on that too."

◇◇◇

I walked down the hallway to the office of the administrator. Connie Simmons had been at Sunny Rest for fifteen years. Like all heads of nursing homes she was buried in paperwork. Even on the good days her life was a kind of lukewarm purgatory between mad families and government compliance. She had the neat dark hair and soft brown eyes of an old workhorse. She always dressed professionally, for success, and to assure anxious families.

Although she was the administrator, she had come up through the ranks, starting as a Certified Nurse' s Aide. She knew the business from the bottom up.

"Morning, Lottie."

"You have a problem, Connie." I quickly told her about the aide's thoughtless remarks. "I'm willing to make this an official complaint. I'll sign anything you need me to sign."

"Good. Most folks chicken out. This isn't the first time her mouth has gotten her in trouble. She's already received two verbal warnings, and one written. Yours is the last one in the chain I need to let her go."

I asked for a piece of paper, wrote out a complaint and passed it to her.

"I'm intrigued that you got through to Mr. Swenson," she said. "That's wonderful."

"Have other people tried?"

"Not when they should have. His first stroke came when he was in prison. It's crucial to have rehabilitation right off the bat and he didn't get it."

◇◇◇

On the way back to the office I kept thinking about the sound Herman had tried to make. The hopelessness of his condition. His family had been killed before there were Miranda laws in place. Everyone had assumed he had done it. He had not had a good lawyer. I remembered his reaction to the aide's words. Not anger, not rage, but profound despair. Helplessness in the face of injustice.

My reaction to cruelty is to go for the jugular, despite the fact mine takes an incredibly civilized form. And I did people in all by myself. I didn't ask others to do my dirty work for me. I hadn't gone home and bawled over that aide's remarks or written Connie an anonymous letter.

I got her fired like a Roman and a man.

Chapter Twenty-One

Back at the office, Josie called just as I opened the third anonymous letter. Sent from Michigan, with no return address, and no signature as usual.

"What's up, Lottie?"

"What do you mean, what's up?" I cradled the receiver between my cheek and my shoulder to free my hands. "Let me put you on speaker. I don't want to mess up this envelope." She tells me that forwarding my cell to my office landline so I can keep on multitasking is neurotic, but I think Josie is bossy as hell.

"You're not making sense."

I laughed at her wariness, punched the button, and replaced the receiver on the cradle.

"I got a call from Keith yesterday and he's very worried about you."

"You what?" I laid down the letter without reading it. "You tell me what's up. Why would Keith call you without talking to me first? Directly. Like husbands are supposed to."

"He didn't know how to talk to you. That's why. He told me about the new job. He's afraid you're working too hard and…"

"Let me guess. He doesn't like the nature of my work. Is that it?"

"Yup, that's basically it, kiddo. He's afraid you'll get…"

"Killed, maimed, or raped."

"That's about the size of it." Josie said, "He didn't want you to think he was trying to…"

"Control me. He thinks he should be a sensitive twenty-first century sort of guy instead of his true Arthurian self. He hates to tell me what to do, but he would love to tell me what to do."

Josie laughed. "There now. I'm so glad I called. I'll call him right back and let him know we had a little chat just like I promised and you understand perfectly. Any message you would like me to convey to him?"

"Yes. Please assure him this is basically a desk job I've taken on for Sam Abbot. Tell him I'll leave the shoot 'em up stuff to the big guys. Tell him that as my sister and my psychologist you think I'm doing splendidly."

As she was speaking, I removed the letter from the envelope, then caught my breath.

"Lottie, are you still there?"

"Hold on a minute while I finish reading this."

> Some persons families are full of lies and conceal murders and blood. How far do you want us to go in telling our family story?

"I can't believe this."

"Lottie?"

"Sorry. I'm reading the strangest letter. It's just now dawned on me something might be wrong with the sender." I told her about the other two. The use of mail drops. The attempts to conceal the sender's identity. Then I read her the one I had just received.

"How strange."

"Isn't it? Keith should worry more about me working here than working for Sam."

If the sender was concealing something terrible, I needed to address the issue in my column. These stories shouldn't be incriminating or obscene or humiliate family members. I would discuss libel, and cover territory I hadn't considered before.

"Any luck on finding Zelda's killer?"

Judy came, stood in the doorway and listened to my sister. Embarrassed that Josie had no way of knowing another person was hearing our conversation, I looked at Judy in apology, picked up the receiver and switched off the speaker.

"None. In fact, I've been very preoccupied with another murder."

Aware of Judy's disapproving glance, I quickly outlined the circumstances of the Swenson murder, then hung up.

Why should Judy be upset over my telling Josie about the Swensons? "So out with it. What's bothering you?"

"Everything," she said. "Mom's death. Dad's health. And you."

"Me?"

"I don't understand why you're not spending more time trying to figure out who killed Mom. That was the whole idea of your taking the job with Sam."

I started to tell her Fiona had an iron-clad alibi for that night, then stopped. I had not checked with Sam to see if this information needed to be kept private.

"Why are you so preoccupied with the Swenson murders? Everyone is talking about it. Margaret is furious with you."

"Margaret? Why would she be mad?"

"She says you were hired to write these county history books, not run a murder investigation out of the historical society."

"The books are right on schedule."

"Tell that to her, not me. I want to know what you're doing about Mom. You promised you would do your best, and you've spent hours and hours on something else." She dissolved into tears.

"What's happened, Judy?" Clearly, something had set her off.

"I got this call from Fiona last night. She wants to come over and collect all the Rubidoux's things that Mom had stored."

"She can't do that." I reached for Judy's hand and squeezed it. "Under Kansas law, all your mother's possession belong to your father. Unless there's a will stating otherwise."

"I told Fiona off, again. Said I'd have her arrested if she sets foot on the place. But I need to start going through all of Mom's things, and just the thought of it hurts. I wish there was someone besides me. Dad can't. I thought with me home he would start coping. But he's not. Now I'm worried that Fiona will come sneaking around when I'm not there."

Heartsick, I knew she was right. "I'm not going to let her," I said. "Not because of what you suspect, Judy, but because Fiona has so little regard for other person's feelings. What is thrown away, sold, or kept should be Max's decision, not her's. She would go through your place like Sherman through Atlanta. I have a hard time standing up to the woman. Max wouldn't have a chance."

"He's not well, Lottie. I'm worried sick."

"I would love to help you sort if you'll have me."

"That would be wonderful."

"I know a little bit about antiques, rare books, vintage clothes. Things that might bring your father some money if he chooses to sell them."

"Thanks. Again. You've done so much already."

"I'll come to your house tomorrow. We'll get William or Margaret to fill in here."

Again, I was able to work both sides of the streets. As Judy's friend, and at her request, I would be able to examine anything and everything, but as a sheriff's deputy I would have needed a search warrant and probable cause just to walk through the door. I was in an ideal investigative position. This part-time Deputy Dogg jazz worked like a charm.

◇◇◇

It rained the next morning. Rain on the plains was rarely Liza Doolittle gentle. It usually came with thunderstorms and ranged from fiercely throbbing to torrential. A rare treat, this steady, peaceful rain softened the outlines of buildings and blurred the blisters of peeling paint on the St. Johns' house.

Judy answered the door on the first ring. "Is this a good day for attic work, or what?"

"Perfect. Do I smell bread?"

"Cinnamon rolls. I baked them myself. I've rounded up some boxes and markers and made a fresh pot of coffee. We should be able to carry everything upstairs in one trip."

I steadied a stack under my chin and climbed the stairs, following Judy's lead. She switched on the lights.

"Oh my," I said, setting down my load. "Oh my." Seeing a pile of Wonder Woman comics and a box of "little big" books, and an old Barbie, still in the cellophane windowed box, I knew at once the St. John's attic was a gold mine.

There were racks of vintage clothes, old trunks galore, stacks of old books and magazines, two dressmaker's dummies, old tables, lamps. There were stacks and stacks of picture frames. I saw five open boxes of dishes. We saw three boxes labeled "to be sorted."

Judy and I looked at each other and laughed.

"I didn't know it was this bad."

"Judy, honey, it's not bad. It's good. Some of these things are worth a lot of money. But we're going to do this right. Use proper techniques instead of running around yelling 'Eureka' like two crazed miners. It's going to take more than one day. Weeks in fact. Whew!"

"Where do we start?"

"By putting everything in groups of like types before we open anything," I said. "All the trunks together, all the boxes of old books together, all the old clothes together. Then we'll begin the real work. I don't want you to discard anything until I've looked at it first."

"You're kidding."

"I'm not. In fact, you're going to be getting a crash course in assessing historical artifacts. We mustn't throw anything away that would bring your father some money. Nevertheless, I don't want a professional appraiser in here until we go through everything first ourselves."

It took us a couple of hours to do the preliminary grouping.

"This does make a little more sense," Judy said. "Now, what?"

"Dishes, first," I said. "They're easier, for one thing. I'll look at them for commercial value, then I want you to see if they have some sentimental value for your family."

I opened the first box and held up three old white coffee mugs. "These mean anything to you?"

She shook her head.

"Garage sale then."

Judy put them aside, then put some plates in the same place.

"Hold it. Those plates are depression glass. Worth at least $60.00 a piece. If I'm not mistaken, that little sugar bowl is Czechoslovakian glass. It will bring around $200.00."

"Wow. I had no idea."

"Most people don't." Then with growing wonder, I realized the box held over a thousand dollars worth of dishes.

After we finished with the glassware, cooking items, and old cutlery, we moved on to old newspapers and magazines.

"Judy, I don't want to rush this process. You've got the general idea of how to go about this now. We must be careful. I'll give you some reference books, and you can look up everything as you sort. Okay?"

She pushed her fist against her mouth, blinked back tears. "My dad. All this money. I'll be able to get help for Daddy."

"Why don't you take a couple of weeks off. I'll stay at the office. It will make William and Margaret happy to see me with my nose to the grindstone."

"I don't want to screw this up."

"You won't. I won't let you. With a good reference book, you can do a great job. While I'm here today, we'll move onto the trunks, because the information in there is harder to assess."

Trunks take the most time, but I also knew they might contain things that were important to Zelda.

"We'll start here," I said, spying one trunk as less dusty than the others. I opened it with a feeling of reverence. I would be looking into another person's life. It was indeed Zelda's own personal trunk. A sectioned jewelry tray contained her high school class ring, her old sorority pin, and medals for various musical activities. Mostly vocal, I noticed.

I picked up a little enamel clown from an assortment of costume jewelry. "See this? It looks like pure D junk, but it's a fine piece of early art deco. It's a good example of things people pitch unaware."

A faint scent of lavender wafted from dried flowers scattered in lace-edged linens. Packets of letters from Max rested beside gold frames cradling miniatures of ancient Rubidoux.

"Paper Direct®. This isn't old," Judy said removing a shallow box. "It comes from a computer company. They make supplies for laser printers." She pulled off the lid. Inside were blank sheets of cheap white paper.

"Twenty pages here," she said, quickly counting them. "Not a word on any of them. Why would Mom keep plain typing paper in this trunk?"

"Hard telling."

"Lottie, look here." Judy held a single piece of paper up toward the light. "Look. There's that rose again. Reversed."

I scrambled to my feet and stared at the paper. "You're right."

"There's a connection with this rose and the story Mom wrote. I know there is."

Chapter Twenty-two

Frustrated, Judy put the paper back in the box, and we turned our attention back to the trunk. I saw a pile of journals at the bottom and felt a rush of adrenaline. I opened one. "Clarissa Roubidoux. Judy, that's your great grandmother. Her diary!" My hands trembled with excitement. "What a find!"

Eagerly, I removed them from the trunk. I glanced at another stack, which had been placed next to them, and looked inside. "These belonged to your grandmother, Melissa." Quickly I checked to see if Zelda had kept journals and diaries also. She had.

My mind raced. In my head, I began writing articles based on the journals of three generations of Western Kansas women. Sociology. History. Women's studies. And if Judy did this too, we were talking about four generations. The information would be priceless.

I sneezed, overwhelmed by the old dusty odor of decaying paper. A rectangle of faint light through a high window illuminated a hat stand holding a Victorian straw with a droopy mauve rose. Rain fell softly and our quiet voices echoed across the ancient collections.

Judy opened a baby book. "It's mine," she whispered. "Look at these pictures, just look. My hair, a little lock of my hair. And look what Mom wrote. See how happy she was."

"Let me check her journal, Judy, for the same time period." I looked through the old books. Zelda had dated them and used the same grey linen, maroon edged books throughout her life.

I would never withhold a journal or a diary from a family, but they can be a real can of worms. Descendents should read every word. Not just skim a couple of pages, decide their parents' marriage was a sham, and good old mom was on the verge of leaving daddy most of the time. Or decide mother hated her life when she was simply premenstrual, and the dust was blowing that day.

I wanted to know if Zelda's private journal matched the emotions depicted in her baby book. I located the entries clustered around Judy's birth.

Judy reached to the bottom of the neat chronological stacks. I quickly calculated the dates.

"How wonderful. She started when she was in grade school," I said. "Did you know this, Judy?"

"Yes. She always wanted me to keep a diary, too. I knew she did this, but I didn't realize what having her diary would mean to me now."

I skimmed over the early years but read enough to know that the twins had a troubled relationship. Clearly, Zelda had struggled all her life to keep from being run over by her manipulative sister. I read through Zelda's early housekeeping entries and then found more emotional ones.

> "Fiona is pregnant. I would give anything, anything to have a baby. I know she and Edgar have had their troubles getting pregnant, too, but I might have known she would be the first. I wish it were me. I wish it were me."

There was a long gap between entries, as though she was ashamed of what she would be writing if she were honest. Then:

> "I got to see him, hold him. They've named him Brian and Fiona is acting like the Queen Mother. I don't care. I just want to be around him. Count his little fingers and toes. She isn't nursing him, says it isn't "modern" and she wants her baby to have the very best,

so I get to give him his bottle. Sometimes I think if I hear her say, 'Poor Zelda' to Edgar one more time I'm going to throw up. Nothing is good enough for her or her little boy. Not the clothes I've made for him, not the presents other people bring him. She always finds a flaw. She even had him out of town in a swanky hospital. She said she wanted to be someplace with the latest equipment just in case something went wrong, but I think it's because she doesn't want anyone to see her naked with her legs spread and strapped to a delivery table and then have to see them on the street later."

Seven years later:

"It's finally, finally came to pass. Max and I are going to have a baby. Thank God in Heaven."

Then:

"When I told Fiona our good news, she looked at me as though I had slapped her. Like she was jealous. Why couldn't she just be happy for me? Just once? "

Then:

"I did not know it was possible for a human being to be so sick."

Then:

"The doctor says I might lose the baby. I'm too wretched to think about it or write about it. He says it will help if I stay calm, but how can I?"

Then:

"They've put me to bed. Total bed rest. Max called Fiona to see if she could help. She said she had many, many other obligations but would do what she could. Poor Max. He's worn out from the store, from trying to help me."

Then:

"I cry all the time after she leaves. She comes to drop off the little meals, which her hired girl has fixed. Today she stared at my stomach, then shed a few tears. But not for one minute did I think she was sorry for me. I think she must want another baby herself. Then she flounced off after reminding me that her pregnancy wasn't easy either. I know it wasn't and we both had to spend a lot of time in bed, but Edgar is so rich. Fiona spent her last three months in California with Edgar's aunt, being waited on hand and foot. She was in a town by the ocean where she got to breathe salt air, not dust. Her bed rest was entirely different than mine. I get to watch my husband work his fingers to the bone because of me."

Then:

"This is the happiest day of my life. I brought my darling little girl home from the hospital. I've hoped and prayed for this moment. I can't believe she's finally, finally here. She's so beautiful and perfect. My cup runneth over."

Seven days later:

"I don't understand why Fiona is being so hateful. I've had Judy home for a week now, and my own sister has not been over to see her yet."

A week later:

"Max finally called Fiona and asked her to come over. He doesn't know I know he did this, but I heard him making the call. I heard him telling Fiona how upset and unhappy I am. I've cried myself to sleep for a solid week. I just don't understand."

Three days later:

"I hate her. She finally came and was as stiff as a visiting archbishop. She stayed twenty minutes. Twenty minutes! And acted like I had given birth to a yard cat, for no more importance than it seemed to have to her. This is her niece! Her only niece! She peered at my little Judy, said she was very nice, asked if I was breast-feeding, then had the nerve to say she looked sickly, like she wasn't getting enough milk. She knew it would worry me to death. Why didn't she stay? When she brought Brian home, I sat with him, rocked him, loved him. I know in a lot of ways, we've never been close, but I'm her only sister, and I just don't understand how she can treat me this way."

"Find something?" asked Judy, looking up from her baby book.

"Yes, I've found something very curious. When I have time, I want to start at the beginning of your mother's journals. As early as she started keeping them. I think there was a lot of tension between Fiona and your mother from early childhood, and through the years it got worse."

She reached for the book. I hesitated. I had to hand this journal over to Judy, of course, but she already hated Fiona. These entries would fan the flames. "Here," I said with a sigh.

At first she skimmed. Her cheeks flamed. Her hands shook. Then she re-read very slowly all the entries from the time before Brian's birth through her own arrival. She reeled, then steadied herself against the trunk as though she were absorbing a physical blow.

"Why would anyone snub a little baby?" she whispered. "I was just a little baby. She had her Brian. Her own wonderful perfect little boy."

"There's got to be something here we're not seeing or not understanding."

"There's nothing to see. Nothing to understand. It's just like I told you. Fiona hated my mother."

It was not the time for me to go into nuances of feelings between sisters. I felt, hoped, that hate was too strong a word. This was, after all, just Zelda's version of events. Fiona's delay could be attributed to something as simple as a head cold. But that thought came from my objective historian side. In my gut, I doubted it. I suspected Zelda's pregnancy affected Fiona at some very deep level. As to the crack about not getting enough milk, I knew it was a decade when nursing fell out of vogue and most babies were bottle fed.

"At least we know how your mother felt about Brian. So it wasn't a payback."

"Oh, Mom just loved Brian. She would have done anything for that little boy."

"That's clear. Page after page shows she just doted on him. What do you remember about Brian when you were growing up? Or Edgar? No one ever mentions Edgar. It's like he's a non-person. How did your mom feel about Edgar?"

"She didn't like him," Judy said. "She thought Fiona had married beneath herself. He was too crude for her tastes. Mom used to call Fiona and Edgar, 'Beauty and the Beast.'"

"And you? Did you like him?"

"Quite a lot, actually." She looked surprised at the memory. "We weren't together all that much. Just on special occasions. Mom couldn't stand the way Fiona always treated us. Like poor relation. Nevertheless, we all got together for Christmas and Thanksgiving."

"So it wasn't like your families didn't see each other at all."

"No, Mom and Fiona were hell-bent on presenting this weird appearance of family unity to outsiders. But I liked seeing Brian and Edgar. It's funny how much is coming back to me. Uncle Edgar was always nice. I remember when Aunt Fiona would launch into her little digs, he would give her one of his looks, but it never shut her up. Then his jaw would tighten. He would ask me if I wanted to go outside and look at cows or something. Fiona wore him down. I know that now."

"He's obviously a good farmer."

"You'd better believe it. Uncle Edgar built up a fortune. Mom may have thought he was stupid, but he's a shrewd businessman. And go figure, he's also a computer guru to half the farmers in this county."

"And Brian? What do you remember about Brian."

"He was absolutely wonderful. Like a big brother to me. That's why I'm waiting until we find something concrete before I go to the police."

"Honey, I am the police," I reminded her gently.

"I wish you had been a deputy the first night, too."

I bit back my opinions about Betty's sloppy interrogation. "You said Fiona and Zelda had a terrible fight the night of the murder. I've assumed it was about withdrawing the story, but was there more to it than that?"

Ashamed, she looked away, then turned toward me. "I'm positive Mom asked the Hadleys for money. She was desperate to find help for Dad. I'm sure you know that."

She sighed, her mouth tense with worry. "He needs an assisted living facility. And that takes big bucks."

I held my arms open and she let me hug her like she was a fragile little doll while I patted her on the back.

She cried, then pulled away and stared at the trunk. "I don't want to believe my mother was capable of blackmail, but from what she said in her phone call, I can't put it out of my mind."

"But you don't know what she was holding over her sister?"

"Not a clue. Mom just said it was high time I knew some things about the family and Fiona should have to pay for everything she's done."

Chapter Twenty-Three

My mind raced. "Sam needs to know about this Judy, even if Zelda didn't live to follow through." Privately, I was beginning to think both sisters were a real piece of work. She nodded and moved to a box of toys. "Tell me more about your cousin."

"Brian was seven years older than me. He showed me bird nests and flowers and took me for walks along the creek. He was kind. He's the only one who's ever been truly kind to me outside of my parents and Uncle Edgar." She sneezed and reached for a Kleenex. "He wanted to be a botanist, you know."

"No! I've never seen it mentioned once in any of his press material. What would make him decide to be a lawyer and a politician then?"

"He didn't decide. Fiona decided for him. I remember there was a terrible hullabaloo over all this. Fiona would not have her darling boy going into a career where he couldn't make any real money. Many of the Rubidoux men have been lawyers. She presented it to Brian as his sacred obligation to carry on the family tradition."

"He's a born natural for the limelight. I can't imagine anyone better at politics."

"Oh, he's political all right," Judy laughed. "Haven't you heard of the Hadley Compromise?"

"No."

"Gateway City has the finest system for choosing up Little League teams of any town around and it came about when Brian was just nine years old. Absolutely no one would pick him when teams were choosing up sides. He dropped every ball that came at him. Couldn't bat either. He didn't have much energy. He and a small cluster of other losers were always chosen last, so he decided to do something about it."

"He was fighting the system when he was just nine years old?"

"Better believe it. He came up with a wonderful method. He asked the coaches to rank all the players, then each coach in turn got to select a number one player, then a number two, and so on. It was fair and merciful. That's why our teams are so well balanced. Thirty-three years later, we're still using his plan."

I smiled. It was the kind of thinking I had come to expect from Brian.

"But why did Brian play at all, if he didn't like baseball and wasn't any good at it?"

"His folks insisted, of course. Real all-American boys played ball. Little League is big here. But it was hard on Brian. Law school was hard on him, too."

"But he made straight A's, Judy. *Law Review* and all that."

"He would be a success at anything he chose to do. I should know. I've had everything terrific he's ever done thrown up to me from the time he was born. But physically, it was too hard on him. There's a gray look about him when he's pushing himself too hard. Look for it. You'll see."

I remembered William's slam the day Brian and Fiona had come to the historical society together, that he looked like he had just come off a three-day drunk.

"He was sickly, growing up. I remember that, Lottie."

"Anything in particular?"

"A bad case of measles. Food poisoning. Boy, do I remember the food poisoning. A bunch of us ate some bad potato salad at an after-school picnic. We all were sick, but he stayed sicker, longer. He was out of school for two weeks. When he was older, I remember him having a bout of yellow jaundice. He got over it, and I don't remember it happening again. But he caught everything. Flu, colds, nothing passed him by."

"He seems to be fine now. He's become a runner, in fact."

She snorted. "Not a chance. Have you seen him? I'll bet if you were a little bird in the trees you would see him walking, not running. Walking slowly, looking at nature."

I laughed. The expectations we have for our politicians!

"See for yourself," Judy insisted. "He's never in anything competitive. Not even golf. Do you know a politician who doesn't play golf?"

I shook my head. I didn't. I knew Brian took a ton of vitamins. The alternative medical people were crazy about him.

I nodded toward the stack of journals. "These are yours, Judy. But please! I would love to have access to them later." I told her about the articles I had in mind.

Judy was unusually quiet the rest of the day, despite my attempts to draw her out. I caught one of her quick furtive glances in my direction. She was up to something.

◇◇◇

On the drive home, I thought about the Hadleys. Despite Brian's suspicions of early Alzheimer's, I suspected Fiona was simply meaner than a snake and always had been. He was just now seeing it. Still, there were those mood shifts, and I had told him we would get the testing done.

There was just one problem. How did you get a grown woman tested for Alzheimer's against her will?

◇◇◇

The next morning, I went to the office early, grabbed an organizer tray from my desk drawer, punched the speaker button, and called Josie to see if her handwriting expert had any brilliant insights into Zelda St. John.

"He thinks Zelda was a very dramatic person."

"Well, duh. I don't need anyone to tell me that." I sorted misplaced paper clips from thumbtacks. "Is there anything else there? Any mental illness? Physical illness?"

"No, none, and this was probably a very good sample. It was lengthy enough to provide a variety of shapes and letters. That's always important."

"I was hoping for something great. Just a minute, I want to shut the door." There was a little movement in the corridor. Currents of air as employees came into the courthouse. The coffee gurgled. My favorite odor. I poured a cup. Just the way I liked it. Black, bitter, obscene. I had hoped the delay would give me time to figure out how to tackle Josie. It didn't. I'd have to do it head on.

"Are you ready for another assignment?"

"Oh, terrific. I've always wanted to be a psychologist by proxy."

"Brian Hadley thinks there's something wrong with his mother."

"From what I've seen, I think there's something wrong with his whole loony family."

I laughed. "He means organically wrong. I told him I would talk to you about having Fiona tested."

"I can't, Lottie. Not any kind of real physical or mental evaluation. It's just not possible without her consent and her full cooperation. Any observations I make without an exam would be strictly guesswork. I leave that kind of voodoo to people on the street. They think they know everything about other people's minds."

"Brian's worried about Alzheimer's."

"The reason he's worried about Alzheimer's is because that's what he knows about," she said flatly. "Everyone suspects Alzheimer's, but there's a number of the dementias or illnesses that produce the same symptoms. How long has it been since she had a complete physical? Brain scans and MRIs would point out anything organically wrong."

"I wish Brian didn't have this election hanging over him. It's putting him in a terrible double bind." I sorted rubber bands by size, then color. "I know he would like to arrange for his mother's testing right away."

"Lottie, have you had a chance to really observe Fiona?"

I recalled the day she first came into my office. "While she was reading her sister's story, I looked at her like she was under a microscope. I watched her hands, her eyes, the way she moved, the way she held her mouth. Everything. I was trying to figure out why she was so upset."

"Good. I know how much you know and see. There're a few illnesses we may be able to eliminate. Not officially, you understand, but if you can remember certain symptoms being present, please have her get help right away. Don't even think about putting tests off until after the election. The reason we're all so frightened of Alzheimer's is that it's one of the dementias."

"She doesn't seem demented or crazy most of the time. I think she's just a born meddler and trouble maker."

Josie laughed. "Probably is. In that case she might have a character disorder. But medically speaking, dementia is simply defined as a decline in thinking function. The term is reserved for cognitive loss that is irreversible. If we can fix this slide and get the patient's faculties back, we use other words."

"I don't want to hear all the other words. I just want to find out what's wrong with Fiona."

"Okay. That day, did she lurch? Wobble? Stumble?"

"Not at all. In fact, I knew it was Fiona coming down the hall by her footsteps. She has this high-toned clickety way about her. Like she's absolutely sure of who she is, where she's going."

"Was there any one-sidedness to her?"

"Like in a stroke? No way."

"Any tremors?"

"No."

"Her eyes, Lottie. Did you notice anything at all about her eyes?"

"They were spectacular. Eyes to die for. Same as Zelda's were, as Judy's are. Blue as cornflowers. Long black lashes. Fiona's lids have probably been done."

"I'm looking for abnormalities here, not a Maybelline commercial. Were the whites discolored? Yellow or cloudy? Was there anything wrong you can remember?"

"Not one thing. I specifically remember her eyes that day."

"Please ask Brian if she's complained of headaches. If not, I would just bet whoever does this exam *won't* find Huntington's or Parkinson's or a stroke. I think we can set Brian's mind at ease a little. A very little, since nothing I'm suggesting is official. Nevertheless, I think you should urge him to get her checked out as soon as possible."

"Based on what you've said, I know he'll want to wait until after the election to have his mother examined."

"Tell him to forget about the election for a while."

"If it's Alzheimer's, he can forget about elections from now on," I said grimly.

The other line rang. "Just a second, I need to put you on hold."

"Sam here, Lottie. I just had a visitor."

Chapter Twenty-Four

I switched to my handset and pressed it tightly against my ear as though it would help to muffle bad news.

"Judy," I said.

"That's right. She's brought me her mother's diaries to establish motive for Fiona murdering her mother. Say's she hated Zelda all her life. She's threatening to go to the press."

"Brian's toast if she does."

"I know that, but legally, we can't stop her."

"She'll stop if we find out who murdered her mother."

"I've done everything I know to do. It's keeping me awake at night." He cleared his throat. "I know I've kind of kept you on the sidelines, Lottie. Didn't take you serious at first. But the information you dug up on the Swensons was first class leg-work. Maybe you can see something I've overlooked. Can you put in more time here?"

I closed my eyes, swallowed hard. "Sure."

I murmured a hasty goodbye, looked around at my ever-growing stack of work, shuddered, sipped my sludge, punched Josie back on line and told her about Sam's call.

"Are you making any progress at all?"

"None. But Sam and I agree if this were a murder for hire, the killer would have used smarter, surer methods than bludgeoning someone. I'm running out of time, Josie. Judy's going to derail Brian's campaign. And Kansas needs him."

"I agree. Oh well. Hell, why not? Send me everything you have about the St. John murder. It would be legal for Sam to use me as a consultant. Since you expect me to be a psychologist by proxy, I might as well be a sleuth by proxy too."

We hung up. Next, I called Brian and urged him to arrange a complete exam for Fiona. He was silent when I described the symptoms Josie had asked about. "Have you noticed any of these things? Headaches? Tremors? Eye discoloration?"

"No, none whatsoever. I'm surprised at what all can go wrong with the human body. I'm sure I would know if Mother were having headaches. She's hardly one to suffer in silence."

He called back two hours later and said he and Jenny had talked it over and he felt as though he had burdened me unnecessarily. While he couldn't thank me enough, he had decided to wait to schedule an appointment for Fiona. No rush. He was certain there was nothing really major wrong.

"It's not a good idea, Brian. Josie made that clear."

He thanked me again, then hung up.

◇◇◇

That evening, I heard the mournful strains of Keith's fiddle when I walked through the door. He played gloomy old-timey songs, "My Darling Cory is Gone," and "The L&M Don't Stop Here Any More." I moved from the kitchen into the living room and watched him play for twenty minutes before he stopped, acknowledged my presence.

"Hungry, honey?" I asked. Like most rural folk, we ate dinner at mid-day. Supper was usually light, improvised.

He shook his head, tucked his fiddle back under chin, then as if worried that he had offended me by his curtness, he lowered it to his side again.

"Unless you've already started something special," he said carefully.

He has brown hair, still thick, although graying. It was mussed now, forming a boyish frame around his serious face.

"No." I smiled. "Nothing special. Soup and fruit."

He started to position his fiddle, then looked mortified and lowered it again.

"I didn't mean to imply you *should* have fixed something special. Don't want you to take it that way."

"Of course not." My tone was light, but I was seething. *I'm not a touchy woman. I'm not like your first wife.* If he started weighing every word, second guessing my every thought, our lives would be impossible.

"I brought some editing home. After I'm done, I'll turn in early." I rose, started toward the stairs, hoping he would call me back.

He didn't.

◇◇◇

The next morning, still miserable over the pall descending on our marriage, I gloomed around the office like an exhausted charwoman. I missed Judy's help, but I wanted her to continue cleaning and sorting her attic. Given her conflict of interests, I was grateful she would be occupied with that task for the next couple of weeks.

By the looks of my desk, I needed to catch up my daily work. I went into high gear. God had given me a good mind. I intended to use it to get my two jobs under control, and find a way out of my marital mess. The most obvious way was to solve two murders, new and old, so I would have time to think about persons other than cold-blooded killers. Persons like warm-blooded husbands.

I flew through the bills and the stories, saving the letter stack for last. I bit my lip, stunned, that I hadn't seen it at once. Another letter, post-marked from Phoenix this time.

> What if the person the family has been hiding is me? What if I've murdered before and will do it again? What if you start uncovering all kinds of trash with your snooping around?

It was as though an icy hand had reached out and clutched my arm. Tickled up goose bumps. Made my heart skip a beat. I, who have always prided myself on my intuition, hadn't had an inkling this person was really dangerous until that very instant. I stared at the piece of paper, got up and locked the office and took the file to Sam Abbott.

◇◇◇

He read them all, smiled and assured me it was someone's idea of a prank.

"It's close to Halloween, Lottie. When you've been around as long as I have, you'd know how to recognize a joke. Someone having fun."

"But what if it's not?"

"It is. I've lived in this county all my life and know about everything there is to know about folks living here. We're not harboring a murderer."

I stared at him in disbelief, thinking of the all the secrets exposed while compiling my books.

"Who do you think murdered Zelda? An alien?" I'd gone too far. Temper flashed in his eyes before he reached for his pipe and delayed. Searching for the right words to instruct a wayward child.

"That's different. And rare. It's never happened here before. It was real. A body discovered. Not pieces of paper."

Thinking of the Swenson murders, I stilled my face.

"You've got to learn to sort, Lottie. Figure out what's intriguing to you as an historian, what's a police matter, and frankly, learn to clamp down on your over-active imagination."

I left, mad as hell, and called my sister on my cell before I went back to the office.

"Josie? Are you up to another professional consultation?"

"If you're up to my bills."

"Remember those letters I told you about? They're heating up." I read her the latest and told her about Sam blowing me off. "What do you think is going on?"

"My head, based on all my training, tells me I agree with Sam. Someone is having a jolly good time pushing your buttons. Someone you know fairly well has a macabre sense of humor."

"What does your gut tell you?"

"My gut says it's worried you're worried. My gut says there's nothing funny about any of this. Not a thing."

"You don't think those letters are just what they appear to be? A cry for help?"

"I hate that stupid phrase." She sighed. "I thought it was the well-known 'cry' before, but I don't anymore. I don't like the tone of this one. Do you have any enemies?"

"No," I said flatly. "I may have rubbed a few people the wrong way, but I haven't made any enemies."

"Think hard."

"I got someone fired at the nursing home," I said tentatively. "She was angry. But, even if she were mad enough, I know she isn't smart enough to be doing this."

"You're not going to like this, Lottie, but I have to ask. Could Elizabeth be doing this?"

"No way." I went rigid. My scalp tightened with despair. "Why would you even *think* that?"

"Don't dismiss the idea too quickly. One doesn't have to be a psychologist to know you're a little touchy about your relationships with your stepchildren. Think about it. If Keith called me to see if I could discourage you, he probably mentioned his unhappiness with your new job to Elizabeth. They do call one another, I assume."

"Yes, and she's very protective of him. But she's not a sneaky person. I think she would call me up and bawl me out. Tell me off for upsetting her father."

"If someone isn't pulling your leg, and if it isn't Elizabeth trying to scare you out of your new job, I like the other alternative even less. The letter says the writer has murdered before and will again."

◇◇◇

That evening, I shoved ground beef back and forth in the skillet, looking at it hard, not meeting Keith's eyes even though he sat a mere three feet away reading his paper. I wished we could recover our former easiness. The distance had begun the day I took the job. I wanted to ask him if his daughter hated me. If I had misread her degree of animosity.

I added cooked macaroni to the mixture, dumped in tomato sauce, and set it to simmer. I started on a salad. He jumped up to set the table.

I dished up. We sat down. He said it looked like rain, and I said, yes, it surely did. He said it looked like everyone was going to have a good corn crop, and I said it sure looked like it. He helped clear. I washed up. He dried.

I ran upstairs, got my pistol and my ear plugs, and went outside. It was deep twilight, and I switched on the yard light. I set up a row of beer cans on a log and started shooting. I heard the back screen door slam. I could feel his massive presence behind me, silently watching.

Bang. The first can flipped into the air. Bang. The second can followed. I whirled around.

"Say something. Set me on the path of righteousness. You know that's what you're dying to do."

"Nothing to say. You're liberated, lady. Got a star on your chest to prove it. You say what you want. Do what you want."

"I don't. I don't. Every breath I draw is dictated by you. I don't speak, act, or do anything without your permission."

We heard each other with obvious amazement. He put his hands on my shoulders.

"You know what you just said isn't true," he said. "Same as I know what I just said isn't true."

"I didn't know you'd mind that much, Keith."

"You did know, down deep inside, or you would have talked it over with me first. That's what hurt the most. Not even talking it over."

He had me there.

"This is the first time since we've married you've ever done anything I didn't like, Lottie. The very first time. And even so, I haven't said one critical word to you about it. Now have I?"

"But you went behind my back, Keith. To my sister. That's what hurts. The going behind my back."

"I was wrong, and I'm ashamed."

I was stricken by his tenderness. It was as though he were handling an exquisite animal whose spirit he didn't want to break.

Tears rolled down my cheeks. "I take it back. I take it all back. Every word I said. You *don't* tell me what to do. What to say. You never have."

"I'm ashamed of calling Josie. I apologize."

"Keith, did you call Elizabeth, too? Tell her how you felt?"

"I mentioned it," he said gruffly. "Why?"

"Just wondered."

He didn't know about the letters I was getting at the office. I decided it was better not to trouble him with Josie's suspicions.

"I think this is a very good night to kiss and make up," I said.

"At last we agree."

Chapter Twenty-Five

The next evening, Keith went with me to a tri-county rally for Brian. The crowd was as big as we could hope for considering the political climate in Kansas this year.

Brian's face tensed as he endured the lengthy introduction. On his right sat Jenny, to his left, Fiona and Edgar Hadley. He spoke for thirty minutes about the farm problem. He pledged to do away with subsidies and promised to investigate the fairness of deficiency payments. It was dull, dull, dull, but it gave me a chance to look at him for a long time.

His eyes were haunted. He had lost weight. Suddenly, I felt very sorry for him. He would probably lose this election. There were too many obstacles for him to overcome. There would be other years, other chances. He was still very young. But from a strategic standpoint, I wished he had waited.

I endured to the end, as did everyone else. Then Keith spotted some neighbors and went off to say hello, and I headed to the back of the auditorium to speak with Brian. He left the building through the back exit before I could reach him.

Fast-moving dark clouds scudded in front of a high-flying crescent moon. The night air was chilly.

A little child came up to him out of the shadows.

"Can I have your autograph? My mom says you're going to be president some day if the people in this state have any sense at all."

He automatically reached toward his breast pocket for a pen, then stopped.

"Later," he said curtly. "I'll do it later. I haven't got time right now. Now run along."

Dismayed by his churlishness, I stayed in the shadows. Brian had always been as gracious in private as he was in public. This refusal to sign a simple autograph was so unlike him I could hardly believe my ears. Slump-shouldered, the child walked away.

Brian walked over to his car, which was parked at the side of the building. I watched as he opened his car door and pulled a flask from the console. He tipped back the bottle and took a deep drink. His hands trembled under the dome light as he screwed the cap back on, and wiped his mouth.

How could I not have seen this? Not have noticed? All the signs were there, and they were unmistakable. If golden boy wasn't an out and out alcoholic, he damn sure had a serious drinking problem.

I recalled the day I had gone to the Hadleys' house, when Fiona had thrown her little fit and Brian had told me how concerned he was. He'd tossed down several stiff drinks in the middle of the day. I had excused him due to the circumstances. His hands had trembled that day, too. I'd assumed it was from anger. As clear as day, I heard again William's words. I remembered Brian's defensiveness.

No wonder he was so often in dark glasses. They were to hide his bloodshot eyes. No wonder he didn't want me to pursue Fiona's physical. It would have drawn too much attention to him. All the symptoms Josie was interested in and had described were ones that fit an alcoholic.

Just win the election, I thought bitterly. They're all alike, and he's no better than any of the rest of them. Just do whatever it takes to win the election.

Heartbroken, I turned, left without speaking to him. I found Keith. "Let's go home."

Not only was I sad over a life being wasted right before my very eyes, I was furious over the time I had wasted on his behalf.

If I had known there was even a hint of this kind of problem, I wouldn't have volunteered to be his county campaign chairman. To some, my attitude would sound cold and bloodless. I didn't care. My struggles with my mother had drained me of all pity for drunks.

I didn't like them.

◇◇◇

The next morning, I edited stories with renewed vigor. Mentally, I composed a little speech to the Hadley family. I now had an ideal excuse to disengage myself from this crazy bunch of people. I didn't want a fiery confrontation with Brian, although it might have done him a world of good. But I wasn't out to do him good. I didn't take him to raise.

My goal had been to get him elected. Now I hoped his hypocritical little soul went down in flames. It might hurt him politically if I withdrew from the local level without explanation, but not much. There was nothing I was going to say or do that the big boys couldn't handle.

Better yet, I fumed, I would put it all in a letter. I reached for a piece of paper with the historical society's letterhead, then changed my mind. I got up, went to my briefcase, and took out a piece of my personal stationary.

The phone rang.

"Lottie? I've been waiting for you to return my call. I couldn't stand it any longer," Judy said.

"Darn, I'm sorry, Judy. I forgot to give you my cell number. What call?"

"I left a message on your answering machine about six-thirty this morning. Before the office opened. Telling you I'd found a letter you weren't going to believe. It'll blow this county sky high. I called early because I didn't want a volunteer to hear me if you had the phone on speaker."

Puzzled, I looked at the message counter on my machine. It was blank. This was the third time now someone claimed to leave a message for me that I hadn't received.

"Just a minute. Sounds like something that should be kept inside these walls." I laid down the handset, and closed the heavy outside door. "Now, what would be so important you would want to call me that early in the morning?"

"I've found the smoking gun, Lottie. The proof that Fiona murdered my mother."

"You've found what?" Blood left my brain along with my police academy training.

"A letter. An old, old letter. Well, a copy actually. Which makes it even better."

Breath returned. Blood began flowing. An old letter wasn't proof of anything. Zilch.

"Explain, Judy."

"One of Mom's trunks had a false bottom. I found it in there. Remember those blank pages we found in the attic? Remember the rose watermark? It's much clearer on this letter. But I want to *show* you, not tell you about it. It's never been about the family history story, Lottie. It's not the handwriting either."

"Judy! What for god's sake?" I wanted to reach through the phone lines and wring her scrawny little neck.

"Come dressed in your Deputy Dog costume so you can arrest Aunt Fiona on the spot."

She interrupted my furious protests that things didn't work like that.

"I've already called her to come over. I want her to actually see me hand you the letter. It's high noon. Fresh horses for me and whisky for my men." Like the hero in an old western, sure of righteous victory, she didn't bother to suppress her satisfaction over the coming show-down.

"Jesus Christ, Judy. Fiona's coming over?"

"You bet. I said her life depended on it. She doesn't know you'll be here. I want to surprise her."

"Don't say anything dumb to Fiona. Use your head. I'll be there in a flash."

Chapter Twenty-Six

Flipping the office sign to "closed," I called Sam as I rushed to my Tahoe. His personal cell phone went to voicemail. "Sam, I'm heading to the St. John's. Judy's asked Fiona to meet her there, and claims she's found a letter tying her to Zelda's death. I want to ward off trouble."

Then worried, I followed that with a call to dispatch and asked Betty Central to radio Sam to meet me at the St. Johns.

"Is it urgent?" Her voice quivered with excitement.

"Just do it Betty."

After I reached the city limits I drove as fast as I dared. Seething over Judy's stupidity in inviting a woman she thought had murdered her mother over to her house, I used every cuss word I'd ever heard Keith use, some of Josie's, and a few of my own. Even though Brian had given Fiona an alibi for the night of Zelda's murder, I didn't trust the woman. Even if she wasn't a killer, she was pure D crazy. No telling what she might do if Judy pissed her off. Dust roiled behind my Tahoe as I tore down the St. John's lane. To my relief, I'd beat Fiona there.

Judy didn't answer the doorbell. When I rang it the second time and she didn't come, I knew something was very wrong.

Judy should have come flying out the door.

Judy should have been tugging me inside.

Judy should have been waving a letter under my nose.

I opened the door and went inside. "Judy?" I started down the hallway toward the kitchen. "Judy?" My voice strained against tight vocal cords. My stomach clamped against a bilious surge. I looked through all the rooms downstairs and went upstairs and looked in Judy's bedroom.

No Judy. I looked in the other bedrooms, went back down the stairs and checked the rest of the house. Mindful of my training, I stepped outside, watching for any movement, hearing every sound. I checked the machine shed. No Judy.

Drawn to the barn, I slid open the door leading to the hay storage area and peered through the dusky interior.

Judy hung from a rafter. Hung like a little sack of seed.

I slowly backed outside, and vomited into a patch of weeds. My teeth chattered. I reviewed the steps for protecting a crime scene. Then paralyzed, I watched Fiona Hadley drive up and park beside my Tahoe.

A nightmare. A waking nightmare.

"Well, bless my soul. I didn't know you were going to be here, Lottie." She was all gussied up in a two-piece blue knit suit with a jaunty fedora hat. "Now what was so goddamn important that my no-count niece would interrupt Tuesday Study Club?"

I looked at her like some dumb animal.

"What's wrong?" She stared at my face as she walked toward me. "Is something wrong?"

"It's Judy."

"Judy?" Her steps faltered, and she glanced at the open door to the barn. She peered through the dusty interior, saw her niece hanging there, and rushed toward her. I grabbed her hands, and held on hard.

She tried to twist away. "Help me," she screamed. "You've got to help me get her down."

"Don't touch anything. Don't do anything."

"She's my niece, you stupid arrogant bitch. My niece. All I have left of Zelda."

"Fiona, stop. It's a crime scene."

"Crime scene? Crime scene? Haven't you got a brain in your head? She's hanged herself, and you're responsible. You encouraged her senseless little witch hunt, and now look what you've done. I tried to tell you. She's always been a mess. A total mess. And you've led her on, with your everlasting probing and slinking around."

"Shut up Fiona, or I'll arrest you for interfering with an investigation. Now get in your car and stay there. Do you understand? I'll have you hauled off. I called Sheriff Abbott before I came. He'll decide if it's suicide."

"Oh, right. In this town it's just as likely good old Yosemite Sam will say it was an accident."

But she went to her car. A direct order seemed to have calmed her.

I heard her sob through her rolled-up window, then Sam drove up. She jumped out, and was at his car in a flash.

"I want you to arrest Lottie Albright for driving my niece to kill herself," she sobbed. "Arrest the incompetent fool. My sister's dead and now my niece. Both of them within a month."

"I want you out of here, Fiona," Sam said. "Is Edgar home? I'll call him to come after you. I don't want you driving in this state of mind."

"I'm not leaving. Not till I see that poor baby cut down off that rope."

"We have work to do."

"We? You're going to let her help with this? Are you crazy?"

He whirled around and flipped his cell phone open. "Edgar? I'm afraid I have more bad news for your family. Judy St. John has been found in the barn. Hanged. Yes. Lottie's here. And so's Fiona. I want you to come get her."

He hung up and walked back over to Fiona. "Get back in your car. Don't touch anything. Don't do anything. Edgar is on the way."

He firmly grasped Fiona's upper arm and escorted her to her Cadillac.

She did not go quietly. "It's all your fault, Lottie Albright. You drove her to it. You won't be able to show your face in this town by the time I'm through with you."

She twisted from Sam's grasp, slid into the driver's seat, and pointedly locked the door. Shoulders shaking, she laid her head against the steering wheel and sobbed uncontrollably.

Then Sam turned to me, with teeth clenched.

"Don't you ever, ever leave a stupid son-of-a-bitching message on my cell phone like that again, Lottie. You either have a situation, or you don't. Our job isn't to 'ward off trouble.' You're either on a job as an historian or my deputy. As an historian you're used to deciding what's important. Evaluating. But, by God, as an officer of the law, I expect you to go by the book."

My face flamed. "I would like to remind you, Sam, that just yesterday, you dismissed letters that I thought were sinister as hell."

"Different situation entirely, Lottie."

"It's not. This started with a letter, too. You said I was supposed to sort before acting. Clamp down on my alleged over-active imagination. No matter what Judy thought, I knew an old letter in a trunk wouldn't be enough to tie Fiona to Zelda's murder, I just wanted to stop her and Judy from getting physical."

"You don't know jack shit, lady. Not about a letter. Not about nothing. Got that? It's not our job to know. We collect evidence. You don't decide. I don't decide. You came here as my deputy. To control a situation. You were an officer of the law when you left that office. I repeat, when you are heading toward people, you've got a situation. Now anything else you've decided to think about a while, before you mention it?"

"Yes." I didn't like ass-eatings, but I could take them with the best. I used to think my dissertation committee members were former SS officers. "Judy said she left a message for me. But there wasn't one, and it's the third time I've run into that situation."

He snorted. "That's curious, but not criminal."

◇◇◇

We walked to the barn. I shuddered, and stared at Judy's pale distorted face. Pretended to be professional, when all my senses were reeling.

"This murder is so obvious the signs would be unmistakable to an eleven-year-old reader of Nancy Drew." Solemnly, he rubbed the side of his nose. "There's sweeps in the dust where someone covered up footprints. Someone carried Judy in here."

He had a faint, sad smile on his face. "Most telling of all are the footprints that aren't here. Judy's. Not a trace of evidence she walked in here under her own steam. Neat trick, don't you think?"

A column of dust moved toward us. Edgar driving at least eighty miles an hour on country roads in his junky old pickup. Crazy careless. He swerved close to Fiona's car, braked, skidded to a stop.

Fiona jumped from her car and ran to him. Edgar hugged her against his chest, they swayed from side to side, then Edgar put his arm around her, left his pickup set, and they drove off in her Cadillac.

Sam called Jim Gilderhaus, and formally asked the FBI to assist. Even though I could only hear one side of the conversation, clearly the agent was aghast that the same family was involved.

"We're not to do a damn thing until they get here. He's going to bring more men this time. Give this place a good going over." Gloomily Sam looked around at the run-down farmstead. Patches of weeds swayed under the blue cloudless sky. A rabbit scuttled toward the shelter belt. We both started as a quick breeze vibrated the wind chimes on the porch.

"Sam, I can give you the time this happened within twenty minutes. Whoever killed her did it right after Judy finished talking to me this morning. Clearly they had reason to expect she wouldn't be discovered until evening, when Max got home from the store. No one knew I was coming here except you and Judy and Betty Central."

"Any chance you were overheard at the office?"

"No. The vault is nearly soundproof after I close the door. And if someone had heard on Judy's end, they'd have known I was coming right away, and wouldn't have gone through with it. They were probably outside watching through a window, waiting for her to hang up."

◇◇◇

Gilderhaus took down every word I said, but his mouth tightened with disapproval at my hopelessly tangled involvement. I was Judy's boss, her friend, and the law enforcement officer who'd discovered the crime. Sun glinted off his silver eyeglasses, as he called to confirm that Fiona had been at the Tuesday Study Club, until Judy called her out of the meeting.

"Now about that letter. Do you know what that was about?"

"No." I told him Judy said the rose watermark was critical, but I didn't know why.

"OK. I want you and agent Mendoza to search for the letter, while the crime team works the barn."

Although we started with the attic and the false bottomed trunk, I was sure Judy would've taken it downstairs. Had it handy, to taunt Fiona, and convince me. We couldn't find it. I knew the killer had taken it, but it didn't matter. Like Sam said, knowing didn't count. My job was to follow procedure by the book, and if I had any doubts on how it should be done, Mendoza set me straight. Her dark eyes scanned like a video camera before we entered any room.

Sam and I spent a long hard day watching experts with resources our sparsely populated county would never have. They cataloged, photographed, bagged, and firmly turned away press, neighbors, and townspeople.

We finally headed for our cars. "That bitch is going to be a real problem," he said. "Fiona's hell on wheels, even when she isn't all het up."

"Don't I know." I got into my Tahoe. He started toward his SUV, then came back and gestured for me to lower the window so I could hear him.

"Just want you to know, Lottie, whether she's a problem or not, no one is going to tell me who I can hire or fire. Especially not Fiona Hadley."

"I have to quit, Sam. This is a high profile case. Lots of attention due to Brian's campaign. It's his mother making all these accusations with his Carlton County campaign manager cast as the villain. Keeping me around will cause you too much grief. It won't work. We can kiss Brian's career goodbye, of course."

His eyes flashed. "So?"

"You may not want me gone, Sam, but Fiona does. I'll resign right away."

"Don't." His eyes hardened. "I won't have it. She'll use that as an excuse to ruin me. Cast doubt on my judgment for hiring you in the first place. She'll go after you too."

Heartsick, I knew he was right. If I left, it might be taken as a sign of ineptitude or wrongdoing on the part of the Carlton County Sheriff Department. Since Sam was the one who had hired me, Fiona would bring him down in a heartbeat. She wouldn't care that he was the finest sheriff this county had ever had or that she would be taking away his livelihood.

"All right, but I'll spend a lot more time at the historical society. I'll work on this by remote. Out of uniform. I won't attract as much attention that way. If you don't mind my mixing the jobs up a little." I tried to sound innocent. Dig free. Our recent flame-out over the letters couldn't have been further from my mind.

His lips twitched, his guile detector quivering at my one-upmanship. There's an advantage to working with old folks who know good and well how the world works.

"Makes sense. We'll do it your way, Lottie."

"First time for my way, huh?"

He nodded. I watched the old man walk off and shivered.

Chapter Twenty-Seven

I didn't get home until after nine. Keith was waiting. I'd tried to call him around mid-afternoon. When he didn't answer his cell, I left bare bones voicemail that Judy was dead and I would be late.

"You've heard? All the details?"

"It's all over town. I've been worried sick." Wordlessly, I just walked over and let him enfold me as I burst into tears, crying over the loss of a woman I'd grown to love like a daughter.

I slumped onto a counter stool at the island. Keith slapped baloney and cheese between two slices of bread. Grim-faced, he handed it to me.

"I can't," I said.

"You can."

Too weary to argue, I reached for it and took a bite. Then I got up reached for Keith again, needing his warmth more than food.

"And to top it off, Sam and I had a fight, honey." I told him about the anonymous letters mailed to the historical society. His breath stopped, his arms tightened.

"That's damn sure not my idea of joke."

"Not mine either."

Then hearing a car coming up our lane, I closed my eyes. The day simply would not end. I would be frozen in this terrible day throughout eternity.

Keith swore, switched on the porch light and peered outside.

"It's Brian Hadley," he said.

"I'm not up to another Hadley."

"I'll talk to him, Lottie. You go on upstairs."

"You will *not*. I kill my own snakes. You should know that by now."

We went to the front door together and opened it. Keith stood behind me, and laid his hands on my shoulders. My soul shriveled as Brian slammed the car door shut. His mouth a razor-thin line, he looked at us hard for a second before he came up the walk.

"Come in, Brian," I said. "I can't tell…"

"You're not going to tell me nothing, lady," he said. "I'm here to tell you. You involved Judy in a kind of work she wasn't equipped to handle. Mom has told me all about the prying she was doing. Now she's dead. By her own hand. We all tried to tell you. But you wouldn't leave well enough alone, would you? Poke and prod, poke and prod."

"Brian, that's not true." I bit my tongue to keep from blurting that it was murder, not suicide. Guilderhaus had asked law enforcement personnel to keep their mouths' shut until the coroner officially announced the cause of death. Not that half the county didn't know already. But after Sam's lecture I intended to behave like a pro. Even if I was dead on my feet.

"Judy was like a sister to me."

"Brian, I know that. She told me how much you meant to her. All the things you did for her when she was young."

"You're off the campaign, Lottie. I should have listened to my mother earlier."

My laughter was harsh, incredulous. Fiona was suddenly an oracle of wisdom? What had happened to the early Alzheimer's?

"As a matter of fact, Brian, you've just beat me to the punch." Keith stood behind me. Ominous, wolf alert. Ready to pounce. "I wrote a letter of resignation just this morning. I didn't have time to mail it before Judy's death."

"Gonna tell me why, Lottie, or are you keeping that a deep, dark secret?"

"Come closer to the light, Brian, I want to be able to look you in the eye when I say what I have to say."

He walked toward us, stopped when he was about six feet away. His complexion was sallow. Yellow. The whites of his eyes were muddy. I glanced at his trembling hands.

"You're the one who's been keeping secrets and now I know what your secret is."

His face paled. The skin around his lips tightened. If it's possible for a human to will his heart to stop beating, the world to stop turning, he did it just then. He was completely motionless. It was as though I had hit him with a two-by-four.

"My own mother was a drunk, Brian. I should have noticed the signs in you earlier, but I wanted to believe." I never took my gaze off him. "It's a common failing in kids who've lived with drunks all their lives. We want so very much to believe, it just breaks our hearts."

I faltered, confused. Even as I was speaking, the expression in his eyes was changing, from shame to a spark of something I could not identify.

"You think I'm a drunk? A drunk?" He threw back his head and laughed.

"I know all about denial, Brian." I wanted to sound brave, self-assured. Keith's hands tightened on my shoulders.

Brian stared at me steadily. I glanced at my feet. Something was happening here I didn't understand. What I did know was I had been in charge and now he was, through some subtle transference of power.

"I've been thinking about a treatment program," he said calmly. "Do you suppose your sister would recommend one? I don't intend to deal with this until after the election. I'm sure you know all my reasons."

I was completely thrown. "Yes, of course, Josie would know who to go to. Brian, I really am sorry. About Judy, about your problem."

"I apologize for my impulsiveness in coming over here."

"No apology necessary. I know how close you and Judy were."

He nodded. "Nevertheless, considering my mother's feelings, it would still be better if you were off my campaign."

"Of course. I think it will a big relief to us both, and I won't have to worry about the press asking questions."

"I'll head back home," he said. "Again, my apologies."

We watched his taillights disappear. Surprised by my sudden surge of rage at Brian's unpredictability, I turned to my rock-solid husband. Relishing his protection, I clung to him like a barnacle.

◇◇◇

The door to my office was already open when I arrived the next morning. Margaret Atchison sat at her desk, sorting the mail. She glanced at me, then looked away.

"I'm surprised to see you here, Margaret. I had planned to close today out of respect for Judy. I came in to round up her personal belongings to take to Max."

She looked up with a stern, sad expression on her face. "They've called a board meeting, Lottie."

"I'm the director of this society and I haven't been told about it?"

She lowered her eyes. "No, it's about you."

"About me?"

"The Hadley family has asked that we relieve you of your duties."

I slammed the storage box down on the floor and caught my breath. "But this is *my* organization. I'm the one who started this place."

"You started it, yes. But it wouldn't be the first time the person who started an organization ended up not being the right person to run it."

"That's ridiculous. We've collected a record amount of information. Our methods are second to none."

"Lottie, I really don't know what's going on. If I did, I would tell you. At first, I was worried your new job would cut in too much on your time here, but I changed my mind. And I never thought much of Judy, but she was doing a good job. Things were going okay."

"I'm going to be in this office more. You can count on that."

Margaret looked at me sorrowfully, and I was stricken with apprehension.

"Maybe you'll be here," she said, "if they let you stay on."

"Let me stay on?" I laughed. Let me stay on this thankless, miserable job? But I knew the job enabled me to live in Western Kansas. I needed work, needed the satisfaction of active research. I needed the connection with the community. More than that, this job was mine, and they were trying to take it from me.

"Won't I have a chance to speak?"

"Oh, I'll see to that. I still have some say-so around this county, but Fiona tells anyone who will listen that you don't have a clue about dealing with people."

My mouth literally dropped open. "She thinks *I* don't know how to deal with people. What pure unmitigated gall."

"She blames you for Judy's suicide."

"I know that, Margaret. How did she manage to crucify me practically overnight? What did she do? Start phoning people from the mortuary?" I ached to tell Margaret that Judy's death was a homicide, not suicide.

"She says there's something worse, Lottie. That's what this meeting is about."

I saw William walk past the door. Grim-faced, his old straw fedora pulled down over his forehead. My heart sank.

Margaret glanced at her watch, stood and squared her shoulders. "It's time for me to go up, Lottie. I'll call down when we're ready for you."

My emotions ranging between seething and heart-sick, I started packing Judy's things while I waited. There were a number of how-to manuals and organizing aids. She'd been determined to do her best.

Sadly, I picked up the one picture Judy had on her makeshift desk: a family portrait of herself, Max, and Zelda. I wrapped it in tissue and carefully placed it on top of her books, where the glass would be protected.

The telephone rang.

"You can come up now," Margaret said. I didn't like the sound of her voice.

Chapter Twenty-Eight

They sat in a hostile circle around the table in the county commissioners' room. Edgar held Fiona's hand. Edgar. I recalled Judy's saying how much she had liked this man, how much he had liked her. He glared at me steadily, his eyes dark globes of hate.

I looked at the circle: Fiona and Edgar, Margaret, William, and my Three Wise Men: Fritz Sprinkle, Bill Loft, and Silas Buchannan. I had given them this name because I could always count on them to bear gifts: wisdom, maturity, and compassion. They were generous and honorable.

Fritz, the chairman of the board was a retired magistrate judge. Tall, leggy as an old flamingo, he and the other two men stood when I walked into the room. The Hadleys and Margaret remained seated.

"Please," I said quietly. "Do sit down. I certainly intend to."

Bill Loft was the only one wearing a suit. He clearly did not want to be here. The weak, sick smile, or his soft, pudgy face signaled that he didn't understand any of this. He wasn't alone. Neither did I. Like most bankers, Bill preferred to conduct business behind closed doors with people he understood. And I knew whose side he would be on if push came to shove. The Hadleys. They banked at his bank. As prominent farmers, they were significant customers: used a lot of money, borrowed a lot, paid back a lot, saved a lot. Banks thrived on the circulation of money.

Silas Buchannon, a retired farmer, and a member of the Parish Council at Keith's church, had sat in on a zillion church fights. He had William's stern sense of duty. He wore blue-grey Dicky work clothes, which to him were considerably dressier than overalls. His wife cut his wiry grizzled hair, and it never looked quite the same from one time to the next. Today, it looked like an old bird nest perched on his long earnest head.

"What's this all about?" I asked.

"How can you pretend you don't know?" Fiona blurted. "Did you honestly think people wouldn't find out?"

I froze. This clearly was something more serious than an objection to my new part-time job.

Fritz cleared his throat. "The Hadleys here say they have proof you took the Custer letter from the Historical Society and tried to sell it."

I felt the blood seep from my face, pool in my feet. The veins in my arms were blue against my ashen skin. "That's ridiculous. I'm a historian. Surely you all know I'm the last person who would do such a thing. Why would you think I had?"

"I got this phone call," said Fiona, "from a curator for a museum in Santa Fe. He'd received a letter from a professor at the University of New Mexico saying you'd called offering to sell a letter in Custer's own hand. The professor was inquiring about its value. The curator called me, wondering how you came by such a document."

"A phone call? You're trying to take my job on the basis of a phone call? This is incredible, Fiona. No one could possibly have my signature on anything, because I didn't do anything."

"There's a fact here," said Edgar.

We all looked at him. As is often the case with persons who seldom speak, when they do, everyone listens.

"The fact is, this letter is missing. No one can argue that. And it went missing on Lottie's watch."

"That's half a fact, Edgar."

Now we all looked at William, who had been silent until then.

"It may be a fact that the letter is missing, but I was on duty that afternoon, not Lottie."

My line may be that I can take care of myself, kill my own snakes, but I looked at William like he was the United States Cavalry come riding over the hill. Who would have thought?

"No one has a key to the main courthouse door except for the janitor, the magistrate judge, the commissioners, and Priscilla Ramsey in case the extension people need in. Several of us have keys to the office, but just Margaret and Lottie have keys to the master file. The Custer letter was there when I locked up the office that evening."

"You can't know that," Fiona snapped.

William shot her a look. "You questioning my memory or my integrity, lady? Old Mrs. Peabody came in just before I closed up. Needed names from some special school records. Margaret was down the hall at an extension meeting, so we fetched her to open the file. I noticed the Custer letter right off when she first opened the file drawer, because Lottie uses bright orange folders for important documents she's going to copy for the State Historical Society. Damned interesting stuff."

"William followed all the rules," Margaret piped up. "It wouldn't be a historical society if folks couldn't read documents. He just had to have someone in there with him."

"I think we all know I follow the rules, Margaret," William said. "Like I was saying, I read what I could before Mrs. Peabody finished, and then Margaret locked everything away again."

Silas cleared his throat. "Fiona, don't you think it's funny that a curator from New Mexico would call you and Edgar?"

A plain-spoken man, like William, he got right to the point.

"'Pears to me that if someone in New Mexico had suspicions, he would call the law. You and Edgar have an unlisted number. How would a feller from New Mexico know what it was?"

"Are you accusing me of lying?" Fiona asked.

"Not right off, no," said Silas. "What I'm saying is, it seems funny someone from New Mexico would call you and Edgar. How would they know to do that? On the other hand, if I lived in this county and wanted to get Lottie in a heap of trouble, I would know you and Edgar were just the people to rile up."

"Did you check anything out?" William asked, "before you called this meeting? Wasted all our time? We're all folks who have real work to do."

I looked at William and Silas. They liked me. They actually liked me. I was surprised at the look of outrage on William's face. Silas' words were harsh, but reasoned. When William spoke next, he didn't bother to pretty up a thing.

"If either one of you had half a brain, you'd know Lottie wouldn't do something that stupid. If she wanted to sell the Custer letter without someone finding out, I 'spec she could have. She would have known how. Another thing is, she's not exactly a pauper. Couldn't have been that much money involved."

"Probably tens of thousands of dollars," Fiona said.

"Yep, probably was," Silas said, "but William's right. Lottie doesn't need that money. Wouldn't be near enough to risk ruining her reputation."

"Lottie spends more money on the historical society than she takes out," William said. "I know for a fact she's brought into the office two computers, a laser printer, a fax, a Nikon digital camera, a photo copy stand, a microwave oven, a digital recorder, a copy machine, and a fancy two-line phone with an answering machine equipped with an extended recorder for taping oral histories. Mighty poor burglar, if you ask me."

Fiona paled. "I'm not making this up," she said. "You're all looking at me like I'm making this up."

The banker looked like he was going to throw up.

Edgar sat there like he had been struck by lightning. Like he was hearing truths he hadn't considered before, but recognized when they were laid out as plain as day.

I finally risked a look at Fiona. She was pale, frightened. A woman who had been through a lot in the last couple of days. Something in her tone of voice convinced me she was telling the truth.

Truth is what I'm about. If she was telling the truth, I wanted everyone there to know it.

I did not like this woman, but for all I knew, she might be ill and right then she was being seen in the worst possible light.

We all knew she was mean as a snake. But historically, snakes have always had a lot to say.

"I think it's time we left, Edgar." Tears brimmed in her eyes as she rose to leave. "I never thought I would see the day when the people of this county would take the word of a rank stranger over a Rubidoux."

"Wait, Fiona." She turned those great tragic eyes toward me. "Please, answer a few questions for me. I would like to know more about that phone call." She gave a proud little nod of assent, but she did not sit back down. "Was it a man or a woman?"

"A man," she said.

"When?"

"Around six-thirty last evening."

"What did the voice sound like?"

"I don't know what you mean."

There are tricks to seizing control, and I know them all. I rose, walked to the head of the table where she had been sitting seconds ago, remained standing, above them all, fists braced on the table.

"Educated, uneducated, accent of any kind? High? Low? Pleasant? What can you remember?"

She moved to my previous place, was joined by a stunned Edgar. Obviously thinking hard, she automatically sat down. I was restoring her credibility through my questions. With any luck, she could save a little face.

"It was a grown-up voice," she said slowly, "not a kid playing a prank. He didn't have any accent at all."

I smiled. Typical Kansas attitude. We're the only ones who talk normally.

"I wish I had recorded the conversation, but I didn't. At first I wasn't paying much attention, then I was too shocked to do anything but listen. He wasn't on the line very long. I started to ask him questions, but he said he had to go to a meeting."

"Sometimes it helps to write everything down, Fiona. I would like you to do that for us right now. What you said, what he said. Everything."

I pushed a legal pad toward her across the table.

"Just try to shut us out of your mind. Play like we're not even in the room."

She nodded and closed her eyes a second, picked up the pen and began to write. It took several minutes. I looked around at their faces. No matter who had started this fight, I had won.

"Thank you," I said, when she finished. "Would you sign and date that, please, for the records here at the society."

She picked up her pen again and did just that. I looked around at the men and Margaret, knowing Fiona's willingness to sign meant something to these people. Same as a handshake on a deal did. Now they all knew Fiona and Edgar Hadley were not lying. Clearly, they knew I wasn't either.

"If you don't mind staying a bit longer, I'd like to read this to all the board members. In case we have questions."

I flashed a brilliant smile at everyone. They had drawn a circle that shut me out. I had just drawn a larger circle that took them in. It was always the best policy if you intended to get anything done.

"Margaret, will you include my next words verbatim in the minutes?"

I, Lottie Albright, am reading a statement from Fiona Hadley presented at a special board meeting of the Carlton County Historical Society called October 15, 2008, to consider an accusation that I, Lottie Albright, stole a valuable document, known as the Custer letter, and offered it for sale to a professor at the University of New Mexico.

The following is Ms. Hadley's statement as to her best recollection of a phone call she received at approximately 6:30 pm October 14, 2008:

I said, "Hello, Hadley residence."

He said, "Mrs. Edgar Hadley, please."

I said, "This is she speaking."

He said, "I don't know anyone personally in your county, but I know your son is running for the senate, and the press reports say you're active in civic and church activities."

I said, "If you're calling to solicit funds, I really must tell you we do not respond."

He said, "No. No."

I really don't recall some of what he said after that because I just wanted to get him off the phone.

Then he said, "Lottie Albright, the director of Carlton County Historical Society, called a colleague of mine at the University of New Mexico who is a Custer scholar and offered to sell him a letter signed by General Armstrong Custer."

I said, "She what?"

He said, "You know about this letter, ma'am?"

I said, "I most surely do. It was stolen."

He laughed then and said, "That's all I wanted to know."

I said, "Wait, I didn't catch your name. There's things I need to know."

I just hadn't paid attention when he first called. I didn't know the call would be so important.

He said, "Sorry, ma'am, I'm due for a meeting."

Then he hung up. We do not have caller ID.

This concludes Fiona Hadley's statement

"Margaret, I'll give you a copy, of course, so you can get everything right for the minutes. Does anyone have any questions they would like to ask Fiona?"

"Can't think of any," said Silas. "Can't tell much of anything from that."

"I can," I said. "I can tell a lot, and I have a friend who is a linguist at Kansas University that can probably tell us a lot more. The use of ma'am is definitely southern, likely from Texas. Few adult males out here address women as *ma'am*. The phrase 'I'm due *for* a meeting' instead of choosing other words, like I'm due *at* a meeting, that's pure midwest, Kansas to boot. I doubt those are the words they use in New Mexico."

They looked at me like I was Moses descending from the Mount with mysterious tablets.

"Any questions? If not, I'm sure the Hadleys would like to get on their way. There's no need to keep any of you here any longer."

William shot them a look, and reached for his fedora.

"After Margaret has all this written down, I want it notarized, then I'm going to make a copy of it for our files and take this right over to Sam Abbot. As you all know, we reported the theft of the Custer letters immediately."

Stunned and stiffly silent, the Hadleys did not look at Margaret or the three men. The radiator clanked and the overheated room smelled of dry dust.

"Edgar, Fiona, despite this turning out a lot differently than you had in mind, I know you were just trying to do your duty. I want you to know there's no hard feelings."

Finally, my voice quavered. Until now it had been firm and fearless. "Please know you have the sympathy of everyone here on the loss of your niece. Good day, all."

Chapter Twenty-Nine

Margaret would be back down when she finished the minutes, and I didn't want to talk to her or anyone else. I hoisted the box of Judy's belongings, paused in the doorway and glanced around the room. I would take the box to Max after the funeral.

One big jolt of memorabilia seemed marginally kinder than trickling back in with stuff I'd overlooked.

Jolted, I saw the letter laying on the stack of mail on Margaret's desk. I set Judy's box down in the corridor, and picked it up. For the first time the postmark was in this state, and from a town seven counties away.

> See what you've made me do? I tried to tell you to leave well enough alone. Told you to stop poking your nose in things that are none of your business. But you wouldn't listen. Now she's dead, and it's all your fault. I didn't want to do it.

Dead? Who could this person possibly mean but Judy? Saliva drained from my mouth. My hands trembled. I had thought these strange letters were from an unhappy, disturbed person, not a murderer. Nevertheless, I'd started a special folder and all the letters were in it along with the envelopes. I willed myself to stay calm, remove that file, put the new letter inside, say all the right things to anyone I met on the way outside, and drive right to Sam's office at a normal speed.

◇◇◇

Sam slowly re-read the letters he'd trivialized before and looked at my office log. He reached for his pipe, coaxed it to life.

"You okay, Lottie?"

"No. If I was in any way responsible for the death of Judy St. John, I won't be able to live with myself."

"No one is responsible for the minds of crazy people, lady. And there's still a chance this person might be messing with you. Exploiting Judy's death to get to you."

"Doesn't hold water, much as I would like to believe someone is just out to torment me."

"How's that?"

"No one's supposed to know officially until the coroner gives his report today that it was murder." I gazed at a slipping wanted poster dangling from his bulletin board. Needing to restore order wherever I could, I rose and pinned it back on straight. "Fiona spread the word around that it was suicide, and all my fault. I know Judy was murdered, you know it, but it's not common knowledge."

"Official don't mean diddley squat. There's plenty of people who knew different when they saw FBI agents at St. Johns. Word gets around fast, and like I told you, this wasn't the most intelligent crime I've ever seen."

"Even so, Sam. For someone to have time to write and send a letter overnight? They had to know."

"By God, now." He rubbed his nose, then held the bowl of his pipe as he listened.

"Josie's wondered all along if my pen pal wasn't living right here in this county. Now I'm convinced they were using a mail drop to cover up that fact, but they would have had time to drive to Stanton yesterday and send this letter to arrive in today's mail."

"I'll turn all the letters over to the KBI today," he said. "Jim Gilderhaus will have an opinion. Count on it. Tell your sister about these right away. She might have some special insight."

I winced. Josie's "special insight" was that my move to Western Kansas had been a waste of a first class brain in the first place.

"I hope we're not putting you in harm's way. Bet Keith's thrilled with all this. I can't even offer you police protection," he said bitterly.

"Sam, I *am* the police. Remember?"

He puffed his pipe and looked at me with a sour smile.

◇◇◇

That evening, I waited for Keith to come home, dreading telling him my work as an historian had taken a darker turn than my job as a deputy.

I met him at the door.

"You look like hell, Lottie. What's wrong?"

"I've been accused of stealing the Custer letter."

Stunned into silence, he took off his denim work jacket walked into the mud room and hung it on a peg, thinking, thinking, before he spoke. "For god's sake, why? That would ruin your life's work. Your reputation. What have you done to anyone?"

"Nothing. And there's worse. Those anonymous letters I told you about might be from the SOB who murdered Judy."

"My God. I wish you'd never…"

"Become a deputy? It's my work at the historical society that's bringing this on."

"Two murders. Now this." He smacked a fist into the palm of his hand, and stared out the window at our leafless cottonwoods before he came over and pulled me close. "I feel helpless," he whispered.

"We *are* helpless. Both of us. But the FBI will take a look at the letters. Sam thinks there's a chance someone is just pushing my buttons."

"Thinks or wishes?"

"Hopes." I lifted my face for a kiss. "I want to stay home with you tonight, but I need to call on Max. Take him some food."

"He's back at the house? Already?"

"Yes. The FBI processed and released the house yesterday, because we've already turned it inside out looking for that letter, and we know Judy was strangled right outside the barn with the same rope used to hang her."

"Poor old Max."

"Come with me? I'm done in. Between the anonymous letters and the Hadleys trying to throw me to the wolves over the Custer theft, I can hardly think."

"You on duty?"

"Nope. Couldn't, wouldn't ask you if I was."

"Good. Then I get to hover. I don't want you out of my sight."

◇◇◇

There were cars parked the length of the lane. Inez Wilson opened the door. Lanky, bird bright, she motioned me inside.

"How's he doing?"

"Just terrible," she said. "Terrible. He won't eat a thing. Won't talk to anyone."

"Let me try."

It was as though there was nothing left of Maxwell. He was a skinny old shell that just happened to breathe because his lungs made him.

On the table were enough cakes, casseroles, salads, and pies to feed an army. I leaned over and kissed his old withered cheek. His eyes clouded with tears. The vacant look in his eyes told me he might as well have been on a desert island.

"Max, would you like me to pick out clothes for the service?"

He nodded and I went upstairs and started through the clothes in Judy's closet. Her bedroom appeared to be unchanged since she'd graduated from high school. The décor was too young, too frilly. She probably didn't have either the time or the money to replace things since she'd moved back.

When Mendoza removed the contents of Judy's little cedar hope chest, piece by piece, she'd admired the embroidered pillowcases.

I settled on a soft coral two piece dress, turned off the light and started down the stairs. I paused and looked back, hoping Judy's letter would somehow glow in the dark. Although Brian had given his mother an alibi for Zelda's death, Judy had been adamant the letter proved Fiona was the kil ler. Proof that was gone now. I knew Fiona hadn't murdered Judy, but I could not be sure she wasn't responsible in some way for Zelda's death.

◇◇◇

Brian gave the eulogy at the funeral. It was sweet. Poignant. Just right. With a few well-chosen words he captured his cousin's wistful personality. He told of Judy's love of nature, their walks along the creek bank, her fascination with dragon flies.

As I listened to him speak, watched his face, I noticed how much better he looked. His eyes were clear, and his hands steady as he held his note cards. He was the epitome of honesty and sincerity. The all-American boy. The entire Hadley family had developed deception into an art form.

I scoffed as I watched. Visine does wonders for the eyes. Perhaps a touch of the hair of the dog to stop the trembling hands. His massive will could keep him together long enough to make a good speech.

At the burial afterward, when they were lowering Judy into the grave, Max looked like he wanted to pitch himself on top the coffin. The funeral was enormous. I clung to Keith's arm as if my feet would give way if I didn't. It was a terrible day, a terrible time for us all. I was bitter that those who would not have given this girl the time of day in real life felt compelled to attend her funeral and feign the deepest mourning.

My own grief was genuine. I didn't know it was possible to feel so desolated over the death of a woman I had known such a short length of time.

Despite my show of bravado at the board meeting, I had not slept well for the last three nights. In the daytime, my startle reflex was on overdrive. All someone had to do was walk up behind me, and I either jumped or dropped something.

Yet the service strengthened my anger. Two murders had been committed in my county. Two. Right under our noses. Two murders, and I was getting letters from the person who very well could have committed them.

I looked around at the sea of faces. Many with black glasses. Cousins to old-time veils. Historically, worn so Death couldn't see you, wouldn't seek you out.

Fiona wept uncontrollably. For show and for the record, of course. She had just watched the biggest threat to her son's career put six feet under. Yet, I remembered her fury the day we had found Judy. On that day I knew she had cared about her niece as much as she could care about anyone she couldn't use.

Fiona didn't have access to the noble emotions that inspired poetry. Her deepest most heartfelt feelings were reserved for herself, but in her own crippled way, I knew she had either cared about Judy more than she had known, or she was deeply frightened.

As was I.

Chapter Thirty

Once home, I called Josie to tell her about the latest letter. "Are you there?" I asked, after a good sixty seconds of silence on the line.

"Just barely," she said. "I don't like the sound of this. Can you send me copies of all those letters?"

"Sure. You don't think it's someone who's trying to push my buttons like Sam thought? Or Sam hoped."

"Not any more. If it's someone living right there in your own county, you're dealing with a person who is very dangerous. Perhaps someone who has killed twice."

"And smart enough to know how to arrange for letters to be mailed from different towns."

"Okay, here's what I think, or suspect. Pick your word."

"Yeah, I know, and all your words are going to be qualified with buts and maybes."

"You bet. I'm *not* a profiler. This is *not* my field. I am *not* a forensic psychologist and I don't want to be one. Ain't gonna be one either, despite your attempts to make me one. I never should have agreed to be a consultant for your little piss-ant county, but you *are* my sister, and I would like to keep you around a little while longer. I think."

I smiled.

"My gut feeling here is your correspondent is not a newcomer, is middle-aged, and has lived in the county a long time. Possibly single or a widower."

"Widower? You think it's a male."

"Funny I would have said that. In the beginning, I was thinking female."

"Why have you changed your mind, Josie?"

"I haven't." She laughed. "It was a slip of the tongue."

"Oh, right."

"They do happen, you know."

"That's not what you've always said before."

"Let's start by eliminating newcomers. Check out strangers, then see if you can gather some gossip for me."

"Gossip is this town's specialty."

"I want to know if someone is disintegrating. If this person holds a job and is in the state I think he or she is in, there would be signs at work. Definite signs of change. They would be noticeable to co-workers. See what you can find out and get back to me."

◇◇◇

A week later, I took Judy's box over to Max St. John. I would visit a while, then let him know about the treasures in his attic. Considering his state before the funeral, I had expected to be let in by a home health person, but that's not what happened.

It took forever for him to answer my ring and longer still for him to recognize me.

I took in his old chino pants. They were food stained and needed washing. He smelled. I wondered if he had had a bath since the funeral. Why hadn't Inez arranged for care? His going to the hardware store every day had been a sham even before Zelda's death. He wasn't thinking, wasn't competing. Walmarted into obscurity.

I didn't give him a chance to turn me away. "I'll bet I caught you at suppertime. Don't let me interrupt. In fact, I'll go right on back to the kitchen with you while you finish. I just came over to bring Judy's things and see how you're doing." Wanting to see what he called supper nowadays, I brushed right past him.

The odor nearly knocked me over. Food from the funeral set on the counter. Meat reeked, cakes and pies were dotted with green fur. Milk clotted in at least seven glasses. Dirty plates ringed the table as though Max had just drug out food at random and eaten his next meal without washing a thing or putting food away again.

Shamed, he stood before me.

"I've kind of let things go, I guess."

I closed my eyes, turned away for an instant, not wanting him to see my tears. I composed myself, faced him.

"It's understandable." I hoped my voice sounded gentle. I couldn't bear to have him think I was scolding. Not after all he had been through. "It's so very understandable, Max."

I moved toward him and held him. He wept silently, shoulders shaking. Wept as though he couldn't make it through another day. I rubbed his back. "It's understandable, but wrong. I'm not going to let you live this way. You need help. You know that, Max."

"I don't care. I just don't care."

"If I were in your place, I'm not sure I would either. But you must try. You owe it to Judy, and I owe it to Judy. I'm going to call the hospital and arrange for you to go into respite care. While you're there, I'll find someone to come in and clean things up. Then we can talk about your coming back. If you want to."

"I just don't care."

"Haven't any of the Hadleys been here? Looking in on you? Seeing if you need anything?"

Angry again, I realized Fiona and Edgar Hadley were still able to make my blood boil. Why in the name of decency hadn't they offered to help this poor old soul?

"Fiona's been here. Said she wanted to go through stuff in the attic."

I closed my eyes and prayed.

Please God, please God, please God.

"She said there was Rubidoux things that belonged to her family. I said she could damn sure have it. Lot of junk. Wasn't doing nobody no good. Not rightfully mine, anyway."

I started to protest, then stopped. Under Kansas law, he inherited all of Zelda's goods. He could give his possessions to whomever he chose. If he had specifically given Fiona permission to take what she wanted, it was a done deal.

Please God, please God, please God.

"Sit down for a minute, Max. I want to check something in the attic myself."

I eased him onto a chair, walked out of the room, then flew up the stairs. I looked around, lowered my head into my cupped hands, and rocked back and forth in anguish.

Stripped. All of it. Stripped bare. Not a trace of the priceless old comics, the trunks, the vintage clothing, the art deco jewelry, the picture frames, the books. Or the journals. Those priceless old journals. Nothing. I slid down the wall to the floor and muffled howls of pure rage.

When I could compose myself, I walked back downstairs. There was no point in making this poor old man any more miserable then he already was. He had never known the worth of the items in the attic, and it would not do him a bit of good to know it now.

"Do you know what Fiona did with everything?"

"Think she hauled some of it off to the dump, kept some of it. Burned some it." His eyes welled with tears. "Don't care. Didn't want to see any of it anymore. She would have gotten it all in the end anyway. Might as well all be burnt now as later."

My soul cried to heaven with outrage, but my face managed a small smile and my hand reached for his, gave it a squeeze.

Ninety thousand dollars hauled off. At least. Enough to provide decent care for several years. I grieved over the money and what it would have meant to Max, and I grieved over the lost history. Would Fiona recognize the worth of those priceless journals, or were they now ashes in the Carlton County landfill?

I took Max back into town with me. I did not have to persuade Dr. Golbert to admit him into the hospital. One look, and he knew Max was in the process of slow dehydration. Then I called Inez Wilson to bawl her out. As county health nurse, she should have arranged for care. Her voice hot with self-righteous protests, Inez argued that Fiona had called and assured her that

Max was doing just fine. Family was family. The Hadleys would look after him.

◇◇◇

I pulled into our lane when a late breaking news announcement came over the radio.

> "At a press conference this morning, Sam Abbott, sheriff of Carlton County, announced that due to the results of an autopsy, the death of Judy St. John, cousin to Senatorial hopeful Brian Hadley, is being investigated as a homicide. While Sheriff Abbott stressed there is no apparent tie-in with the murder of Judy St. John's mother, Zelda St. John, earlier this month, he cannot rule out the possibility at this time. Sheriff Abbott announced that the KBI, once again, would be assisting with the investigation."

Finally. Even thought it was common knowledge Judy had not committed suicide, this would officially put a stop to Fiona's campaign to convince people I'd overstressed a vulnerable young woman. Although it was cold comfort having folks know she had been murdered instead, at least Max was now safely settled in respite care where he would be protected from the press.

Chapter Thirty-One

I spent the next morning at the historical society working both jobs to locate my elusive letter writer. Shamed over his dismissal of the letters to begin with, Sam had grudgingly acknowledged that the positions sometimes intersected, and I was in the best position to know when that was an advantage. In return, I'd sweetly agreed to call him to decide when there was a "situation" looming.

Margaret looked tired when she came in. The murder had taken a toll on everyone. We didn't feel safe in our own county now.

"It wouldn't be a sin, if you took a day off, you know," I said.

"That applies to you too, Lottie."

"I need to keep my mind occupied."

She sighed. "Me too." She placed her purse behind her desk.

I stopped and stretched. "Since we're here by ourselves, perhaps you can fill me in on some things I'd like to know."

"Like what?" She tensed and curled her fists into tight balls.

"Oh, relax. This isn't a sheriffing question. I just want to know more about The Ladies. How do you see them? Or did see them, I guess. In particular, do you know of anything strange going on with Fiona about the time Zelda was pregnant. Some incident? Or event?"

"Funny you should mention it. I'd almost forgotten." She sat with her hands clasped on top of the desk. "Fiona was fit to be tied. Don't know what got into her. I've seen other women turn weepy like that when they had a lot of miscarriages or were infertile, but she already had Brian."

"Still, if she'd wanted a large family, and it wasn't going to happen that might have done it," I said. "Some infertile women are very envious of another's pregnancy. Or it could be simply that Zelda was the center of attention for a change."

"Phooey. Don't you believe it. They were both impossible to deal with. Fiona may be a steamroller, but Zelda had her ways of getting even from the time they were little. When she wanted attention, she got it. She was just sneakier than Fiona."

The cords in Margaret's neck tightened. Her voice tensed with disapproval. Surprised by her animosity, I looked away.

But there was no denying the anguish in Zelda's diary. What a way for two sisters to carry on. I thought about Josie and me. Despite our little verbal squabbles, she was like a second heartbeat. If anything ever happened to her, I would probably die too.

Margaret started filing and I turned my attention back to locating my letter writer. A quick call to the City Office eliminated newcomers. No new utility hook-ups for the past three months. No new subscriptions to our paper, either. No strangers reading the Gateway Gazette in the library.

I listed all the businesses and institutions in the county. Teachers would notice if someone was out-of-whack in the school system, unless my letter writer was a maintenance or lunchroom worker not under daily scrutiny.

The courthouse grapevine is instantaneous. I would have heard about one of us weeks ago. Bank personnel would nail one another in no time. A dysfunctional person would have a hard time keeping financial transactions straight.

After I closed my office that evening, I drove to Sunny Rest Manor. Even given the circulation problems of the elderly, I couldn't imagine anyone being comfortable in the over-heated facility.

I peeked inside the admissions coordinator's office. It was empty. Since the home has an open visitation policy, I went straight to the administrator's office, unannounced.

Connie Simmons was staring gloomily at a stack of papers when I walked through the door.

"Am I interrupting?"

"Nope," she said. "Wish you were. Can't seem to find my start button."

"Start? You should be looking for the off switch. It's about time to head home."

"Can't," she said flatly. "Surveyors coming this month. Sometimes I think the government invents all this red tape to see if they can break us. And if that isn't bad enough, we've got a flu bug starting. Not too many of the residents down yet, but it's disastrous when they all get sick."

I shuddered, imagining the laundry, the stench, the problems with the staff. I gave a weak wave of my hand and tried to smile.

"Have you replaced that rogue aide yet?"

"Sort of," she said grimly. "I have a body on duty here, but she's young and inexperienced and thinks she's too good for the job. She may be right. I don't know. Not many folks want to change old folks' diapers." She laughed at the pleading look on my face.

"Sorry, Connie. I have the world's weakest stomach, but I'm getting better. I think. I managed to get through Judy's murder and do what had to be done without totally disgracing myself."

She gave me a quick sharp glance of sympathy and had the good sense to change the subject.

"What can I do for you?"

"It's a business call, actually."

"Sheriff or historical?"

"You know, I'm not sure anymore. The two jobs are starting to overlap. Is anyone on your staff acting funny? Not like herself?"

"May I ask why you would want to know this?"

"No," I said flatly, "you really can't."

"Well, that answers my first question. It's obviously law enforcement. Not historical." She reached inside her desk for the roster of employees, riffled the stack of papers, picked up a pen and absently began thumping it against the top of the desk as she tracked down the list with her fingers.

"We have a high percentage of young, certified nurse's aides. CNA's, they're called. Some boys, but mostly teenage girls who are earning money for college working after school and on weekends. We're very, very lucky in that respect. The residents adore them. There's raging hormones and intrigues and the whole boyfriend/girlfriend thing. You know, prom dresses and who's breaking up with whom and whose parents are the most ghastly. But all of them are normal crazy. Nothing out of the ordinary."

"Any new hires?"

"One older woman. Rock solid. I've known her all my life."

"The rest?"

She scanned the list again. "Two of the women are widows; we have five divorced or single mothers just trying to make ends meet. The rest are married women. Only three male CNA's. All these people are fine. Just fine."

"Nurses? Any change there?"

"None."

"You'll watch?"

"Of course. How can I not?" she asked dryly. "This kind of question does have a tendency to rivet one's attention on the staff."

"I know, and I'm not out to make anyone miserable."

She looked at her paperwork, glanced at her watch and rose from her chair.

I scrambled to my feet. "It's late, and I haven't been very considerate of your time. Thanks, Connie. I think I'll look in on Herman Swenson again just to say hello, then I'll be on my way."

"Okay. Minerva is probably ready to leave by now."

"Minerva?"

"She's a reader here. Along with Margaret Atchison and Inez Wilson. We have several residents who love to be read to. The three women all come twice a week on different evenings."

I could imagine Minerva volunteering for this one-on-one activity. It would be just like her to make this invisible contribution to the community. Margaret Atchison, with her strong sense of responsibility, *would* find some way to work this in. But Inez Wilson? The queen of commotion? I couldn't see her sitting still long enough to read a book to anyone.

Minerva was just coming out of Herman's room. She stopped in the doorway, leaned against the jamb. She trembled. There was a fine sheen of sweat on her face.

"Minerva? Are you sick?"

She tried to smile. Her color was ghastly. "Dizzy," she said weakly.

"Connie was just telling me about this flu bug."

"I never get it," she said. "Never."

"Well, you seem to be getting it now. You can't drive home in this shape. Do you need to go to the doctor?"

"No," she said. "The clinic is closed for the day, and I would have to see him at the emergency room. I'm not that sick."

"You're chilling, Minerva. Shaking all over. You need to see someone."

She clamped her teeth together and shook her head.

"You shouldn't drive," I persisted.

"All right, I would appreciate a ride home then. If it's not too much trouble." She said this stiffly, in the manner of a person who hates to ask for help in any way, shape, or form.

"Are you kidding? That's what friends are for. Besides, I owe you, Lady. Think of all the information you've dug up for me."

"Just doing my job."

I was just the right height to serve as a crutch. My shoulders were level with her armpit. She steadied herself and I helped her outside.

"Is your pickup a stick shift?"

She nodded.

"Damn. I'll have to take you home in my Tahoe."

"I'll need my pickup to drive to work tomorrow."

"I don't think so." I laughed. Then feeling her tense, I added, "Keith is in town at an Elk's meeting tonight. I'll come back here and wait until it's over. Your stick shift certainly won't bother him. He can bring your pickup by on his way home, and I'll follow in his Suburban."

"Too much trouble," she mumbled. "Far too much trouble."

"It's not. Keith's coming to town tomorrow, anyway. And he can bring me back to my Tahoe."

She steadied herself against the front fender. I opened the door and eased her inside. I walked over to her pickup and got her briefcase. The cab was spotless and shiny. She had even Armoralled her floor mats.

In the bed of her Toyota was standard Western Kansas survival equipment that I, too, carried. Blizzards come on with nightmare suddenness. Minerva, however, won the preparedness prize. There was a sleeping bag neatly enclosed in a nylon sack, a camouflage jacket, a Coleman heater, a shovel, a pick, and flares.

I walked back to my Tahoe and held up the briefcase. "Need anything else?"

She shook her head. I dropped her keys into my purse. She sat totally motionless, her fingers pressed against her temples, speechless, clearly miserable.

She lived five miles out of town in a neat little double wide trailer. Once there, I braced her again, helped her up the steps and reached for the doorknob. The house was locked. I fumbled through the ring for the right key.

Her living room was as impersonal as a mobile home showroom. The walls were paneled with cheap light oak. A small self-assembled desk held a computer with a vinyl cover. There wasn't a paper out of place. She pointed toward the couch.

"No way. You're going straight to bed, where you can sleep comfortably. You might think you're going to be just fine, but I'll call tomorrow morning to make sure you have plenty of groceries."

"No need," she said. "I'll be at work."

"Wanna bet? This is going to put you under for at least three days. Count on it."

"It can't. I've got too much work."

"It will. You'd better call that lady who helps you during tax season and ask her to pitch in."

She groaned.

"Where're your pajamas? I'll heat some soup before I leave." I bustled around, taking over.

"My head," she moaned.

"You probably should have gone straight to the hospital."

"I'll be fine by morning."

In her bedroom an oblong mirror reflected a bookcase headboard with a good reading lamp and an assortment of books. I knew she would not appreciate me inspecting the titles. I turned back her crème chenille coverlet and fluffed her pillows.

One wall was covered with old pictures and yellowed embroidered samplers. An intricate crocheted doily had been placed on a square tall table, beside a small trunk.

I did not comment on her memorabilia. Others might think this was the real Minerva, but I knew better. Our real self usually *is* our mask, the face we present to outsiders. Hers was intensely private. If she had wanted me or anyone else to see all this, she would have had it on display in her living room or at her office in the courthouse.

She swayed as she bent toward her shoes. I quickly knelt, untied her laces for her, and eased her shoes off her feet.

"Do you need help undressing?"

"No." She smiled weakly. "Nightgown on the hook in the bathroom."

I got it, handed it to her, then reached for her over-tinted glasses, but she shook her head.

"I need them to read."

"With your headache?"

"Habit. I don't think I can sleep without reading a couple of pages. It settles me down."

I laughed. "Me, too." I said. "Bet we could have some grand discussions."

"Besides, my head doesn't ache, I'm just dizzy."

I glanced at my watch. "Anything else I can get you before I fix a bite to eat?"

A tear rolled down her cheek from under her smoky lenses.

"Minerva, are you in pain? I've been calling this the flu without really knowing a thing. I really think you should see a doctor."

"I'm so dizzy. I can't stand not being right in my head."

"What you can't stand, dear, is the thought of not being totally competent and in control."

She smiled. "If I'm not better by morning, I'll call him. I promise."

I went into her kitchen and boiled some water for instant soup, made toast, and carried the tray back into her bedroom.

She had propped herself up on pillows against the headboard. Tears trickled as she looked at the tray.

"You've been very kind to me, Lottie."

"Nonsense. This hardly makes me Mother Theresa."

"You don't know. Thank you."

"Anything else before I go back to the manor? Keith and I will have your pickup back here in a flash."

"Nothing," she said.

I turned and headed for the front door.

"Lottie," she called suddenly.

I went back to the bedroom. "There's something you should know."

I waited.

"You have an enemy."

Chapter Thirty-Two

"A *what?*" The term was quaint, ancient. Startling in this day and age.

"An enemy," she repeated. "You know how I feel about gossip. I do not, will not, pass it on. But you need to know that Christine Julep has been telling people she will have your job. She says, an eye for an eye, a tooth for a tooth."

"Who is Christine Julep?"

I was astonished that someone I didn't even know was determined to take my job from me. Or jobs. I wondered which one she had in mind.

"She's the lady you got fired at the nursing home."

"The aide?" I said blankly.

"She says what you did wasn't right. She's been talking."

"Don't worry about it," I said. "She doesn't have any power over me. No one will pay a bit of attention to her, and Connie Simmons will certainly back me. She knows the real story."

"Lottie, you're my friend. You need to understand something, and I don't think you do. You're making enemies. Back off. Quit poking around."

"Zelda's murder? You think I should back off of Zelda's murder?"

"Zelda's and Judy's, and all the other research you're doing right now. I hear things. People are talking."

I looked at her carefully. There were things I wanted, needed to know. For instance, just who, specifically, was so critical of my research and just what research did she have in mind? Were the Hadleys causing trouble again? But there was no point in quizzing Minerva when was sick and upset.

Her face was white and strained. It could have been her guilt over passing along trouble as much as her flu. I reminded myself that when one is ill, the head is sick too. In fact, if she hadn't been coming down with something, I doubted she would have made so much of Julep's ridiculous threat. Things that seem normal and manageable by day loom ominous at night.

"I'll think about this, Minerva."

I left quietly, called Keith to meet me, and decided to pop in on Herman Swenson while I waited.

◇◇◇

He sat in the dark, slumped in his wheelchair. Slack-jawed and miserable, tied in with cloth restraints.

"I think you need a little bit of re-arranging again," I said brightly.

I got behind him and pulled him up in the chair. He grunted his thanks.

"I thought you might be watching the game tonight. Or do you still follow football?"

His eyes flashed. I looked around the room.

"Guess it would be a little hard, wouldn't it? Without a TV. Sorry. That was thoughtless of me."

Ashamed of having prodded a wound, I sat trying to think of something to say. I was probably the only one here who knew he was once a marvelous athlete. Certainly the only one who knew he enjoyed football. Nursing homes are populated mostly by old women.

"Excuse me, I'll be right back." I went to the central activity room. A dozen women were watching a romance movie on the only TV.

I went back to Herman's room. Behind him on the panel of lights and switches was a cable hook-up.

"We have an extra TV at home. It even has a VCR. It belonged to Keith's dad. I'll bring it in. No point in just letting it set."

The look on that man's face. It will stay with me until I die. Like I had offered him a cup of water in the desert. I stared at his restraints, longed to cut him free. But I knew restraints were for the protection of patients.

Still, I was suddenly depressed. Whether from the sadness of seeing the loneliness of Minerva's life or this man's profound misery or my bewilderment at the sheer hostility of the forces gathered against me, I couldn't say. Tears welled up in my eyes.

He saw.

"I don't know what's come over me. Mind if I borrow a Kleenex?"

I blew my nose and sat back down. "There's folks who think I'm doing things I didn't do. Worse, I don't understand any of this. I just don't understand."

If I had wanted compassion, a sympathetic ear, someone who truly understood, I had it. All the sorrow of the world was there in his face. All the empathy I needed.

"I shouldn't be burdening you with all this, it's inexcusable. My troubles are nothing compared to what you've been through. I'm so sorry, so terribly sorry. For all that's happened to you, Mr. Swenson. That you are here. That you lost your wife and your darling boy. That you lost your baby."

Tears trickled down his cheeks. I rose, grabbed another Kleenex, and dabbed at them gently. "Just look at us," I tried to smile. "Aren't we a sight? Don't we make a pair?"

I stroked his withered old cheek, and he tried to kiss the palm of my hand. This gentle old man liked women. Was at home with them. Not a violent person. I knew in my gut, my heart, my brain, that this man would not have committed those terrible murders.

His face twisted. "Ba…ba…ba…" Puzzled, I strained at the guttural sounds. "Ba…ba…ba…" They were followed by a click, then a gush of air. Shaking, his face reddened. "Ba…ba…ba…" Then the click again. It didn't make sense. "Oh please," I said. "I didn't mean to upset you."

He stiffened. "Ba…ba…ba…" Then he made a half circle motion with his hand, his index and ring fingers pressed against his thumb. I looked at him dumbly, tried to understand. He breathed in harsh puffs. I whirled around to call the nurse.

She came running in, took one look, and asked, "What happened?"

"I'm not sure."

"I'll get a shot." She rushed out of the room.

He slumped, defeated, back into his usual slack posture. I pulled up a chair and patted his hand. "She's just going to get something to help you relax. You'll be just fine. I know you were trying to tell me something. Something important."

He groaned, tried to make the sound again.

"I'm sorry I didn't follow up on my promise to get those speech tapes, but I will. I've been busy," I said drily. "A wee bit preoccupied. When we get your TV hooked up, we can watch them together. Until you learn to make the sounds, you can at least point at them."

I waited for the nurse to come back, then rose to leave.

He clung to my hand as long as possible. No mistaking what he was trying to communicate through that.

It was naked hope.

Chapter Thirty-Three

When we returned Minerva's pickup there were no lights visible in her house. Not wanting to wake her, we left the keys in the ignition and drove the Suburban on home.

Keith drove me to my Tahoe the next morning. "Thanks, honey," I said, when we reached Sunny Rest. This was his second trip to town in less than twelve hours. His face was grave and he had hardly spoken on the way in.

"Is something bothering you? Other than me expecting you to act like a taxi driver, I mean?"

"No. I've been thinking about how selfish I am with my time. It wouldn't hurt me to visit old man Swenson. Or watch a game with him from time to time. I would hate to be his age and never see another man."

"He'd love it. Absolutely love it. Thanks, darling." I fished for my keys, and waved as he drove on to the feed store. I loved being married to a kind man. Totally open, he operated in the sunlight.

Minerva's pickup wasn't there when I swung into my parking spot at the courthouse. I ran up to the third floor. Elsie Spodes, the elderly lady Minerva called on to help out from time to time, sat at her desk.

"Is Minerva doing all right? I told her I would check on her this morning. I tried my best to get her to a doctor."

"She says she is fine," Elsie rolled her eyes. "Fine enough to dictate a bunch of instructions at any rate."

We both laughed. Reassured, I went back down to my office. My curiosity about the rumors Minerva had heard could wait a couple of days until she recovered.

Mail Call. Priscilla Ramsey was taking care of the distribution, and I saw the letter at once. I waited until she finished talking about Martha Stewart's latest decorating advice before I eased her out the door.

I used gloves this time.

> Do you want to die.? Haven't there been enough deaths in this county? A long line of murders. You know what you have done. Stop or you're next.

I closed my eyes, swallowed, called Sam Abbott.

"We have another letter, Sam. Get over here right away." I slammed down the phone.

Minutes later, he walked through the door.

"The postmark? What about the postmark?"

"Denver, this time."

"Go some place, Lottie," he said. "Just leave."

I looked at him incredulously, then gestured at all the work I needed to do. I started to speak, but he gave me the look, then cut me off.

"Leave all this to the KBI. They're the pros. We're not. This should get them in gear again. Don't want to hear none of your long smart reasons why you can't leave. Just want you to get the hell out of Dodge." He left.

I reached for the phone, called Josie, told her about the latest letter and Sam's order.

"Well, good for him," she said. "He's finally seen the light. The letters have changed, Lottie. In the beginning, the writer went to a lot of trouble, using mail drops, disguising the point of origin. Now they're losing it, and getting a lot more dangerous. It all adds up to the same thing. You're seriously over your head. Got that?"

I winced at the anger in her voice.

"So what do you want me to do? Roll over and play dead?"

"It's where you're going to be, if you don't watch your step. Someone is threatening to kill you. Has that sunk in yet?"

Soberly, I stared at a stain on the ceiling. Curiously enough, it hadn't. Zelda and Judy had been murdered. But it didn't seem real to me that my own life was in danger.

"You're overdue for a visit. You need a break."

"I know I do."

"I'll pamper you," Josie coaxed. "Breakfast in bed. You can stay up all night and watch old movies. Eat bon-bons. Get drunk. Read trashy novels. Anything."

Despite her attempts to keep it light, I was touched by her fretting.

"I'll need to round up help." I sighed, thinking of the burden this would put on the volunteers. After rising to my defense, William had become increasingly gruff. As though he resented being forced into showing me kindness. However, I knew I could count on him. Duty, you know.

"When are you coming?"

"Right away. Be there day after tomorrow."

◇◇◇

As I packed, I felt cheated out of the pleasure I usually took in the onset of winter. The leisure of holing up in our wonderful house, with a warm fire, the odor of bread baking, good music, Keith next to me in his oversized leather chair. We could go all afternoon, buried in our books, barely speaking, just smiling foolishly over the deep peace we felt in one another's presence.

This evening, however, there was no peace to be found anywhere. Grimly, conscientiously, like a child forced to confess her sins, I told Keith about the newest letter and the personal threat. I told him of Josie's fears we were dealing with a very dangerous person. I looked away from his sharp glance and the sick anguish on his face. For the first time since we had been married, I felt like fleeing from my husband. Not from his rage, but from his pain.

"Well," I said brightly, "any questions?"

"Nope. When are you leaving?"

"Right away. Tomorrow."

He nodded. "Good." The word came out in a puffy little explosion of relief. "I want you out of this town."

I melted. "Oh, Keith, try not to worry. I am sorry. About everything."

He reached for me and pulled me against his giant chest. He stroked my hair like I was a puppy, then suddenly tightened his hold so fiercely I struggled to breathe. We swayed from side to side.

"If anything happens to you."

"I'm not quitting, Keith." The words gushed from me. Hung between us. Astonished, I recalled the words of E.M. Forester. "How do I know what I think until I say it?" "Sam needs me. This county needs me."

He stiffened, then relaxed his hold on me and stepped back. Abruptly, rudely. Almost as though he was pushing me away.

"Tell me what I'm supposed to do." He looked at his hands. "Just what am I supposed to do?"

"Just love me," I said simply.

He nodded, but his eyes were haunted.

"You don't have to like any of this, Keith, but I'm not quitting."

"Got that the first time. You don't have to draw me a picture."

"You'll get over it, Keith." But I knew by the sudden fury in his eyes, he would not.

We weren't going to talk. No point in it. Thinking couples can work it out is for the very young. We both knew better. This marriage would never work very well for either one of us. It would have if I had stayed the same person. But I had not. I had changed.

Not blinking once, I met his gaze and held it. Knowing he was not seeing me as a woman, or his wife, but simply as a human being. We lived a lifetime in that glance, and came to know the mature secret joy to be had in a marriage when one stops trying to make it work.

He nodded so slightly I nearly missed the movement. My heart leaped with joy at the quiet pride in his eyes. We were bound by devotion to our thoroughly unworkable unreasonable lovely marriage.

"You win," he said softly.

"I'll finish packing."

Chapter Thirty-Four

Josie has two homes: a townhouse near the University in Manhattan, and a large A-frame on Tuttle Creek. I pulled into town early the next afternoon and retrieved the key to her apartment from over the door. She had a two o'clock class to teach and had told me to let myself in.

I quieted Tosca, who barked frantically at the intrusion. The foyer opened into an elegant living room. Creamy white woodwork accented an exquisite array of art objects. Oriental rugs gleamed on oak floors. An enormous bay window overlooked a small patio. However, one's eyes were immediately drawn to a majestic black grand piano, where my sister kept her heart.

Once inside, I hauled my suitcases and my briefcase into her guest bedroom, changed into sweats, and poured myself a very large glass of wine. I flopped into her best reading chair, picked up the latest issue of *Opera News* and fell deeply asleep.

When I awoke, it was early evening. I heard her moving around and sat up abruptly.

She looked at me and lit a cigarette.

"It's my own home," she said crossly, shoving her lighter back in her pocket.

"I didn't say anything. Besides, they're thinking of legalizing suicide here in Kansas. Shall we start over? Hello, Josie."

"Hello, Lottie."

"You look wonderful. Is that new?" I eyed her cinnamon-colored silk suit.

Amused, she let smoke drift from her nostrils. It would be impossible to keep track of Josie's new clothes.

"You look like something the cat drug in, and by the way you've been sleeping, I'd say you got here just in the nick of time."

"For what? A lecture?"

"No, for me to save your life."

"Not you, too."

"Keith been giving you a hard time?"

"No more than I deserve. I really am in somewhat of a pickle."

"I would say that's the understatement of the year. You've lost weight, Lottie. Ten pounds? Fifteen?"

"Not that much, surely." I looked at my body, surprised I hadn't noticed. For the first time in five years, we were exactly the same size.

"I had planned to take you out, but I've changed my mind. You don't have the energy to move. I'll order a pizza. Do you want to go back to sleep or talk? It's up to you."

"I want to talk. I've got to talk to someone besides Keith. It worries him too much. And God forgive me, last week, I even bared my soul to a poor old man in a nursing home. I need to talk to you as my sister, and I need to talk to you professionally."

"So you're finally willing to admit you need a shrink."

"Oh, please. Spare me. But I'm starting to think half the county is out to get me and I don't know if I'm cracking up or if it's the truth. I've got so much to tell you I don't know where to start. I'm so glad to see you, Josie."

We smiled at one another in pure delight.

"Oh, goody, I get to tell you what to do for once," she said. "You're going to start with a long bath in my Jacuzzi. The pizza will be here by the time you're finished. After I get some food in you and you've settled down, you can tell me everything."

◑ ◑ ◑

After we'd eaten, Josie put on a Chopin CD.

"Why don't I start with murder number one? Zelda St. John."

"Have you made any progress at all on that?"

"None. Judy swore Fiona Hadley was responsible. She claimed to have proof. But whoever killed Judy took any proof she had. Fiona had alibis for both Zelda's murder and Judy's murder. She was home with her son and her husband for the first murder; she was at a women's club meeting during the second."

"That doesn't preclude her hiring someone."

"That's true, Josie, but you said yourself Zelda's murder was a crime of passion and so poorly done that it couldn't possibly have been a murder for hire. Fiona knows how to find good people for whatever she wants. I'm betting any murder she arranged would be professional."

"What a smashing testimonial to someone's abilities," Josie said drily.

"Yes, isn't it? But it's the truth. The woman is phenomenal."

"Who does the KBI think did it?"

"At first they thought Zelda's murder was a random act of violence during a burglary. But two murders? The same family? During a senatorial campaign? Now they're forming a task force."

"And Sam. What does he think?"

"Sam thinks it's someone she knew. He never did believe it was a burglary, because there was no forced entry and no signs of disturbance at the doorway and a person couldn't get past their two German shepherds unless Zelda called them off. They usually ran loose."

"Do you think there's any basis at all for Judy's accusations?"

"Yes. Because she was so very, very sure. That's what's driving me crazy. I know Judy believed she had something that implicated Fiona in Zelda's murder. However, Fiona couldn't have been involved in Judy's. That's one fact I'm dead sure of. She was in full view of thirteen women until she left, and I was already at St. Johns when she arrived. No one would have had time to arrange a darn thing from the time they knew I was supposed to meet Judy and the time I got there."

"How did Fiona look? Act?"

I told Josie everything I could remember about that terrible day. Fiona's rage, her grief, my and Agent Mendoza's search for the mysterious letter.

Thoughtfully, Josie swirled the wine in her glass, then rose to insert new CDs in the changer. When she sat back down, I could see a subtle change in her scrutiny from that of my sister, to that of Josie Albright, clinical psychologist. She was now watching, evaluating, measuring.

Attempting to deaden her professional attention, I blurted, "Did I tell you about the old Swenson murder, Josie? I'm working on that, too. For the sake of this darling old man."

"Now that's entertainment. What else do you do for fun nowadays? Read forensic journals?"

"I know. I can't believe the turn my life has taken."

"I have questions, and there's one I want to clear up right now. Could anyone have known you were meeting Judy St. John the day she was murdered? Overheard you?"

"Maybe, by lurking outside the office with an ear pressed to the door. It would be the only way. Besides, a person wouldn't have had the time to arrange anything. It wasn't twenty minutes from the time Judy called until I got there." Tosca raised her head from Josie's lap and looked at me with interest.

I laughed. "All ears, aren't you, precious?" Disarmed by the wine, the beautiful room, a full belly, the rich tones of her stereo system, my wariness melted and I leaned back into the lush sofa.

"Judy didn't have my cell number, and even if she'd had it, you know what service is like on the farm. But it worried me when she said she'd called before the courthouse opened that morning and left me a message. I never got it."

Her eyes brightened. "What did she say in the message?"

"She said she'd told me about a letter." Jolted, I shot upright. "She said she'd called early because she didn't want to risk a volunteer overhearing."

"We're going to start with one little mystery at a time. We'll work up to the real stuff gradually. What kind of answering machine do you have?"

"AT & T."

"So do I. Let me try something." She reached for the phone and dialed the number of the courthouse. "Testing. Just checking." She replaced the receiver, then went to her bedroom and got her purse from the closet. She dug out her wallet and flipped through cards until she found the AT & T instructions.

"The default access code is #10. Have you ever changed it?"

"No."

She re-dialed the courthouse number and put her own phone on speaker so I could listen. When my voice instructed the caller to leave a message at the sound of the beep, she punched in #10. A mechanical voice announced, "You have one message." Then it continued with, "Testing. Just checking."

Shocked, I stood and reached for the code card. I hadn't changed the default retrieval code. I studied all the enhancements. "Anyone, at anytime could listen to my messages from any phone anywhere," I said. "Anyone. If they knew the access code."

Josie dialed once again with her cell speaker on, read the menu on the card, punched in a new series of numbers, and deleted the message she had just left.

"So that's how. At least three people have told me they left messages I never got."

"Now we can clear up mystery number two," Josie said. "You're not cracking up. Half the county really is out to get you."

Chapter Thirty-Five

When I didn't laugh, she shot me a hard look and refilled my glass.

"Now for mystery number three. How does the Swenson murder fit in with any of this?"

"It doesn't. It just gives me something to do in my free time."

She laughed. "Well, tell me all about the old man. He sounds far enough in the past to be safe. It would be a very good idea to put the St. Johns women out of your mind for a day or two. Tomorrow after I see my clients, we'll go on out to Tuttle Creek. You can just stare at the water. It will do you a world of good."

I told her all about the entanglements of the Swenson/Champlin families and how Herman Swenson came to be convicted of the murders.

"How tragic."

"You'd know how tragic this actually was if you could meet him. He had a miserable excuse of a lawyer. Didn't help himself. Didn't defend himself. Said it was all his fault. All of it. But he never actually confessed to the murders. Then he had this terrible stroke."

I told her how I had connected with the old man through his love of football, about his attempts to speak to me.

"I'm going to take some speech tapes back to Gateway City. He was trying to tell me something the other night, Josie. I know he was. About his family."

"I can't imagine why I thought it would be more relaxing for you to talk about this murder instead of the others." She reached for her cigarettes, and took her time lighting one. "If anything, this is bothering you even more."

"It is. It's just so unfair."

"He had normal interactions with the community before this happened?"

"As nearly as I can tell. There were meetings, events."

"Something is wrong with this picture all right. And the sister-in-law? Rebecca, was it?" I nodded. "Where did she go after her sister's death?"

"I don't know. There wasn't anything in the paper. And they used to put everything in the local news section. The lawyer who handled Swenson's estate is dead, but his son took over his practice. He'll have his father's old files and they'd have sent Rebecca the check from the sale. I'll call the office first thing tomorrow morning and ask Margaret Atkinson to run down that address."

"No, no, no. Tomorrow you're going to relax, damn it."

"Can't."

"Won't, you mean." She dragged me from my chair and I batted at her in mock protest as I stumbled to bed.

◇◇◇

The next morning after Josie left I took my coffee outside to her patio and tried to enjoy the beautiful blue sky and the smell of burning leaves. But I jumped out of my skin when a car door slammed and sent my cup flying. I swept up the glass.

Action was my favorite antidote for free-floating anxiety. I marched to the phone, called Margaret Atchison and asked her to track down Rebecca Champlin. She called back around noon.

"Greg says Rebecca Champlin moved to Topeka immediately after the auction. That's the good news. We know the town. The bad news is that any monies or papers requiring her signature were sent to a post office box. No physical address."

I groaned. "Thanks, Margaret."

"We've had a number of genealogists in." Her voice was stiff with disapproval of my flight to Eastern Kansas. "Minerva is back on the job, but Patricia Ramsey is out along with about ten others. William and I have managed to escape the flu. Good thing, too."

Her refusal to offer any information about the St. Johns was a subtle reprimand that I usually concentrated on the wrong things. Like murders instead of the history books.

After I hung up, I went outside again. What would I have done in Rebecca Champlin's shoes? I'd have moved from Carlton County. Too many terrible memories. There would be work available in a city. And anonymity. A place where people wouldn't be bringing up the tragedy day after day.

Rebecca had a lot of money for those times. The inheritance from her parents and money from the sale of her farm. She would have been Emily's heir, too, but that wouldn't have amounted to anything. The bank would have had the first claim to any proceeds. Nevertheless, Rebecca wouldn't have had to work at all if she didn't want too.

On the other hand, I mused, maybe she would have wanted to live in the country. Rebecca had always lived on a farm, chose to keep on living on a farm after her parents died. But if I were in her shoes, I wouldn't have wanted to work a farm. The financial risk was too great, I would just have wanted to live on one. I would have looked for a house with some surrounding acreage. About forty acres would be just right.

I may have had trouble relaxing, but I didn't have any trouble thinking, and thinking isn't bad when one's intuition is out of whack. But try as I might, I couldn't actually enter Rebecca's mind.

Surely something went terribly wrong for this woman. One didn't just drop out of everything during high school without a reason. I suspected health. However, I didn't know if she'd actually quit doing needlework or just stopped exhibiting in the Carlton County fair. She might have entered in other counties. Perhaps she was tired of going up against her sister every year.

One thing was very clear. My head was now abuzz with my "other" murder. The Swensons. Now *it* was starting to drive me crazy.

It would be well worth my time to go to Topeka and look up the records of real estate transactions for that year. Then it occurred to me that just because she had her mail sent to a post office box in Topeka wouldn't necessarily mean she had moved there. She could have lived in another town and picked up her mail in Topeka. But if she did that, it would be because she was trying to hide her identity.

Would I do that if my sister and her children were murdered? I might, I decided. If the press was prying all the time. Before it happened, she had become a recluse. But she had come out of her shell after her parents died. Why had their deaths made a difference? She'd become a terrific businesswoman, prospering from raising and selling hogs.

I glanced at my watch. Too late to zip over to Topeka today, and I had an appointment with Josie's speech pathology friend at three o'clock. We would head to the lake after that. I picked up my coffee cup and went back to the kitchen.

My cell rang.

Thinking it might be Keith, I answered on the second ring.

"Sam Abbott here, Lottie."

"What's up?" I knew it was something important for him to interrupt my visit.

"Just wanted to tell you not to rush home. Take your time. Zelda's murder has been solved," he said bitterly.

"What?"

"According to the Neanderthals at the KBI, they are now convinced Zelda was murdered during a random burglary. Yesterday, someone used her bank card in Denver to make an ATM withdrawal. Far as they're concerned, that ties it up with a neat little bow."

"But wasn't there a video? All of those places have videos, don't they?"

"Get this, the person wore a ski mask and a camouflage suit. Which means our thief is smarter than the average bear."

"Everyone in Western Kansas has camouflage," I said, "but the ski mask was a nice touch. So is deflecting the search to Denver."

"That person knew he was being videotaped. He knew the KBI would be keeping track of credit card transactions. That kind of stuff is common knowledge nowadays. He's no dummy."

"The KBI was set up."

"Dumb bastards. Doesn't take much," he said.

"What if it's our letter writer?"

"If it is our letter writer," he said, "that's good evidence our pen pal really is a murderer instead of a teaser."

My throat was dry. I licked my lips. The last letter had said I would be next.

"I'm coming home, Sam."

"No point. You can't do anything. I'm so mad the KBI is pulling out I could spit nails. We're going to be right back in the dark ages without their resources."

"What about Judy?"

"You ain't going to believe, this. They don't think there's any connection between Zelda's murder and Judy's murder."

"More reason than ever for me to come back. I'll talk to Jim Gilderhaus myself."

"Won't do no good. Jim's not the problem. He agrees with me. It's his higher ups who're ordering him off the investigation. So stay in Manhattan. You'll just wear yourself out back here. You need the rest."

"I'm not getting any, Sam. When I'm not thinking about the St. Johns, I'm thinking about the Swenson murders."

"Wish I had never told you about them. Wish I had never hired you on in the first place."

Men. If Sam and Keith had their way, I would be wearing an apron and making strawberry jam.

"I'll be there tomorrow. If I didn't have an appointment with a speech pathologist I'd leave today. Josie isn't going to like this. She was planning on going to the lake."

"Sorry I had to make this call, Lottie, but I didn't want you to hear it on the news."

◇◇◇

By the time Josie finished with her last patient and came through the door, I'd collected the tapes I needed for Herman and was already half-packed.

"You're not leaving?"

"Sorry, something's come up. I'm going back to Western Kansas right now, and psychologists aren't permitted to throw tantrums."

To my surprise, she didn't bother with a reply. She put up her briefcase, crossed over to the piano, and trailed her fingers across the keys. Then she lowered the lid over the keys, picked up her cigarette case, and turned it over and over.

"Lottie." I looked up at the worry in her voice. "I know it's too late to ask you not to be involved with this. You know Keith is worried sick and that isn't enough to stop you. You're not going to listen to me much. A little maybe. But I want you to consider what I'm going to say. Please?"

I nodded, suddenly swept with a wave of sorrow, like I was afflicted with an incurable disease causing enormous distress to my family.

There were tears in Josie's eyes. "I've been consulting with a friend of mine. He's on staff at Washburn and was, in fact, formerly a profiler for the FBI. Here's what he has to say. He believes you are dealing with a multiple murderer. You and Sam are not mistaken in that, no matter what the KBI thinks. This person is extremely intelligent. You know that already. And dangerous. It's a terrible combination. For some unknown reason you've pushed this person to the edge."

"Me?"

"You. Not the St. Johns. You. That's what he thinks."

"I just don't understand. It doesn't make sense."

"I've shown him everything, told him everything, and he's positive it's something you're doing. Or saying. Or not saying. You, Lottie. You."

"I've been over everything in my mind a thousand times."

"I know that. He has an idea for smoking this person out."

"What?"

"Your only contact is through your column, right?"

"Right."

"He wants you to use it. Coax this person into writing a family history. Everything that's said will help us. Can you do that? We'll be looking at every word on this end."

I was hopeful for the first time in a month. Later I would remember that wild hope I felt then and on the long drive back across Kansas. With my hope and my naive confidence I was equipped to deal with the Devil.

Chapter Thirty-Six

I made another call for family stories in a quarter-page ad in the Gateway City Gazette. The text was fourteen-point script, Garamond type, bordered with an antique scroll design. At the bottom of the ad a notice referred readers to additional information in my column.

My column was entitled, "They Need to Know."

> Are you tired of reading family histories that seem like fairy tales? Have you delayed writing your own story because it's "too grim, too shattering." Too contrary to perceptions of idyllic life in a small county?
>
> THEY NEED TO KNOW. I'm urging everyone who has refrained from writing his or her story for any of the above reasons to make the effort. For your sake, and for our sakes. We need to know.
>
> This column will appear on a daily basis for the next two months. It's not necessary to write the whole story at once. We will be happy to print a small section you can supplement from time to time.

It took three days. The letter came from Tulsa, Oklahoma.

> "I was a very special child. My mother loved me. We waited every day for my father because our lives would be perfect when he came to us. I never got to meet him because he was killed in the war.

You can print this. Do not print the P.S.

P.S. My mother taught me not to flinch. She did not like it when I was unhappy."

That was all. This stilted little letter. Loaded. One didn't have to be a psychologist to know how. I closed my eyes for a minute, slowly reread it, and called Josie.

"I want to look at it," she said. "Fax it right away."

I did, and she called back fifteen minutes later. "I talked with Harold Sider, the professor I told you about who used to be with the FBI. In tomorrow's column ask her what made her flinch."

"Her? You think it's a she?"

"Harold does. I don't. But then I'm not a profiler. He's the expert, so let's go with his assumption. However, we both agree there's too much leeway for mood changes by the time your questions and her answers are printed in the column. We want to keep pressing her. Harold has an idea for that, too. Are you on the Internet at the office?"

"Sure. I mostly use Microsoft Outlook at home and on my laptop, but we're on America Online here at the office because more people are familiar with it. Researchers can use services like Family Tree-maker Online and get into the state historical society's databases."

"Super. We know all these letters were printed using a laser printer, so here's hoping our poison pen pal is computer literate in other ways. Put a notice in your column saying people can email if they like. Assure the readers you'll only print what they want."

"Can you trace anything that way?"

"No. But you can save and forward the letters to me immediately through AOL. The goal here is to track emotions. That's all we're after right now."

I glanced at the clock. "Okay. If I hustle, I can make tomorrow's paper."

◇◇◇

Right after the *Gateway Gazette* came out the next day, I hurried to my computer and accessed America Online. "You have mail," announced the mechanical voice.

There were eight messages listed. Annoyed at having to read through four pieces of junk email, I read them anyway, to make sure I wasn't tossing something important before I forwarded the trash to TOSSPAM. There were three requests for historical information. When I clicked on the last email, I gasped. My pen pal. At last I had a name. AngelChild. *AngelChild*

> What made me flinch? It was not knowing what she wanted when she came toward me. Usually she hugged me and told me I was her darling little angel child. But if she didn't like the look on my face, she would slap me instead. Then she would tell me how ungrateful I was and lock me in the closet until I was grateful. I don't mind being in the closet. She is not in the closet with me.

I forwarded it to Josie then called her.

"The last sentence is written in present tense through the eyes of child," she said. "Not from her vantage point as an adult. She must have been terrified."

"It makes me sick just to read it."

"I'll show it to Harold, and we'll let you know the next step."

Too fidgety to go through my regular mail while I waited for her to call back, I took a folder of stencils from the supply shelf and began tracing letters for a display. It calmed my hands, if not my mind. Josie called back five minutes later.

"Harold wants you to try to make her respond right away. If you can't, she may be at work and can't risk using the business computer. It might mean she's emailing from her home. Every bit of information helps."

I thought hard about the next question.

> "Didn't your teachers notice anything wrong? They are supposed to be trained to recognize child abuse."

I sent the message and stayed on-line. For the rest of the day, I listened eagerly for the mail announcement, but it never came.

It was waiting the next morning.

> Don't you ever, ever criticize my teachers. You don't know anything. I loved school. Mother didn't want me to go to school. I didn't want to either at first, but the truant officers made me. When I got there and saw what other children did, what they were like, what they knew, I understood what I was supposed to do. With my mother, I never knew. That was the worst part. The not knowing.
>
> I talked mother into ordering the right clothes, because if things weren't right, the men might come around again. They might take me away. Everyone felt sorry for the poor widow woman who had lost her husband in the war but they would not feel sorry for a mother who wouldn't let her darling little girl go to school."

I quickly typed.

> Which war? World War II? Korea? Vietnam?

There was no response. I reconciled myself to waiting until morning again. My pen pal was female. Harold was right. Since she had not come online during the daytime, we could be certain this was a working woman. She had used the words "truant officer," an older term. She was not young.

I was a bundle of nerves. At the office, at home that evening, I jumped at shadows and started at the slightest sound. Keith was at the neighbors, seeing to a dog that had been hit by a car. I felt like a teenager who had watched too many re-runs of *Halloween*.

Hoping hot chocolate would help calm me, I then swore like a dock hand when I dropped the cup on the floor. At least cleaning up the mess was something I could handle.

Determined to do something productive, I finally scrawled a note to Keith and left for the Sunny Rest Nursing Home for my promised visit to Herman.

I lugged in the combination TV/VCR I had promised him and soon had it up and running.

"No football on tonight," I said, after checking all the channels. "Besides, I brought those tapes I told you about. We might as well get to work." I slipped the cassette into the slot. We listened to the dull introduction, then he studied the sound patterns.

"Do you think we can figure this out?"

He nodded. I focused on the section of tapes illustrating the "AB" words. He nodded. His eyes were bright.

"Ba-ba-ba," he mumbled. "Ba-ba-ba."

"B-a-a? Like in sheep," I asked.

He shut his eyes in despair.

"Ba," he repeated.

"Long A? Are you trying to say a long A?"

He nodded.

I tried words. "Bad? Back?"

He flushed with frustration.

"Let's go through the alphabet."

He nodded again.

"Baby? Are you trying to say baby?"

If he had been a puppy, he would have wiggled out of his chair. Now I knew what he wanted to say, but I didn't have the slightest idea why. He began the clicking sound again. It was a little easier this time, because I was looking for a word that would make sense with baby.

"Can you open your mouth a moment? I want to look at where you're putting your tongue."

The tip was curled forward touching the top of his palate, near his front teeth. I put mine in the same position and started down the alphabet again. Very quickly I zeroed in on the "cl" sound and mimicked the roundness of his mouth.

"Clothes," I said. "You're trying to say baby clothes."

He nodded and nodded and nodded, then let out a slight expulsion of air. No longer excited, he had the quiet pride of someone who has completed a long, hard journey.

"But I still don't understand what you want me to know."

He gave a little shake of head and smiled. "Oh, you think I can figure it out, do you? Just like that? Well, you're right about one thing. I'll bet I give it my best shot."

I glanced at my watch. "Better be going. I can't tell you when I'll be back. I'm busy at the office right now. I'll leave instructions at the desk for working with these tapes."

◇◇◇

Keith's Suburban was in the garage. He sat at the island sipping a cup of instant soup and reading the *Wall Street Journal* and ambled over when I walked into the kitchen.

"That's not enough food for you," I said. "Let me fix you a sandwich."

"I'm okay."

He gave me a weak smile and I answered with one of my own.

"Yeah, we're both okay," I said bitterly. "Just super. This mess wouldn't be so bad if I could leave you out of it. You've lost weight, too, and I'm so terribly sorry to be worrying you, Keith. But this is a small town, and after this *thing* is over the chances of anything dangerous ever coming up again in my lawbreaking career are so remote that…"

"Shush," he said gently. "Just don't talk about it." He kissed the top of my head, smoothed my hair back and caught my face between his large strong hands, tilted it so he could look me fully in the eyes.

"Haven't you noticed? We get along much better if we just don't talk about it."

Chapter Thirty-Seven

It was Friday. Boots and Levis day, which suited me just fine. As I dressed, I winced at the stranger in the mirror. Circles under her eyes. Saggy jeans.

I settled down while driving to work. Overhead, a flock of geese V-d their way south, and I saw three pheasants in a fence row. We were starting corn harvest in Western Kansas. The air smelled like money. Gathered bounty.

I had just rounded the three-mile corner when an announcement came over the radio.

> Senatorial candidate Brian Hadley became ill at a rally in Wichita last evening. Hadley started swaying at the lectern, and, according to those in attendance, began making a bizarre series of unconnected remarks. His publicist, Myron Caldwell, immediately rushed on stage and asked the organizers to call an ambulance. Hadley was taken to Wesley Medical Center for treatment. A spokesman there stated that Hadley was suffering from exhaustion and had contracted a flu-type virus. He will be released today and plans to return to Carlton County and spend several days with his parents. His schedule will be curtailed until he returns to health.

Sick or dead drunk? Furious with this egotistical alcoholic who would not admit or face up to his problem, I missed my turn, braked abruptly spraying gravel, and then backed to the intersection.

I tried to put him out of my mind. It was none of my business. Not anymore. But all of the events of the last month were congealing into a dark lump somewhere in my stomach.

When I got to the office, I logged onto AOL, clicked on the mail icon, and pulled up a message from AngelChild.

> We told everyone she was blind. When she had to go out in public, she always wore dark glasses and used a white cane, but she could see all right. Momma saw everything.
>
> I kept myself neat and clean and did everything just right and never, ever missed school. Even when mother tried to trick me into staying home I didn't miss school.
>
> I was very smart and all the teachers liked me. I did not have friends. If I had gone to slumber parties, they would have wondered why I didn't have them to my house. Momma didn't have to go to parent-teacher conferences because she was blind.
>
> P.S. I missed school when I buried her. But I had a perfect attendance record until then.

My throat tightened as I reread the last line. In one of her letters she had written about "a long line of murders." I hadn't known what she meant at the time. I did now. I forwarded the message at once, then phoned Josie.

"Lottie. We've absolutely got to locate this woman."

"I thought women weren't supposed to be serial killers."

"This isn't the same as a serial killer. She may have killed more than her fair share, but in her mind there's a reason. None of these people were random victims killed for the thrill of it. They seem to have been a threat to her in some way. I'll call you right back, with our latest and greatest plan."

It was a quiet day at the courthouse. I had plenty of real work to do. It steadied me somewhat. The phone shrilled like a banshee an hour later.

"Carlton County Historical Society," I said. It was Josie.

"Lottie, can you set up AOL to reply to AngelChild on your laptop or home desktop?"

"Well sure, but Sam wants it to go through my server here and my off-site backup in case we need to file charges. He doesn't want some lawyer to accuse me of altering dates."

"Oh God." She paused. I heard another voice in the background.

"Would it be possible for you to stay in the courthouse tonight so you will know the moment a message comes in?"

"It can be done. I'll have to pull a few strings, but I can do it."

"We want you to reply immediately. Harold thinks she might mail right back, and if she does, it will be more spontaneous."

"My questions will be more immediate, too."

"Harold wants you to have police protection while you're there."

"Honey, I *am* the police. Why does everyone keep forgetting that?"

"Can't someone stay with you?"

"No. What a mess. The letter saying she killed her mother changes everything. Most of the time my two jobs are a dream situation, but sometimes I'm walking a tight-wire and this is one of those times. Keith would be here in a flash, but now this is police business and the wrong person could jeopardize our prosecution later."

"Lucky me. I'm the lone professional consultant. Sam? Can't Sam be there?"

"Nope. One-horse town. No extra personnel. He'll be on duty, covering all the rest of the county. There's the city police department, but they don't know anything about any of this because it wasn't in their jurisdiction to begin with.

"Harold and I are thinking about coming out."

"Don't be silly. I'll be just fine. What do you think? She's going to reach through the screen and grab me?"

"No, but she'll know where you are. If you email right back, he'll know you're at the courthouse. If she lives in this county, pure logic will tell him you're there alone. I don't like it."

"He again, Josie? Freudian slip?"

"Did I really say *he*?"

"You did. 'He'll know you're at the courthouse.'"

She was quiet for a moment. "There is a masculine *feel* to this person. I've said that all along. This person is extremely cunning. What worries me is the possibility some of what's being sent might be a disguise. Close enough to the truth emotionally, but physical facts switched."

"To throw me off?"

"Exactly. The reclusive mother has a ring of truth, but maybe they told the teachers she was crippled instead of blind. The right clothes could have been overalls instead of dresses. That kind of thing."

For the first time I felt like I was totally over my head.

Chapter Thirty-Eight

I got permission from one of the county commissioners to be in the courthouse after hours. He gave me an extra key for the use of the historical society. I was spared explaining anything to Keith as he was out of the house when I got home.

Grabbing a sleeping bag, my travel kit, and some fruit, I left a note saying I had to be on duty, not to wait up. He could reach me through the sheriff's office. Which was the truth. Sam knew where I was and why.

The massive stone courthouse looked sinister in the moonlight. Leaves on the ancient cottonwoods flashed silver in the night wind. I shivered, hair rising on the back of my neck, as I unlocked a side door.

Once inside my office, I did not turn on my light until I had closed the door tightly. The heat had been turned down for the weekend and the room was chilly. I arranged my sleeping bag, my little sack of food, turned on the computer, and thought about all Josie had said. Push a little, but don't scare off AngelChild. A ticklish balance.

Finally I typed:

I'm so very sorry you had to ruin your perfect attendance record.

I waited. There were far more important issues than her attendance record, of course. Serious questions I wanted to ask. Like, did you kill your mother, darling? But I was trying to establish a rapport. A rapport with a crazy woman. Or man.

She had ignored my question asking "which war." Was it because she didn't want me to get a fix on her age?

The old pipes clanked. There was a snake-like hiss in the corridor. I rose, opened my door a crack and risked a peek. It came from an old radiator at the end of the hallway. The maddening hum from my ancient overhead fluorescent light sounded like a distant plane. The odor of wax and Pine-sol permeated the air. I sat back down and stared at the chipped green and white tiles on the floor, the institutional green walls, the mismatched cabinets and desks.

I didn't have to be here. I wanted to be home. All I had to do was walk away from all this. Back to my lovely house and my warm husband. AngelChild wasn't one bit crazier than I was.

Around ten o'clock, she came on line.

> Thank you. I was very proud of my attendance record. I had to bury her, you see. All by myself. The ground wasn't frozen yet, but it was taking too long to dig only at night. So I had to miss a day of school. I didn't want a neighbor to see a light in the yard at night. Besides, at night I always had homework and I didn't want to get behind.

That was all. I forwarded it to Josie. She called back shortly.

"Harold's right here beside me, Lottie. Good job. You got a lot of concrete information. Her mother died in the fall, because 'the ground wasn't frozen yet.' We know she had neighbors. Try to get more."

"Okay. I'll see if she is actually at her computer."

More exhilarated than fearful now, I typed:

> It must have been hard for you.

Fingers crossed, I squeezed my eyes shut. When I opened them again, a new message appeared on the screen. For the first time, she was coming back in real time. Responding instantly, just as we had hoped.

> It was the worst day of my life. I had never missed school before.

I blinked. Burying her mother wasn't the worst part of the day. It was missing school.

> What was the best day of your life?

She typed:

> The day I turned eighteen and I wasn't a minor anymore.

I drew a deep breath.

> How old were you when your mother died?

The screen was quiet for a few minutes. Then:

> Just sixteen. That's why I had to bury her all by myself. I couldn't let anyone know she had died. Funerals, burials cost money. They would have made me live with someone else, but I could take care of myself. They would have snooped and snooped and found out about the money.

My hands shook as I typed:

> Did you kill your mother?

The answer came back, lightning fast:

> I know what you're trying to do. You're trying to trick me. You're next.

I closed my eyes and pressed my fingers against my temples. I had pushed her too far. The phone shattered the silence. Assuming it was Josie, I started talking before the caller could speak.

"I've blown it. Too fast. Much too fast."

"Sam Abbott here, Lottie. I need you to come with me to the Hadleys."

"Can't do it. My letter writer is on-line. I don't dare stop."

"This is more important. We got a 911 and I want a woman there with me, just in case."

"A 911. Did they say why?"

"All they said was that it was an emergency and they needed an ambulance. I don't want Betty Central to go with me for obvious reasons."

"For obvious reasons," I echoed.

"The ambulance is on the way, and just in case, we need to be there, too."

I closed my eyes, knowing I couldn't hold up if the "just in case" was another murder.

"Sam, I can't leave here. Not now."

"There's no one else, kiddo. Just you."

I looked at the screen. It was blank. She had signed off.

"Okay," I said bleakly. "Chances are she'll never speak to me again, anyway."

"I'll be there in a flash and pick you up."

I hung up, reached for my coat, locked the room and headed out.

◇◇◇

All the lights were on. An ambulance blocked the circular drive. White-faced and trembling, Fiona opened the door before we could knock.

"What are you doing here?" she snapped.

"You called 911, lady," Sam said.

"I wanted an ambulance. Not the police."

"Well, you're getting the whole enchilada. Two for the price of one. What's the trouble?"

"It's Brian," she said. "Something happened. He started breaking things. Saying things." She was in a bathrobe. Without make-up, she looked years older. She pressed her fist against her mouth, and tears streamed down her cheeks. Edgar stood in the hallway and watched the EMT's load Brian onto a stretcher.

Sam gazed around the foyer. A dented brass pot from an overturned uprooted ficus plant lay on the slate floor next to splintered rungs of a walnut chair. Brian was yelling, writhing on the gurney. One of the technicians drew some liquid into a syringe, held it up to the light to eye the contents, ejected a drop, then turned, plunged the contents into Brian's arm.

"I'll get dressed," Fiona said curtly. "Edgar and I will follow the ambulance to the airport."

"The airport?"

"He's ill. Can't you see that? We're flying him to Denver, where there's top-notch doctors."

"All right," Sam said. "That's your privilege. Looks like this is strictly a medical problem, but we wanted to be sure."

Fiona nodded stiffly. Edgar still had not spoken, and a glance told me he didn't intend to. They wanted us gone. Once again, I regretted having seen this family when they were so vulnerable.

"Now what in tarnation do you suppose *that* was all about," Sam said finally, on the drive back.

I turned from the window where I had been staring at the moon-lit landscape. Sam's craggy old features were high-lighted by the glow from the dash.

"I don't suppose. I know. I tried to tell Brian he needs treatment. Not that a drunk ever listens. D.T.'s, that's what. You were just seeing a man in a full blown episode of delirium tremens."

"Brian's a drunk?" He took his foot off the accelerator for a split second.

I told him about the hidden bottles, Brian's sullen refusal to give a kid an autograph at the rally.

"Who'd a thought it?"

"Not me, Sam, and I can spot one a mile off. He had me fooled."

"Guess this finishes off his career."

"Yes, I guess it does."

I turned my face away so Sam couldn't see my tears. Brian was a dead duck, but it didn't give me one whit of satisfaction.

Ashamed at the anger I'd harbored, after seeing a magnificent man in such a pathetic state, I thought about what he might have been, should have been.

"Do you want me to take you home, Lottie?"

"No, my car's back at the courthouse. I'll check back in on my poison pen pal before I go home, but I think I lost her when I left." I filled Sam in on all the details of the email exchange.

Back inside my office, I glanced at my watch. We had been gone over an hour. Thinking there would be no more activity that night, I rolled up my sleeping bag and collected my bags and headed for the door. Then I paused, just to be sure, and touched a key on my computer to de-activate the screen saver.

The words were in caps, bolded and underlined:

<u>WHERE ARE YOU? YOU'VE ABANDONED ME. I WAS GOING TO TELL YOU AND YOU LEFT ME. TELL YOU EVERYTHING. I KNEW I COULDN'T TRUST YOU. YOU'RE LIKE ALL THE OTHERS.</u>

She had broken. I'd missed my chance. Balloon-light, my head tried to fathom the implications of bungling this opportunity.

My fingers trembled as I typed:

> Please, oh, please. There was an emergency. I had to leave. I want to keep talking with you. Don't stop.

There was no response. Fifteen minutes later I called Josie and told her what had happened.

"I just hope we haven't lost her for good," she said. "What she's already told you might have satisfied her urge to confide. It may have been enough. Not enough for us, of course. But enough for her to feel better."

"Oh, no, what incredibly rotten timing."

"Yes," she said softly. "Incredibly rotten."

Chapter Thirty-Nine

Normally I sleep late on Saturday. I love waking up to birdsong outside our cheery yellow bedroom, love the dazzling blue brightness of the sky from our second-story balcony.

But this morning, I was wired. After Brian's collapse I had stayed at the courthouse until three o'clock in the morning. Nothing I said lured AngelChild back online.

Furious at having alienated her, after a scant hour's sleep, I cleaned.

I scrubbed bathtubs and showers and floors and went after spots like I was the ghost of Lady Macbeth. Keith watched me all morning.

I was heading toward the kitchen windows, bucket and squeegee in hand, when his voice rang out.

"Stop it, Lottie."

I spun around, inadvertently thrusting my squeegee in front of me like it was a lance. "You're wearing yourself to a frazzle."

Deep lines, new ones, creased his forehead.

"Come here," he said gently and beckoned with his fingers like he was coaxing a mad pet dog out of a corner.

I looked at my squeegee and tried to laugh as I propped it up beside my bucket. Then I covered my face with my hands and burst into tears. He scooped me up like I was a sack of feathers and carried me upstairs.

"Right out of *Gone With the Wind*," I said.

"Not quite, sweetheart, but I *am* going to undress you and put you to bed. The ravishing can wait until you're in better shape. We're going to have a long, long talk. You're going to stay in that bed for the rest of the day if I have to lock you in your room. I want you to tell me everything that's going on."

"Okay. You're a clear thinker, Keith. I want your opinion. Sometimes I overlook things that are in plain sight, and you never do."

"And you see things I can't see," he said.

"No, I don't see. I *know* and then I have to find evidence to back up what I know. Josie says with you and me, it's sensation versus intuition."

"Well, let's see here. You've told me about two murders, an accusation that you stole the Custer letters, missing messages on your answering machine, a vanished letter that links Fiona to Zelda's murder, threatening letters you've received at the courthouse and that the leading senatorial candidate is a drunk. Wonder what you're holding back?"

I laughed despite my exhaustion, swallowed hard, told him I had spent the night alone at the courthouse, and was called away to an emergency at the Hadleys. I told him about our AngelChild sting.

"Son-of-a-bitch, what were you thinking? What was Sam thinking in letting you be there alone?"

"No, you think Keith. It had to be me there, and Sam and I and Betty Central are it."

"I could have been there."

I closed my eyes. "Sweetheart, I was on duty. A deputy can't take her husband along for protection."

He flushed.

"And other things keep gnawing at me. I want to know what Judy found. That alone is about to drive me crazy. She said it was a letter. A copy of a letter actually. It only makes sense that Judy's murderer took it or destroyed it. Now if you really want to help, think. I need someone who can help think."

With Keith concentrating on details rather than scolding me for endangering myself, a tight wire inside snapped. I had the sensation of floating softly to the ground and my ground was always Keith.

He rose and walked over to the entertainment center built into the bookcase and flipped through some CDs. He selected Vivaldi's Four Seasons and adjusted the balance on the player. Then he came back, kicked off his shoes and stretched out beside me on top of the quilt.

"I make a top-notch detective, don't I?"

He drew me close. "I don't have any bright ideas. It's not exactly my calling, either."

I rolled toward him and laid my head on his chest. He stroked my hair. "I hate to worry you."

He inhaled sharply. "You can't stop me from worrying. It's in my job description. In the marriage vows as I recall."

"Is not." I punched his shoulder.

"Make a deal with you, Lottie. Keep me posted on everything and I promise I'll treat you like a professional. And I damn sure can help keep you in better shape. I'm upping the household help starting Monday morning. You've got more important things to do with your time than scrubbing floors."

"Elizabeth will think I'm a wimp," I mumbled.

"Yes, she will at that."

I didn't remember Keith leaving the room. I did remember waking up around seven o'clock and eating a sandwich. That night, I dreamed about a woman in black trying to coax me across a swamp. She was beautiful and compelling, and the surface of the water was lighted by luminescent gases that shifted and glowed. I yearned to follow her, but at the side stood Zelda and Judy. They were gesturing frantically, warning me away.

◇◇◇

The next morning, I made a three-egg western omelet, added two slices of toast, an orange, and a pot of coffee. I used my Fiestaware. Cheered by the splash of orange and gold and aqua

I carried the food out to the patio where I could watch the birds.

The sky was pale grey, charged with energy like a blank computer screen. I groaned at the image of a computer. Suddenly chilled despite my wool socks and flannel shirt, the food stuck in my throat. Despair over having lost AngelChild swept through me like a Kansas dust devil across a field.

Grimly determined to banish murder from my mind, I went back to the kitchen for a thermos of coffee and grabbed a wool comforter from the hall closet. I adjusted the stereo to the outside speakers. Too edgy to bear the emotionality of bluegrass, I ran upstairs for the Vivaldi CD.

Back outside, I draped the quilt over one of our white resin loungers. Keith's daughters hate our tacky lawn furniture, but I don't. It's the perfect in-your-face material for the wind, the dust, Mother Nature's assaults on our rural courage, day after day. I sat down in my nearly indestructible recliner, pulled the blanket around me, sipped my scalding coffee, and dared whatever to come and get me.

Keith was at Mass. He never missed. It felt good to be home by myself. I smiled at the finches balanced on the edge of the bird feeder. A rabbit appeared at the edge of the windbreak. It darted in, then out, then disappeared back into the dense cedars. It's lovely, having real acreage.

The view from our backyard is framed like an elegant golf course with grass down the center and a wonderful collection of shrubs, flowering trees and flowers flowing down the sides. My mums were a riot of gold and bronze and maroon.

My internal computer bleeped. Error. Error. The mums needed transplanting. I hadn't gotten around to it yet. So much for my stab at tranquility. When I'm worried, minor things nag. Take on too much importance. Josie says I'm prey to free-floating anxiety and I should get over it. I sighed. I knew I should call Josie. See if she and Harold had any more bright ideas.

I hadn't returned some overdue library books. Hadn't folded the wash. Hadn't been back to visit Herman. I decided if I ever got enough energy to get out of my chair in this lifetime, I would perhaps go to the nursing home and visit Herman Swenson. Of all that was going on in my life, he seemed the safest.

Then I thought about the baby clothes. Another damned mystery. What was I supposed to know? Understand? Like bobbing for apples, just when I was on the verge of sinking my teeth on a thought, it went back under.

Later, I would give credit to Vivaldi. As the music proceeded to the autumn movement, it came to me with a flourish of trumpets and cellos with dazzling clarity.

Baby clothes. Baby clothes.

I knew. I knew. In my very bones, I knew.

I threw off the comforter, ran into the house, got my keys and dashed to my Tahoe. The key to the front door of the courthouse was still in my jacket pocket.

◇◇◇

Inside my office, I flicked on the computer. While I was there, I wanted to see if AngelChild had emerged again. However, my mind was on another time, another person. Triumphantly I pulled out my file on the Swenson murders. I pulled out the original note the bank had held on Herman Swenson's property, and then the bill of sale. I compared them. I was right. I made copies for myself and Sam.

Seeing that there was no new email, I switched off the computer, stuffed the Swenson file and the print-outs from AngelChild in my briefcase, locked up, and tore over to Sam's office.

He was dozing in his wooden swivel chair, hat atilt, and covering half his face, feet propped on his desk.

"Wake up, Sam. I'm bringing you good news. Tidings of great joy and all that."

"Huh." Startled, he jerked awake.

"I have proof positive right here that Herman Swenson did not murder his wife and son."

"What?" Fully upright now, he fumbled in his desk drawer for his glasses.

"Proof, Sam. Solid proof." I pointed to the deed and the bill of sale. "See anything funny there?"

"Nothing except how pathetically detailed all the early bank notes were. Buckets, tea towels counted. Even the forks and spoons listed. We've talked about that before Lottie."

"On the original bank note, there was an enormous list of baby clothes. Emily was a superb needlewoman. She embroidered stacks of clothes for Johnny before he was born and for all of the babies she miscarried and for the babies yet to be born. Now look at the bill of sale after the murders."

He stared at the paper. His hands trembled. "That man has been locked away for years. What have we done?"

"Yes! It's what is not there, Sam. No baby clothes! Not a single article of baby clothes listed in the bill of sale. Whoever took those baby clothes murdered Herman Swenson's wife and son."

"And the baby," Sam whispered. "The baby."

Chapter Forty

Sickened, he coughed from a sudden intake of smoke.

"The baby needed those clothes," I said.

His Adam's apple bobbed.

"The baby's body was never found because it wasn't there, Sam. Someone took that baby."

His hands shook as he tamped fresh tobacco into the bowl. The first match died out, then another. It took several. I didn't mind. There's some news so terrible you can only inhale it slowly. One toxic breath at a time.

"We've had an innocent man locked away all these years."

"Yes, all these years," I said bitterly. "He lost his bank. He lost his farm. He lost his wife. He lost his son. He lost his baby. Then he lost his natural life. We've kept him locked away all these years."

"None of this is proof of Herman's innocence." He thrummed his fingers on the desk. "We'll need solid evidence."

"I know that. But it certainly is grounds for reasonable doubt."

"You betcha. I'll have the case reopened. Everything scrutinized using new forensic methods. None of this was available fifty years ago."

"In the meantime, I'll start looking for the real murderer. I'll begin with the assumption that baby was born alive."

"What vicious son-of-a-bitch could have done such a terrible thing?"

"Yes, a terrible thing. Strange, isn't it, that people didn't have a bit of trouble believing Herman did it. Wouldn't have been because they were prejudiced against bankers, would it?"

"I believe you," said Sam. "Everything you're saying. But for once, I know better than you where to start looking. No one could hide a baby in a county of this size. No one. So we're going to start looking for someone who moved away right after the murders."

We both said the name at once.

"Rebecca Champlin."

"She moved to Topeka," I said. "Right away. She said she couldn't stand to live any longer in a county where she had experienced so much heartache, but there certainly could have been another reason."

His quick eyes flashed agreement.

"I'll bet I know who can tell me about Rebecca. Herman Swenson."

"Thought he couldn't talk."

"He can't, but he managed to get the baby clothes information to me. It will be interesting to see what he knows about his wife's sister. Herman dated her first. Before he started going with Emily. Hard to believe the hell-hath-no-fury thing could go to such extremes, but who knows? There was something wrong with that woman. I'm sure of that."

"Got that right," Sam said. "She was crazy as a bedbug if she did this."

"Whoops, there. Now who's jumping to conclusions?"

"Not much of a jump. This is going to be like finishing up a jigsaw puzzle. Even so, it'll have to wait. We have a more important job right now."

"Don't I know," I groaned. Reaching for my briefcase, I pulled out the messages from AngelChild.

He read them quickly, then once again with painstaking carefulness. "This should be a real eye-opener to the KBI. I tried to tell the stupid, inept bumblers…"

"Don't antagonize them."

"Don't plan to. Butter won't melt in my mouth. Just want to show those ignorant bureaucrats what real detecting looks like."

I laughed. "Those so-called ignorant bureaucrats have all the tools, the resources, the equipment."

"Yeah, but they don't have our secret weapon."

"Which is?"

"You, Lottie."

"Why, Sam, thank you," I stammered. Ridiculously pleased, I felt myself blush.

"No, I mean it. I'm blown away at the stuff you've unearthed with academic methods. We're going to postpone going to the KBI with these printouts."

"We have to turn over information."

"We will. After we're done collecting it. There's no rule I have to parcel it out bit by bit. If I take this to them now, they'll want to take over. Probably put their own people online."

"They can't do that. AngelChild is too sensitive. She would know in a heartbeat it wasn't me."

"I know that, but the dumb bastards won't."

He was right. I glanced at my watch. "Keith will be getting home from church any time now. Since it's Sunday, theoretically AngelChild should be home, not working. Since I slept most of the day yesterday and didn't try to get in touch with her, she's had a whole day to settle down. I'll go back in this afternoon and try again. Over my husband's dead body, of course. He'll want me to rest."

"Dead bodies are my specialty now," he said gloomily. "They used to be yours."

◇◇◇

I laughed with delight when I saw her black Mercedes parked in the driveway. Josie sat at our resin table with Keith and a stranger. Tosca, yipping happily, tried to corner a toad at the edge of my flower beds. I parked, ran to Josie and hugged her hard.

"This is Harold Sider."

"I feel like I know you." I smiled and shook his hand. He had a cocker spaniel's soft brown eyes. Too kind for a law enforcement officer, ex or otherwise. I saw the St. John's Bay label on the navy cardigan draped over the back of his chair, glanced at his khaki Dockers, his scuffed loafers, and trusted him. Serial killers probably did, too.

"To what do I owe this unexpected pleasure?"

Josie squinted at me hard. "You look terrible. What have you done to yourself?"

I stiffened. "Haven't you ever once in your whole over-privileged life started off with hello? What are you doing here? Did you drive four hundred miles just to insult me?"

"Not this time. I'm taking over, Lottie."

I looked at her blankly. My life? My husband? My job?

"The thing with AngelChild," she said gently. "Harold and I have talked. You've done a terrific job so far, but we want to be in charge of the email. He's a forensic psychologist, I'm clinical. We're the A team."

I started to protest, then stopped. I was a pro too. At historical research. Part of professionalism is knowing when someone else could do the job better.

"You're right," I sank into the chair beside Keith. Eyeing me with relief, he reached for my hand and gave it a squeeze. He stroked my forearm.

"I don't want to put you in harm's way," I said.

"Not to worry. Harold will be right beside me in your office."

"Whew! Talk about the cavalry showing up." From the looks on their faces, they were surprised at my reaction. I held up my hands.

"Did you think I would risk blowing this? That I'm too egotistical to step aside? But Sam has to know you two are stepping in. I'll call him right now. I was going back to the office this afternoon."

"We called Sam just before you drove up," Harold said. "He said you'd just left. We couldn't do this without his clearance. He's all for it."

"The sooner we get started, the better," Josie said. "We've both gotten two-day replacements for our classes and I've called my patients. If we can't get what we need in two days, we'll cry uncle."

"I suppose you're going to pass yourself off as me."

"But of course. With the weight you've lost, it'll be a snap."

I looked pointedly at her coal black hair.

"Covered," she said. "I thought of that. I'll comb in a few streaks of temporary silver frost."

"How will you explain Harold? People aren't used to seeing a strange man in my office."

Harold edged forward on his chair. "I'll pose as a computer guru guiding you through a new program. New configuration. It's a plenty good enough explanation if someone comes looking for you and sees me sitting at your sister's side."

"And what am I supposed to do in the meantime?"

"How about hanging around the house?" Keith asked. "Taking care of yourself for a change. Eat, sleep. Minor stuff like that."

I ignored my husband. "What a gold-plated opportunity. I know exactly what I want to do. I'll go to Topeka and retrace the life of Rebecca Champlin."

Keith groaned.

"Two days to concentrate on Rebecca! I can discover the secrets of the universe in two days. And before I leave, I want both your impressions of this woman."

I told them about Herman and the baby clothes. Harold's eyes widened with surprise.

"You didn't know how good Lottie was, did you?" Josie said.

"Since she's your sister, that hardly surprises me. It's amazing how the past affects what's happening now."

"Thanks to one and all, but I'm not angling for compliments. Before I leave, please look at all the information I've accumulated. I want your expert opinions about Rebecca Champlin. What you think, what you suspect."

"From what you've said, I'd say you're right in wondering about this woman's health problems," Sider said. "You need to get her past medical records."

"If I have a lull, I could ask for information," Josie said, "You couldn't, Harold, without setting everyone in the county abuzz, but I could."

"Don't even think about asking for Rebecca's medical records," I said. "Stick to your main murder. Dr. Golbert would know in a heartbeat you're not me. Besides, right now, I'm just looking for evidence that might support my ideas. Hello," I coaxed. "I need to focus on something else while I'm gone. Not just sit around. Help me out here."

Harold nodded and Josie gave in.

"If she killed her sister and nephew and stole a baby, she was clearly psychotic," Josie said.

"Doesn't mean she acted irrationally," Harold added.

"A newborn baby would have needed medical attention," Josie said.

"Not unless there was something terribly wrong," said Keith. "Lottie says she was a farm woman who raised hogs. She would have known a lot about birthing that would apply to humans."

"But surely she took the child to a doctor at some point," Josie said.

Keith was thoughtful. "Maybe not. These were the years before inoculations or regular check-ups of any kind, and no government oversight whatsoever."

I glanced at my watch. "We need to get started. All of us. Oh-oh. You'll have to be seen driving my Tahoe, Josie. I'll have to take your Mercedes. Hot dog."

"Hot dog, hell," she muttered.

"It's the breaks, sis."

Harold grinned and Keith rolled his eyes.

Chapter Forty-One

By two o'clock I was on my way to Topeka. Once there, I checked into a hotel with all the executive amenities. I tested my wireless connection and emailed to my own computer at the historical society to see if Josie was online. I got an immediate reply:

> We've sent two messages, and AngelChild hasn't responded. We're afraid if we push too hard, we'll lose her for good. I wish you were still in town.

I typed back:

> There can't be two of us sitting there in the courthouse, remember? Folks are supposed to think you're me. The real test of that will come tomorrow if someone wanders in and asks you to find information about their family tree.

From Josie:

> Let's hope that doesn't happen.

I stayed on-line. Josie or Harold would send me IMs and forward AngelChild's messages. If AngelChild didn't bite by eight o-clock the next morning, we didn't expect to hear from her before evening. Harold believed the person worked, and was still stable enough to show up.

Josie phoned.

"We'll cool it for several hours. We want to see how she responds to suspense on her end."

"Okay. I'll take a shower and order room service. Flash me if she breaks in."

The shower was quick and hot, the food mediocre. I had just propped myself up against all the pillows the room had to offer when my laptop beeped.

What did you do after your mother died?

AngelChild responded:

> I bloomed. I was valedictorian. I should have been surrounded by family congratulating me. I turned eighteen two weeks before graduation. I told everyone my mother had died very suddenly and we would be burying her in Western Kansas. No one knew she had died two years earlier. See what she made me do? I'm an honest person down deep inside. She's made me lie all my life. It was supposed to be different for me.

Bingo, I thought, *she's given us a magical bit of information. She was valedictorian.* When she said the burial was in Western Kansas, it implied that she was then living in Eastern Kansas. I knew how to locate Eastern Kansas valedictorians.

In an earlier email she had said her father was in the war. Someone had carried Judy into that barn. Carried her and lifted her. That person had to have been strong and in decent physical shape. AngelChild's father could possibly have been in World War II. It was the earliest war to make any sense. Assuming it was an American war.

To be on the safe side, I would start ten years after that time and cover a ten year span to find the names of all the valedictorians in all the high schools east of Salina.

While I was gloating over this information, Josie flashed back an instant message:

> There's my ticket in. I'm going to find out why she felt she was *entitled* to a different life.

Jobs! What we do for a living has everything to do with how we think, what we look for. Josie zeroed in on AngelChild's psychology, I was concerned with old high school records.

She typed quickly:

> Harold just warned me to wait for that kind of probing. He says let her go while she's on free flow. He doesn't want me to ask any questions at all. Just show empathy.

AngelChild continued to type. It was coming like a river now:

> After her "burial," people made all over me because I was an orphan. So brave. If they only knew how brave I had been all my life. They couldn't touch me. Couldn't do strange things to me or put me with strange people because I had reached my majority.

A date, a word, I pleaded. *Just one. That's all I need.*
Josie typed:

> I know how brave you are. It must have been very hard for you. I wish I could have been there for your graduation. I'm sure you were beautiful.

She typed:

> I really was beautiful. I bought a brand new dress and looked just as nice as the other girls.

Where did you buy the dress, I pleaded silently. *Give me the name of a store.*

Josie wouldn't know to ask that kind of question. If AngelChild had bought it through mail order or some little general store, it could be any town in Kansas. If it were a Penney's or a Sears it would be a medium sized town, but if by some stroke of luck she had bought the dress at a store like the old Pellatiers here in Topeka, it would give me a very specific town and date.

Josie risked a question:

What was your dress like? I wish I had been there to see you.

Immediately from AngelChild:

It was stunning. A red sheath. Momma would have hated it. She said I was a shameless hussy to seek out clothes that showed off my body. But it wasn't clingy. She said I should never wear red with my coloring. Never. I didn't care. I wanted it. It was very expensive, and I bought a pair of high heels to go with it. They were my first, and I had a hard time walking across the stage. But it was worth it. No one had ever seen me look like that before.

The screen was silent, and I took advantage of the lull:

Josie, we've got her. She graduated in the sixties, and she's a redhead.

She typed:

Isn't that a bit of leap?

I responded:

Nope, you're concentrating on psychology, and I'm looking for facts. Jacqueline Kennedy's sheaths were all the rage, and even though she popularized low heels, trends hit Kansas late in the clothing cycle. Women wore pointy-toed high heels a lot longer out here. And redheads were always cautioned about wearing red.

Then AngelChild was back:

I was free. Everyone knew I was going to college. I bought a car. I had missed out on driver's ed, so I had to hire a private instructor. But I didn't care. Everything was worth it.

Then Josie made her mistake:

There were two years from the time your mother died and you reached eighteen. What was the first thing you did when your mother died?

AngelChild responded:

I looked in her trunk. The trunk I had never been allowed to open. Then I understood everything. You're trying to make me crazy again. You'll pay for this.

The screen was silent. Josie waited ten minutes, then phoned.

"Blew that one," she said. "That time was too loaded for her. My guess is she's done for the night. When she had a little time between sessions before, she came back. Harold's betting she will again."

"Tomorrow, I'll hit the research center and zero in on May newspapers published in Eastern Kansas during the sixties and look for a female valedictorian wearing a sheath. I won't be able to see the hair color, but I can narrow it down. Her hair will show up as grey tones."

"Fantastic!"

"Will be if I can come up with a name."

"Get some sleep, Lottie. Harold and I are staying right here just in case. But we're able to take turns. You have a packed day ahead of you tomorrow, and you need your rest. If she comes back online, we'll call you."

◇◇◇

I awoke early the next morning. Too impatient to wait or waste a precious second, I decided to learn what I could about Rebecca Champlin before the Kansas State Historical Society opened.

I drove across town to the courthouse. Luckily, in addition to Topeka being the state capitol, it was also the county seat. The records would show if Rebecca had bought a small farm somewhere in Shawnee County. If what Sam and I suspected was right, she'd moved with a tiny baby. Ripped from her sister's womb.

When the register of deeds brought me the county books, I quickly flipped to the pertinent months. I traced down the columns of property transactions. Nothing. No Rebecca Champlin. Disappointed, I scanned earlier, then later months.

I had been so positive she had moved to Topeka. So sure she'd bought a small piece of land. Coveted privacy. Especially if she was trying to raise a small baby.

I went to the treasurer's office and requested property tax records. No Rebecca Champlin there, either. Perhaps she had changed her name. That would make sense, and it would make my job a lot harder. I glanced at my watch. The research center would be open now. Time to look for my redhead.

Once again, I shoved the vindication of Herman Swenson to the back burner.

Chapter Forty-Two

The vast research center of the Kansas State Historical Society is in the same building as their state of the art museum. I had to put my cell phone, purse, any pens, and notebooks inside a locker before I went inside the main room. Only pencils, a few pages and a laptop were allowed inside, and my laptop would be opened and inspected when I left. Despite these precautions, persons somehow managed to smuggle out documents. I presented my credentials at the desk, and headed back to the microfilm.

So many towns. So many newspapers. East of Salina is considered to be Eastern Kansas. That half of the state, where Josie and I grew up, has water and trees in abundance. The people are softer, less judgmental. Pioneers used to say there was no Sunday west of Junction City and no God west of Salina. We're big on self-reliance in Western Kansas.

I made a copy of the state map and asked for microfilm, county by county. I plugged my laptop into an outlet as I intended to work straight through until closing.

All research takes time. Tedious, achy time. It's donkey work. There are no short cuts. I loaded the film, forwarded to the month of May, then realized all the graduates were in caps and gowns. There was no way to spot a sheath dress. I would have to read copy and research all the female valedictorians. Reel after reel, paper after paper, for four hours. My eyes hurt. My shoulders ached.

Schools began consolidating after the fifties. Before that, small high schools had graduating classes of twelve to twenty students. I scanned through male valedictorians with flat-tops and listed the girls along with their counties.

Nowhere. Nothing. Reel after monotonous reel.

The research center closed at four-thirty. I took all the film back to the desk, retrieved my possessions, and reluctantly headed back to the motel. Too tired to dress for dinner, too melancholy to want the isolation of room service, I wheeled into a McDonald's and ordered a calorie-laden Big Mac value meal.

◇◇◇

Back in my room, I called Josie.

"Nothing," she said. "But we were expecting that. We're sure she works and is doing this out of her home, so prime time will be evening. Harold says probably before midnight, because she'll have to work the next day. He thinks she's a sensible person, who values her job."

"I ran into a dead end here. With both projects." I told her I suspected Rebecca Champlin had changed her name and that it would take a lot of time to track her down. "No luck spotting AngelChild either, but I'm only a third of the way through the counties. How did your day go, otherwise?"

"As in, how did I spend my summer vacation?"

"Something like that."

"I was busy," she said. "Quite a few people who work in the courthouse stopped by. A Minerva, can that really be her name? dropped off some deeds."

"Yes, Minerva is the county clerk."

"I met William, by the way, whom I knew by reputation."

"Oh, boy."

"Actually, I liked him quite a lot. And Margaret Atkinson. She came by too."

"Whew. If you talked to those two and neither one knew you were a substitute, you were perfect. What did they want?"

"I had the feeling they were both checking up on me/you. They asked questions about the progress of the books."

"Undoubtedly," I said.

"You'll be thrilled and amazed to know you/me made a fabulous impression. At the time they were both there, Harold and I were busy compiling a list of all the people who have *not* turned in a family history."

"That's a great idea."

"Isn't it? I'm willing to bet some folks right here in this county are going to be very conspicuous by their absence. When you get back, we'll take a hard look at the list together."

I turned on the bed lamp. The dim bulb was god-awful for reading. But the blue and mauve décor was comforting after a long day of sitting on a straight-backed oak chair.

"I'm in for the night. Here's hoping AngelChild is in the mood to chat."

"I want to know about that trunk," said Josie. "What was in that trunk that her mother would have kept hidden away? She said she understood everything when she opened the trunk?"

"When do we start?"

"Harold says we're ready. It's time."

"See if you can talk him into waiting another half hour. I want to shower and call Keith to give him the number to the main desk at the research room because I can't take my cell inside. Even though I'll have my laptop, internet access is limited to data bases. I'll have housekeeping bring me some extra filter packs for the coffee pot. Then I'll be set."

Twenty minutes later, I flashed her a message. I was ready too.

Josie typed:

I love trunks.

No question, just a statement. We waited and waited.
Finally AngelChild logged on:

My mother's trunk is my most prized possession.

Josie typed:

> Some people keep trunks for a very long time.

AngelChild:

> I've not only kept it, I've added to it.

Josie, immediately:

> The trunk must have been very special.

AngelChild:

> It's everything. The trunk is what gave me the courage to buy my red graduation dress, buy my car, go to college. I would have been loved. It was my heritage. There were papers. Newspapers. And pictures of my father. A strong handsome man. Pictures of his arm was around my mother. Smiling, like he adored her. She's smiling too. Pushing my brother in a swing.

I closed my eyes. Was she reading happiness into these pictures? How had a war destroyed this family's joy? If there had even been a war. Perhaps what AngelChild believed was a family myth.

> There's a picture of a rocking horse. I wanted a doll. Mommy won't let me have a doll. Not ever.

Josie flashed a message to me:

> Something's happening. The diction level is starting to slip. She's becoming more childlike. For our purposes, that's just fine.

AngelChild:

> I want my mommy. I want my daddy. I hate you for making me remember all this.

Then silence.

Josie phoned. "We're so close, Lottie. So very close. She's just about to break."

"The woman she's describing in the pictures doesn't sound at all like the woman she grew up with. What happened to her mother's mind? What happened to her father?"

"I suspect she knows," Josie said. "I think she knows everything."

"Earlier, she said it was the war."

"Maybe so, more than one woman hasn't been able to handle a war. You might as well get a good night's sleep, Lottie. There's a pattern, here. Harold doesn't think she'll come back online tonight, but he'll sleep here anyway, and I'll go back to your place. I'll relieve him tomorrow morning, so he can grab a nap and a shower."

"Okay. Tell Keith if either of you need anything."

"He's been great. Couldn't ask for a better host."

"If anything unusual comes up, page me at the research center tomorrow."

◇◇◇

The next morning, I glanced at my alphabetized list, asked the man at the main desk for more microfilm and began where I had left off the day before. By ten o'clock, my shoulders ached and my eyes were starting to blur.

"Lottie Albright, please come to the main desk."

Startled at hearing the page echo through the microfilm reading room, I jumped up too suddenly and knocked a reel off the table. I picked it up, put it back in the re-shelving tray, and hurried to the main desk.

"Lottie Albright?"

"Yes."

"There's a call for you in the business office." He pointed toward the room. A secretary steered me to a phone with a blinking line.

I picked up the receiver. "Lottie Albright, here."

"Lottie." It was Keith. My knees went weak and my stomach lurched when he hesitated. Why would he hesitate? What was the matter?

"It's Josie, Lottie."

Chapter Forty-Three

I couldn't speak, couldn't breathe.

"Someone tried to kill her on the way into work this morning. They've Life-Watched her to Denver."

I swayed, braced myself against the desk.

"It's my fault," I moaned. "All my fault. They thought she was me. How could I have let her take my place? What happened? How bad is it?"

Again, there was that terrible hesitation. "It's very bad."

"Is she going to die?" My heart exploded with pain.

"She's no longer in immediate danger," he said quickly.

"What then? What? Her hands? They haven't hurt her hands, have they?" Josie would never, never be able to stand being unable to play music. It would kill her.

"No, it's not her hands," Keith said softly.

"Her face?" Bizarre crimes filled my mind. Josie would just hate being scarred, disfigured.

"No, not her face, Lottie." If it were possible to hear someone swallow over the phone, I was hearing it now.

"What, then?"

"It's her mind, sweetheart. They fractured her skull. They left her for dead. She's in a coma, and there's a good chance…"

Finishing for him, "that they ruined her wonderful, wonderful mind. A chance they've destroyed her!"

"Yes. That's about it. The doctors aren't sure how this will go."

I blinked back tears. "I'm coming home right away."

"I don't want you driving in this state of mind," he said.

I glanced at the secretary hovering anxiously in the doorway. "No point in that anyway. I'll catch a plane to Denver."

"Great. I'll meet you there. Harold Sider went with Josie's medical flight."

"I need to get Josie's car back to her apartment."

"Don't worry about that. Harold Sider will find someone to help."

"I'll leave the keys here at the front desk. This place closes early. They need to be here by four-thirty. I'll take a cab to the airport from here. My room is on an American Express card. It's still open. Please ask whoever gets her car to check out for me and collect my things."

Only Josie, my Josie, would have recognized the rage behind the icy calmness of my voice. If Keith lived with me for a thousand years, he would never be able to hear it.

"Okay," he said, his voice relieved at my sensible efficiency. We hung up.

"My sister has been in an accident," I explained to the secretary. "Is it all right if I leave some car keys here and use your phone to call a cab?"

She nodded. "Of course."

I made my call, went back to the reading room, put the film in proper order, and placed it in the reshelving rack.

I picked up my still open laptop and carried it to the front desk.

"I need to ask you a very special favor."

The secretary vibrated with helpfulness.

"Do you have a hotspot I might use? One for your employees perhaps? My laptop has a wireless card, and I need to send an email. But I really don't have time to go back to my hotel."

"Of course," she said quickly. "But there's no need. You're welcome to use one of our staff computers, you know."

"Thank you, but I want all mail records recorded on mine." No one would ever see this message but me and AngelChild.

She led me into a private research room and tactfully closed the door behind her.

Only then, did I loosen my deadly self-control.

I stared at my white hands as I loaded Outlook and typed in her AOL address. The blue veins looked like earthworms trapped in ice. I would have a few minutes before my taxi arrived.

AngelChild, I'm alive. Alive. And I'm going to kill you.

The moment I typed the words, I knew they were true. Josie had always been frightened by the cold ruthlessness of my anger. She says it will get me into trouble some day.

Blinded by tears at the possibility I wouldn't be saying "Josie says" ever again, I began to type words so foul, so evil, I would not have thought I was capable of such filth. I hoped they scalded her to death.

I sent the message, put the laptop in my briefcase, and went downstairs to wait for my taxi.

◇◇◇

Keith met me at Denver International Airport. He had aged ten years in the last two days. Wordlessly we clung together.

"How is she?" I asked.

"The same," he said. We hardly spoke on the drive from DIA to University Hospital.

◇◇◇

I gasped, then closed my eyes when I saw the network of tubes snaking from her body. I forced myself to see what the monster had done. Josie, the most intensely alive of any person I knew, now looked like a plastic contraption. My chest tightened with pain. I walked over and squeezed her hand.

"You're going to be fine," I said fiercely. "Just fine."

It was all my fault. It should have been me lying there. I spun around, and fled sobbing from the room. Keith followed me to the intensive care lounge.

We spent the night there, dozing in recliners, taking turns at Josie's bedside. I did not want her to be alone. Die alone. By the next morning, there was no change.

Dawn was cheerless. Yellowed light like old gauze streaked with bloodstains. Keith returned from the cafeteria with coffee, handed me a cup.

"She may be in this shape for a very long time, Lottie," he said in the corridor outside her room. "We have to face facts."

"Tosca," I said. "Who's taking care of Tosca?"

"I took her to the vet's," he said, glancing at me sharply, as he cautiously sipped from the Styrofoam cup.

"Please, honey," I whispered. "Please. I don't want to talk about it. Not yet, not now. Let's talk about the Chiefs, the election, the stock market. Anything else. Not her. Not now."

"Okay," he said. "We are going to talk about food, though. When did you eat last?"

I looked at him blankly.

"Just what I thought. I'm going down to the cafeteria right now and bring you back something. Even a sweet roll would be better than nothing."

"All right." I stepped back into Josie's room and resumed my vigil.

My cell rang. It was Sam. I brought him up to date on Josie's condition.

"Everyone thinks it's you, Lottie. The media assumed that right off the bat. There were good reasons for us not to correct that impression. You're safer this way. If AngelChild knows you're out running around, she might be tempted to try again."

I started to tell him she *did* know it was Josie, not me, she had nearly killed, through the email I sent from Topeka. Without understanding why, I didn't want Sam to know that just then. I could always call him back after I'd had a chance to think. He told me again how sorry he was my sister had been hurt. I thanked him and hung up.

Glancing at Josie, her beautiful face swathed in bandages, a part of my soul started to rise like deadly swamp gas.

I understood then why I had withheld information from Sam. I wanted it to be between me and AngelChild, and no one else.

I intended to kill her.

Chapter Forty-Four

AngelChild knew it was Josie lying there. There would be a message waiting for me on the computer back at my office.

For an instant, I was swept with shame at my shrewdness, my cunning, and I yearned for the check Josie had always provided. But I was dealing with a mind so savage we all seemed helpless before its murderous brilliance. Like moths, we kept flying into the flames and dying. Someone had to put an end to her.

When Keith brought my roll and orange juice, I surprised him by eating it all.

"I've been thinking," I said, "I don't want Josie to be alone, but you're right about the length of time this might involve." Relieved that I was starting to plan, to cope, he squeezed my shoulder in approval. "Why don't I take the Suburban home and get some clothes, and make some arrangements for Tosca. She has to be miserable at the vet. Margaret loves dogs. I'll bet she'll keep her. When I get back, you can go on home and I'll be prepared to stay."

"Good idea, honey. Your Tahoe was totaled, of course. You'll need to pick out a new one while you're here in Denver."

"Okay." Then ashamed, I closed my eyes. Murder on my mind. Cold-blooded murder, and he was that easily duped. But then, only Josie would know.

I blazed home like a wild fire, watching for cops, but passing everyone in sight when I could. I drove straight to the courthouse. There was no moon, but as I hurried toward the door, sporadic gusts of wind buffeted the leaves on cottonwood trees and they glistened and swayed in the starlight. I went straight to my office.

The tell-tale beep was waiting for me the moment I booted up.

"You have new mail," stated the mechanical announcement.

AngelChild had typed:

> You have no right. I know who your family was and the kind of money they made and where you come from. You don't know what it's like for some of us. I didn't want to hurt you or your sister. But you gave me no choice.

I checked the date on the message. It had been sent late last night. After Josie had been taken to Denver. After I had sent my message twenty-four hours ago.

Ignoring what Josie had said about losing her for good, I typed:

> You're a cold blooded killer no matter how you try to pretty it up. A killer. Do you understand that?

Words immediately filled the screen:

> I'm not. That's what I can't make any of you understand. I'm not. You're making me do these things. All of you.

I had to find her. I typed:

> Tell me who you are.

Tell me who you are, I thought desperately. I had to know. I waited for three hours. There was no reply. Profoundly exhausted, chilled at the thought there might not ever be another message, I switched off my computer and drove home.

◇◇◇

The phone jarred me awake, calling me from a nervous bug-infested dream.

"Hello," I mumbled. "Keith! Has there been any change? Has something happened?"

"No," he said quickly. "Not that."

"What time is it?"

"Eleven o'clock."

"In the morning?" I groaned. Given the time I had spent in bed, I should have felt rested. Instead, I felt as though I had been clubbed.

"Josie's breathing easier. Her color is a little better. She's not out of her coma, but something's better, I can see it in the doctors' faces."

I closed my eyes, gave thanks.

"Margaret Atkinson called to ask how you were doing. She said everything was fine at the office except every time they tried to use the computer, the email announcement kept breaking in."

"None of the volunteers can get into my email without the password."

"I called Harold Sider, and he thinks it may be a real breakthrough. "

I shot up in bed. "In what way?"

"Harold thinks AngelChild knows it's not you here in the hospital. If so, how does she know?"

Because I told her, I thought. *That's how she knows.*

"He's worried sick about you. So am I. The big change is that she's emailing in the middle of the day. He says we can't give Margaret the password to your program because she would be privy to information that could compromise the prosecution's case later on. He doesn't want to risk having evidence thrown out. If we send Sam in to read your email, everyone in the courthouse will want to know what's up."

"Sam's not very good with computers anyway. Wouldn't do us one whit of good to send him over if there's a situation beyond email."

"Surely you know this isn't my idea," Keith said bitterly, "but Harold and Sam have talked, and they want you to walk into the courthouse, bold as brass, and put an end to the charade and retrieve those messages. Everyone will know it's Josie that was hurt, not you. Honey, I'm scared to death this will force her hand."

"I don't care," I said. "I don't care who knows. She's sending mail in the middle of the day. She's breaking down. It's okay, Keith. Let's get this whole mess over with. The sooner, the better."

"Harold and I have made arrangements with a private security company for your protection. Carlton County doesn't have the resources to safeguard an egg. Two of his friends will be at the courthouse around five-thirty this evening. After you retrieve what you can from that bitch, wait for them there. They'll drive you back to Denver. I don't want you on the road by yourself."

◇◇◇

A ghost drifting through the walls couldn't have caused more commotion in the courthouse when I walked through the front door.

Inez Wilson grabbed my hand at once. "Lottie, I don't understand."

"The press got it all wrong. It was my sister, Josie, who was hurt," I said. Employees popped their heads out of their offices, and I gave the same explanation over and over again.

Margaret Atkinson started with fright when I walked in. Even after I told her about me, about Josie, she had trouble accepting it. People kept coming to the door, buzzing about like gnats. The story of the killer accosting the wrong sister made the rounds in no time. Finally, I told Margaret I needed computer time and would close up myself.

"You shouldn't have to work under these circumstances," she said.

I managed a weak smile. "I'm not. I'm just grabbing a few things up before I head back to Denver. I'll close up, and you can go ahead with the volunteers you have scheduled for tomorrow." It took another fifteen minutes to ease her out the door.

I hung up a do-not-disturb sign, entered my password, and clicked on the message from AngelChild:

> Don't you understand? You were going to ruin my son. My only son.

I stared at the words. Read them over and over. *My son.* Judy had said it was Fiona. Said she had proof. I clenched my fist, twisted it against my mouth and howled silently. The St. Johns. This was about the St. Johns and Hadleys. *Why wouldn't we believe Judy? Why couldn't that waif of a girl make us understand?*
She typed:

> Zelda found the letter, that prideful, stupid letter. It should have been burned years ago. It never should have been written in the first place. Never have been left for Zelda to find. But I was so proud. Why did you have to come into this county and start that wretched project and ruin everything? Ruin my son. Yes, I killed them. Both of them. Zelda and Judy, and it broke my heart. But if I had to, I'd do it again.

My hands shook as I typed:

> It's over, AngelChild. I know who you are.

I had my hard evidence. My confession.
Just then I got a call from Keith.
"She's taken a turn for the worse, honey. The doctors want you to be here. Your security escort will be there in two hours. Are you packed? Can you leave from the courthouse?"
"Yes," I said woodenly. I turned off my computer and walked over to the wall safe and took out my gun. I studied the smooth blue steel of the barrel, the cross-hatching on the polished wooden handle. Gunmetal was always cold, even in a warm room.
Two hours. It would be easy to kill Fiona and get back to the courthouse in two hours. With luck, I would be on my way to Denver by the time the body was discovered. No one would suspect me. I could be with Josie, knowing the woman who had

hurt her was dead. She would not hurt anyone again. I would be at peace.

Every fiber in my body revolted. My mind could plan, anticipate, but my soul was horrified at how easily I could think like a killer. Just a week ago, I would have sworn no circumstances could reduce me to such a state. Just a week ago, I would have given this information to Sam Abbott at once. I put the gun in my purse, and winced at the weight. The deadly burden.

My sister was dying.

Then anger gave way to grief. I shuddered at how close I had come to losing control. I took a deep breath, reached for that part of myself that would make Josie proud.

For Josie's sake, I would not kill this woman like a gunslinger in a two-bit Western.

For Josie's sake, I would not spend time in prison.

For Josie's sake, I would go through all the proper channels.

But I knew who AngelChild was. Before I turned the printouts over to Sam and Harold Sider, I was going to pay Fiona Hadley a visit.

She would not be facing Lottie Albright, officer of the law, but a sister with a broken heart.

Chapter Forty-Five

Brian's car was there. It didn't matter. I didn't care who heard what I was going to say. Not bothering to knock, I opened the front door.

Brian shouted at Fiona. They wouldn't have heard me if I had used a battering ram to break in. From my vantage point in the foyer, I could see everything. Brian's face was highlighted by the setting sun. His skin was sallow, his eyes yellowish and bloodshot. His hands trembled as he waved some pages at Fiona.

Fiona's hands were raised, shielding herself from his anger. Blue eyes pleading for compassion as he spit out the words.

"I've found it. I know what you were trying to hide. What you've been hiding all along. I know what Aunt Zelda found."

"Why couldn't you have left well enough alone? You've been like a bloodhound snooping and snooping. I would have told you eventually. At the proper time."

"Never. You'd have gone to your grave without saying a word. I kept digging because you hurt three people I loved. Uncle Max, Aunt Zelda, and Judy. They were the ones who loved me for myself. You trashed Judy every chance you got. You never missed an opportunity to belittle your own sister. And Max! Poor lonely old man."

He wiped perspiration from his upper lip, and swatted back a lock of hair.

"I love my uncle Max. The forgotten person. You never gave him a thought, did you? Well, I visited him after you cleared out his attic. He tried to tell me it didn't matter, what you'd taken. But he was sick. Sick to his bones. That's when I knew something was wrong. I've lived with your intrigues all my life. I knew there was something you were trying to hide. That's when I started to look in earnest."

"Liar, liar," Fiona said, her voice soft and taunting. "What a pretty lie. Someone who doesn't know you as well as I do might believe that's why you kept digging, but we know better, don't we?"

Dazed, he shook his head and waved the letter.

"How could you have kept this from me? This is why you didn't want Judy working at the historical society, isn't it? You were afraid she knew about this. I could just kill you for this."

"You don't mean that, Brian. Please say you don't have it in you to do that. Tell me you're not a murderer."

"I don't know what you're talking about." His voice was low, dangerous. "What kind of lies have you concocted this time?"

Scarcely breathing, I moved behind the massive door leading from the foyer to the living room and peered above the middle hinge.

"The murder of your aunt, your cousin," said Fiona.

I could hardly stand. The blood flamed behind my eyes. *Not Brian. Not Brian.* AngelChild had been covering for Brian all along.

"You're crazy," he blurted. "Absolutely nuts. You're capable of anything, anything. Including smearing me. I know that now. Is there blood on your hands, Mom? Something too terrible for you to talk about? Even with me? Your darling fair-haired boy. The apple of your eye?"

"I'm your mother. How can you say such things?"

"You're not my mother," he shouted. "Not my mother. I'm holding the proof of that right here."

"Brian, darling. That's not true. Not true. I am your real mother as surely as if I'd given birth to you. There's things you don't know. Things you don't understand."

I was too stunned to feel fear. That's why Fiona had been so hateful to Zelda after Judy's birth. She was consumed with jealousy that her sister had produced a child and she hadn't.

"I would have shown it to you some day. Son, everything I've done, was for you. Everything. Zelda saw that letter when she was snooping around and copied it. I should have burned it at the start. But I was so proud, so proud of what it had to say about you. About your birth parents. Then she tried to blackmail me. At first I didn't think she had the nerve. I laughed at her. It would have been my word against hers, and everyone knew she was half-crazy."

"I still don't understand," he said. "I can't follow your schemes. Your plots. I never could. What would this letter have to do with Aunt Zelda's story?"

Fiona's voice was dull, heavy. Her magnificent face sagged. "When I saw her story, I knew my sniveling sister had actually copied this letter, just as she said. The one you are holding. The stationary has a watermark."

Brian stared at the pages he held. "A rose?"

"After she copied the front of the letter, with all the details of your birth, Zelda turned it over and copied the blank back side. The watermark showed there too. It's fainter. But it's there."

My mind reeled. Fiona had seen the rose. Not at first, but the second time she read the story. I understood now that Zelda had copied the rose watermark from that letter onto blank white paper, then wrote her family history story on that paper. But I wasn't any closer to knowing what was in the letter.

Fiona raged at Brian. "At first, I could hardly believe my eyes. For all I knew she had a whole supply of that paper stashed away. The blackmail would never end. My own sister was going to sell you down the river. That's why I had to get all of her junk out of Max's attic after Judy died. Before Lottie started snooping."

She was right about the stashed supply. I recalled the box of blank paper with the rose watermark in Max's attic. Judy had obviously found Zelda's copy of the letter Fiona was protecting.

"Was it worth a murder? Two murders?" Brian's voice caught.

Fiona shrieked and pressed her fingers against her throat. "I did not kill my sister or Judy. How dare you? How can you have lived in this house all these years and think such a thing? Brian. I know what you're hiding. What you're trying to cover up."

He looked at her sadly and shook his head. "Still the actress, aren't you? Still think you can manipulate anyone and everyone."

"I'm telling you the truth," she said slowly. "The truth."

"There's something else you kept from me."

He walked over to a box on the sofa and opened the lid. He took a piece of cloth from the box, slowly unfolded one of the ancient yellowed pieces of old linen and pointed to the embroidered initials.

"Did my real mother make these? Do you know who she is? These initials, ECS. Who do they stand for?"

I swayed and clutched at the door frame.

Emily Champlin Swenson. The missing baby clothes.

"It's your father's fault. Your father," wailed Fiona.

I slipped back to the open front door, started the Suburban, and drove back to town like I was pursued by demons.

"All your father's fault," she'd said. Edgar Hadley. Was Edgar the murderer? Was AngelChild a man as Josie suspected? A man? The uncle Judy had adored? Confused and exhausted, my mind whirled. The St. Johns, the Swensons. The murders were connected.

Brian was far too young to be the missing Swenson baby, but then where did those clothes come from?

I was suddenly jolted by another thought. Was Edgar the missing Swenson baby?

Panic stricken, I glanced at the clock. Just an hour left before my escorts arrived. But it was time enough to print out AngelChild's confession, take it to Sam and tell him what I'd seen and heard.

I yearned for Josie's wisdom and her wit, her ability to sort through complexity. Nothing made sense. I could think on the way to Colorado.

Back in my office, as I waited for the printer to warm up, Brian's face swam before my eyes. His chin with the adorable cleft. His boyish freckles. Those earnest gray-blue eyes. And his mouth. His sensitive mouth. Everything about him said trust, trust, trust. I am integrity. I keep promises. I walk miles to return pennies. You're safe with me.

He was not Edgar and Fiona's son. Either Brian or Edgar or Fiona had murdered Zelda St. John to keep her from revealing this fact. Somehow, some way, Brian's family was connected to the murder of Emily Champlin Swenson and my poking around into this old scandal would ruin him. I thought he wanted to conceal his drinking from me, but alcohol was the least of his problems.

The janitor stuck his head in door. "Time to close up, Lottie."

"I need a few more minutes. I'll lock up."

"Don't forget. Outside too."

I finished, turned off all the equipment, snatched up the papers, ran out the office, and secured the lock on the front door. Five after five. Barely enough time to get these printouts to Sam before my escort arrived.

I jumped in the Suburban, turned the key and nothing happened. The battery was as dead. I looked at the light switch. I had left the lights on. I pounded the steering wheel in frustration.

I looked down the street, then thought I saw Edgar Hadley's pickup passing through the intersection. My heart beat as fast as hummingbirds' wings.

Had he seen me at his house and followed me? He could easily have been in the barn or another out-building. I had to stay calm. I couldn't get back into the courthouse.

Relieved, I saw Minerva in the back parking lot. I hollered at her.

"Trouble?"

"You'd better believe it," I said tersely. "I left my lights on."

"Need a ride?"

"If you don't mind." I struggled to sound normal. "Margaret told me you bounced right back."

She shrugged. "I was out three days. It seemed like a lifetime."

"Let me grab my purse and briefcase then drop me off at the Sheriff's office." I wanted Sam. Right now.

I got in her pickup. Hearing a familiar noise, I turned, then froze. Edgar was driving toward us, just three blocks away. He wouldn't be looking for me in Minerva's Toyota, but I couldn't put her at risk. We'd have to pass him to get to Sam, or drive in the opposite direction and circle back. Remembering the gun rack in the window of his pickup, I played it safe.

"On second thought, take to me the Total station first." They'll jumpstart me." I willed her to hustle. Drive away. Anywhere. Before Edgar arrived and realized my car was dead. I'd call Sam from the station, and he could pick me up.

She glanced at her watch. "I have an errand to run."

"I really am in a hurry."

I looked through her rear view window at an assortment of fertilizer, lime, and shovels.

Edgar's pickup pulled into the curb at the front parking. I ducked out of sight until I heard him pass.

"Dropped my keys," I mumbled to Minerva.

She drove to the east edge of town and kept going.

"Told Doc I would drop these things off at his garden. It's on the way."

We would damn sure be safe there. Silently swearing at her adherence to lists, I tried to smile. I reached for my cell phone to call Sam, but it was out of service range.

I kept looking behind us, checking for Edgar, as she drove on for three miles out to the area known as Groendyke's Woods. I thought of what Josie had said "Look for the person who has not turned in a family history."

Edgar Hadley. Not one word had been turned in about the Hadley family and they had lived in the county since homestead days.

Suddenly, I heard his pickup in the distance, coming up fast. Someone must have seen me leave with Minerva, and told him we headed east.

We were coming to the turnoff, the lane sloped sharply in a deep draw. The area was hidden from the road. I risked a glance at Minerva. We would soon be out of danger.

Please God, I prayed. *Just a few more yards.*

We turned into the heavily rutted, winding path that bumped into this area. I took a deep breath. Groendyke's Woods was like a little hidden valley and Doc's garden was famous. She drove past the little incline, which led over the ridge onto his ground.

"Missed my turn," she said. "There's a place on up a ways where I can back in and out."

She was driving too fast. We hit a large rut. It was like falling into a trench. The jolt knocked off her glasses.

I saw her eyes. They were a brackish yellow. Like a swamp. Foul and diseased.

I couldn't swallow, couldn't think, couldn't breathe. Couldn't look away from her eyes.

With the eyes revealed, the features intact, I knew I was looking at Brian Hadley's mother.

I knew who had murdered Zelda and Judy St. John.

Chapter Forty-Six

Frantic, I reached for the door handle. My stomach plunged. She pulled me back with hands strong enough to rip the pelt right off a rabbit, then quickly snapped the automatic childproof locks.

My head swam. I had to think. Had to act. My redheaded valedictorian, right here all along. I could not look away from those terrible, brackish eyes. Brian's eyes. Brian's eyes were a lesser version of whatever was wrong with this woman. But they were the same.

"Take a good look," she snapped, pulling me closer to her. "It's a pretty sight, isn't it? Jaundiced like an old decaying turnip. Under a microscope you'd see the Kayser-Fleischer Rings. I had to look at eyes like these most of my life. They're my mother's eyes."

"I don't understand." I choked back sour liquid coming from my stomach. The taste of pure terror.

"I have Wilson's Disease. So does Brian. These eyes are just one of the symptoms. Wilson's can make you crazy. Brian was doing fine with treatment. Just fine until you kept him under your spotlight, day and night. The press dogged him until he couldn't even go to the doctor when he was supposed to."

Dizzy with shock, I stared at her eyes. They were the reason she wore dark glasses. His eyes were why Brian had started wearing dark glasses. Not to cover up his grief over his aunt's death, not to disguise what I had mistaken as drunkenness. The glasses were to hide this hideous color.

"You're AngelChild, and you're the Swenson baby."

"Oh, yes, I'm the Swenson baby, the infamous Swenson baby. The woman I called mother was really my Aunt Rebecca. I hated her even more when I went through the trunk and found out what my life should have been like."

I swallowed and recalled the trunk I'd seen in Minerva's bedroom. Josie had told me to look for a person who was disintegrating. I had ignored all the signs. Minerva's dizzy spells I had assumed was flu, her weepiness the night I took her home. The things she'd said that weren't like her at all. The missed work.

At last, I knew what had been wrong with Rebecca Champlin. It was Rebecca, Minerva's aunt, who had had this disease, not Emily. I remembered Rebecca's eyes had been veiled or concealed in some manner in all the pictures I'd seen after she stopped her activities in high school.

"It's why you doctor in Denver, isn't it?" I blurted. "Not because you don't like the doctors here, but because you need very special medical treatment."

I started thinking again. I had to keep her talking.

"It's why I do everything. Everything. It's why I have to have a hairstyle that makes me look like an old hag. I can't have a beautician cut my hair because I don't dare take off these glasses for a cut and a shampoo. It's why I type everything. I can't trust my hands to write a decent note. They shake."

"And Brian, poor Brian has the same problems," I said. I knew now why Brian didn't sign the autograph for that little kid the night I thought he was drunk! He had missed treatments and couldn't trust his handwriting. So many pieces were falling into place.

I recalled Judy telling me about Brian's clumsiness, the dropped balls, his aversion to sports when he was in grade school. His jaundice. This disease was why Fiona had him flown to Denver the night Sam and I went on the 911 call. Our local doctor would have known at once he wasn't having DTs.

"But Brian couldn't have hidden it forever," I said.

"Oh, yes, he could. He could nowadays if you had left him alone. My son. That marvelous man is my son! I saw to it my son had the best. The best adoptive family, the best education, the best medical treatment. I spent my childhood with a crazy woman, a murderess, but I saw to it that my son had the best." She was quiet for a moment. "It's hereditary. Although Rebecca actually had the disease, Emily was a carrier."

Twilight now. Furtively I glanced around, saw no escape. *Delay, delay*, I thought.

"Brian's wonderful," I said.

"At first, it broke my heart when Fiona claimed my wonderful son was her own flesh. She was not the prize I thought she was. I worked for Kansas Adoption Services after I got out of college. I was pregnant when the Hadleys' application came through. They were from Carlton County. The county where I should have been raised. They were rich. She was a Rubidoux. I saw to it that Brian was placed with this family. Then I moved here, where I could keep an eye on them."

"If Fiona had said he was adopted from the beginning…"

"If. But she didn't. She was too proud to admit she couldn't conceive. I attended his school activities, watched him debate, heard him speak. Heard her claim it was due to his heritage as a Rubidoux. I learned to content myself with standing in the crowd watching, whispering in my heart, my son, my son."

Abruptly, she opened the door on her side and dragged me outside. When my feet hit the ground, I tried to twist away, but she hooked her arm around my head in a choke hold and yanked my arm behind my back.

Dizzy with pain, I tried to think. She would kill me.

"You can't possibly get away with this, Minerva."

"You wouldn't listen," she said. "You would *not* listen. I tried to tell you, tried to warn you. I couldn't even get the board to fire you."

Shocked, I sagged against her.

"You're the one who stole the Custer letter. The one who set me up. You made that so-called New Mexico phone call, didn't you? How?"

"I have a phone mechanism that disguises voices."

There was no mistaking her pride, her smugness. What had Josie told me repeatedly? That I was dealing with a diabolically clever person. High I.Q. Very, very organized. Very, very ruthless. Capable of compiling exquisite plans.

"And Zelda's story? The missing story?"

"I burned the goddamned thing, what do you think? Should have been the end of it. If it hadn't been for you and Judy, it would have been."

She started dragging me toward a enormous three-acre thicket of dead tree branches and brambles.

She was going to kill me! Did she think I was just going to let her kill me without a struggle?

I braced my feet and gasped when she jerked my arm high. I had to use my brain. I was no match for her physically.

Delay, delay. My escorts would be at the courthouse soon. "Why didn't Rebecca get help?" I yelped with pain as she yanked my arm tighter.

"They didn't have good treatments back then. And she was a single woman with a baby to explain. She was crazy, not stupid."

We were nearing the thicket. The men would see my car. I knew, of course, I had been set up. Minerva had turned my lights on, run down the battery.

"You won't have enough time. Keith will be worried. Someone will come."

"Shut up."

"You won't have time to dig a grave."

"I know exactly how long it takes to dig a grave. It took much longer to dig Rebecca's than yours. She was a very large woman."

She had already dug my grave. A person capable of executing detailed plans, Josie had said. *Somewhere in that macabre skeleton of trees was my grave.*

We were at the very edge of the bramble woods now. She stopped to catch her breath. I tried to shut out the pain, gather my wits. I had enticed her into emailing me for the sake of setting the record straight. Perhaps the same appeal would work again.

"Before, before you do this, I want to know. What was in the letter you sent with Brian?"

"I wanted Fiona to know that this baby's mother was quality," she said. "When I knew the Hadleys would be adopting Brian, I searched all of Topeka for stationary worthy of that letter. Back then, I didn't have this tremor. I wrote it with my finest penmanship on stationary by Eaton called *Love Letters*. It was perfumed and exquisite and had this lovely rose watermark." Minerva's voice quivered.

"I told them I was very intelligent and extremely talented. Not that starkly, of course. I chose each word with great care. Then I added that Brian was actually a descendent of one of the Lees of Virginia. I wanted them to raise Brian as a very special child. I put all my expectations into that letter."

"A Lee! With Fiona being Southern, no wonder she raised the child like he was next to the Almighty. No wonder she kept that letter."

"Then God help me, I could not resist sending the collection of the baby clothes my mother had embroidered for me. My real mother. The clothes she had intended for me." Her voice caught. "Rebecca had kept them all in a special trunk."

"And Judy found the letter?"

"She found the copy Zelda had made. Judy intended to give Zelda's copy to you and Sam. My original was safe with Fiona. God knows that bitch would never show it to anyone, but she'd kept it, of course, because it said her son was a Lee."

There was little daylight left. Soon my escorts would arrive, find the Suburban and notify Sam. Soon people would be searching. I had to keep her talking.

"Why did you kill poor Zelda? I understand that you killed Judy to keep her from taking the copy to Sam, but why Zelda?"

"That day Fiona went running out of the courthouse I knew something was wrong."

"We were watching the clouds," I said. "And I had left my office unlocked."

"Zelda's story was lying on the floor where Fiona dropped it. I saw the watermark. I knew Zelda printed her story on copied sheets from the backside of that letter. To Fiona, it was simply proof that her sister had the guts to go through with the black mail. But I had notarized deeds, signed hundred of documents for the county. I was afraid Zelda had recognized my handwriting and knew I was Brian's mother. My son was running for the senate. Everything would come out then. Everything."

A coyote howled in the distance, sending a shiver up my spine.

"That's when I made my stupid, stupid mistake." Minerva's voice softened with remorse. "I went to her house that evening after Max had left for the Lion's Club. On impulse. It wasn't like me. But I had to know! She let me in and I could tell she hadn't connected me to the handwriting, the letter, anything. So I just told her I was there to get a contribution for Sunny Rest's literacy program."

"Why did you kill her then? If she didn't know?" I blurted out the question, hoping the agony in my voice wouldn't stop her from telling me the rest.

"We chatted. She went to the bedroom to get her checkbook. I waited next to her piano with all those pictures of Judy. And Brian. She and Max were always crazy about Brian. She came back into the room. Looked at me like she was seeing a ghost. It was the picture. If I hadn't been standing with my head at the same angle as Brian's in that picture, she would never have known."

I closed my eyes, opened them. Waited for her to go on.

"I'll never forget her words. Never. 'So it's you,' she said. 'You. A Virginia Lee, my foot. Well, I'm calling a halt to this whole charade. I'm going to the paper tomorrow morning.'"

Minerva's voice faltered.

"Fiona had been there earlier that evening, you see, and they had gotten into this flaming fight. Zelda was so angry she'd lost all thought of blackmail. She wanted revenge instead. Wanted to get even with Fiona for years and years of slights. I tried to talk to her, but she just laughed. I started toward her and she got scared and ran into the bedroom and I guess you know the rest."

"Does Brian know you're his mother? Does Fiona know?"

"No." There was a new weariness to her voice. "Only Zelda. Only I knew the horror of the story the press would uncover if they started digging."

"Fiona wanted to cover up the adoption," I said, seeing it all now. "Brian wanted to cover up Wilson's Disease. You knew the stakes were much larger. You wanted to hide old murders."

Minerva was breathing harder now. She was seconds away from dragging me into the woods.

"Herman Swenson is your father. Your own father. Don't you care? How can you stand to let that poor man go to his grave letting everyone think he killed his wife and his son and his baby?"

At last I had hit the spot I had been probing for.

"Don't you think I know that?" Her voice sank to a whimper, as though she were drained of all energy. "He'd have been a wonderful father. Emily would have been a wonderful mother. Instead I was raised by that creature."

"No wonder he's the one you read to in the nursing home"

"I wanted to know what he was like. What I would have been like."

"It's not too late."

"Shut up. It's too late for everyone but Brian. I'm not going to let you ruin Brian."

"Brian's father. Who was Brian's father?"

"Just a man I met. I wanted to lose my virginity. I wanted to know if I could feel. Be normal."

"And were you?" I asked cruelly. "Are you?"

She gave another vicious tug on my arm. I was close to passing out from the pain.

"Shut up. What do you know about doing without a mother and a father? You know nothing. Do you know what I did first? The very first thing after I shoveled the last load of dirt over Rebecca?"

"No, Minerva. I'm trying to understand. Really trying to understand," I sobbed.

"I looked in the trunk. The forbidden trunk."

"The trunk that's in your house?" She kept coming back to it. Now, and before as AngelChild.

"Yes. She had never let me see inside that trunk. But I knew where she kept the key, and I looked. And I found my baby clothes. Layer after layer of baby clothes. And newspaper clippings. Then I knew where she had gotten me. She killed my mother. Her very own sister. I was robbed of a real mother who would have loved me. And a big brother. I would have had a real brother."

She's talking, talking. Wants me to know. Hope flickered. Perhaps at some subconscious level she didn't want to kill me.

If I could just find the right words.

"Minerva, don't do this. For Brian's sake, don't do this."

I had found the wrong ones.

"This *is* for Brian's sake," she cried with new determination. "Don't you know that yet? It's for his future."

"Oh, Minerva, he's already struggling to keep himself together. I thought he was an alcoholic."

She whirled me around and slapped me hard across the face. In that instant, when she let go of my arm, I tried to run, but she grabbed my arm again before I could turn, then kicked me in the stomach. This time I fell to my knees, dizzy with pain.

She let go long enough to pick up a limb, raised it over her head. I tried to get to my feet, but managed only to twist aside far enough to take the impact of the blow on my shoulder, instead of my skull. She hit something. Something tore. My arm was finished.

I fell back full length and hoped she thought I was unconscious. She began dragging me into the thicket. I was wild with pain, but I did not cry out. My only chance would be to catch her off guard.

Eventually, she would have to go back for the shovel, the sacks of lime. It would take her a while to cover her tracks. That's what the rake had been for. To rearrange this carpet of leaves.

I was dead weight. She was exhausted. Her breath was now coming in hot ragged gasps. She could drag me only a few steps at a time before she had to stop and rest. She dropped me abruptly.

I knew we had reached my grave.

Chapter Forty-Seven

Was she going to shoot me, knife me, or bash in my head?

Whatever she was going to do, she would do it right now, before she went back to the pickup for supplies.

Please God, I prayed. *Let me live.* My timing had to be perfect.

Remembering what Sam Abbott had taught me about the danger of hesitation, before she could experience the giddy intake of breath from knowing she had reached her destination, I rolled toward her ankles, and yanked on her right arm, tumbling us both over into the open grave.

She landed hard, face down. I was on her back. Before she could catch her breath and push up, I got to my knees on top of her flattened body. My left arm was useless. I could only brace myself with my right arm. It was not enough to leverage myself out of the hole.

Her face still pressed into the damp earth, she groped behind her and grabbed my ankle. My blood froze. I was injured. She was not. It would all be over in a matter of seconds.

But it was Friday. I was wearing my cowboy boots. I kicked her head with my free foot. Kicked her three times.

Once for Zelda.

Once for Judy.

Once for Josie.

She was as still as a corpse. I stood fully upright on her back. Bracing my right elbow, I heaved myself out of the grave. Dizzy and terrified, I wobbled to my feet and stumbled toward the edge of the thicket. My tongue swelled in my dry mouth. I plunged forward, the hair prickling on the back of my neck, as though she could rise from that grave, fly though the air, and grab me.

I reached the edge of the clearing. Her Toyota was only three hundred yards away.

I could hardly breathe. I knew I had to get to the pickup.

I opened the door and dropped into the driver's seat. The damned stick shift. My left arm was too injured to manipulate controls simultaneously. The seat was too far back to brace myself well. When I finally got into position to turn the key and hold down the clutch, there was a sickening whir, whir, whir, like an old engine makes on a cold morning. Frantically, I tried to reposition myself. The engine was getting weaker.

I tried to calm myself. I counted to thirty. When I turned the key again, there was a dead click.

I trembled violently, and knew with sickening certainty it was not from fear. Pain surged and I tasted blood.

My hands shook as I reached into my purse, glanced at the "no service" bars on my cell, then grabbed my gun. I tucked it into the band of my jeans. I had to get help, and there was only one way out. Down the road, the same way we came in. I shut my mind against the thought I might not have enough time.

Dizzy with shock, I got out and started down the road that was little better than a rutted path. I heard an occasional car in the distance. I reached down and picked up a limb to steady myself. I willed myself to push against the pain, the terror. Felt my blood pressure dropping like a rock in a lake. I had to get help. Had to make it to the road.

If I didn't, I would die.

I staggered across the little culvert. I was close. Only twenty more yards and I would be over the little hill that obscured this area from the highway. If only I could make it to the side of the highway.

Any day but Friday and this road would be scarcely traveled. But it was high school football night. Everyone would be going to the game. Lots of people coming and going.

I heard a sound behind me. A twig snapped. Minerva was not dead.

Not dead.

She was coming for me.

I clamped down on a sob, on any sound at all.

Her progress would be slower than mine because she was trying to move quietly. She was skirting the edge of the clearing and I was using the road. But I was hurt and she clearly had not been hurt enough.

Not nearly enough.

My gun was useless. There was too little light for a long shot. Even if I made it to the highway there was no guarantee someone would see me before she killed me. She would know I was headed for the road. She would stop at the dead pickup. She would know a lot.

What she could not know was that I was slowly bleeding to death.

I couldn't let her know that. I pressed on toward the highway, as though I had not heard her. I was nearing the rise. I knew she would try for me before I reached it.

She would not know about the gun, but it was too dark to shoot.

I heard a sound about ten yards away. Then dead silence. I knew she had stopped, cold afraid I had heard her.

Spurred by panic, I knew I had one chance. I groaned to let her know I was injured. Injured and easy prey. Groaned like I was too wiped out with pain to be aware of what was before or behind or below or above.

I dropped to my knees. An irresistible target. Hurt. Terribly hurt.

Now she did not bother to hide herself. She walked steadily toward me.

When she loomed right before me, I raised my gun and shot her. Three times.

Once for Zelda.

Once for Judy.

Once for Josie.

I hoped she was dead. I hoped I would live.

I dragged myself down over the rise.

There were cars coming. I saw there were two cars close together. One might stop if there was the safety of another close by. I thanked God this was Western Kansas. Farm country where people were used to looking, seeing, noticing.

Dazed, I heard Edgar Hadley's pickup. Saw him pull over, jump from the cab. Start toward me.

Blackness. I swirled down into velvety blackness.

Chapter Forty-Eight

Blinded by an explosion of light, I squeezed my eyes tight against the pain. I heard voices.

"She's awake," Keith said. There was an odor wafting across the room. Jasmine. Roses. Heavenly. Something in me loosened, let go of terror. I knew I was smiling despite the torture of moving cracked lips and bruised flesh.

I slept again. Hours later, when I could bear to open my eyes again, Keith's face was flanked by people in white.

"Josie," I murmured. "Josie."

Keith was by my side in an instant. "She's fine," he said. "Just great, Lottie."

"I already know that," I whispered.

Then I fell into a deep dreamless sleep.

"How did you know?" he asked, the next morning after I devoured a breakfast large enough for a harvester.

"I smelled Joy Perfume and figured she had sent you or some-one else out to buy it. I knew everything was all right. Only a very conscious Josie would insist on her little luxuries while lying in a hospital bed. She had to have been out of her coma to send you off shopping. I doubt if even I could get you to shop for me," I said ruefully. "So where are you hiding her?"

"On another floor. We'll put the two of you together as soon as you're out of intensive care. You've got a busted rib and it punctured a lung."

"Josie's here. Right here in this hospital?" But of course they would have flown me to Denver.

Later that morning, I was pronounced fit to be moved and transferred to her room.

"It's for smokers, you know," Josie said. She sat on the edge of my bed, her eyes bright with tears.

"Is not." I laughed, then winced at the pain. I reached for her hand and patted it. We leaned toward one another, foreheads touching. I stroked her hair and felt her shudder.

"I'm so sorry I got you into this," I murmured. "So terribly sorry."

"Just hush. I'm fine. *And* we caught a murderess."

◇◇◇

"You have a visitor," Keith said.

Elizabeth walked through the door, bearing flowers.

"I hear you've been blooded, Lottie," she said. Her voice was solemn, respectful.

"It's been quite an ordeal," I said. She glanced at Josie and flushed. She walked over to her bed.

"I owe you an apology. I'm terribly sorry for my behavior the night you were at our house. Please forgive me."

There was no mistaking Elizabeth's sincerity.

"Of course I accept your apology," Josie's voice dripped with sugar. "Put the whole incident out of your mind, please. That's certainly what I intend to do."

"Thank you. You're being very gracious."

Keith beamed. Elizabeth came back to my bedside. "There's so much I don't understand, Dad. Edgar Hadley found her? Brought her to the hospital?"

"Yes."

"Why was he looking for her?"

"According to Sam Abbott, Edgar had seen our Suburban parked in his driveway, and when he went into the house, he asked Brian and Fiona what Lottie had wanted. When Brian realized what she might have seen or heard, he went tearing out of the house. He wanted to track Lottie down and ask her not to take his allegations against Fiona too seriously. He wanted his mother to have a decent lawyer before she talked to anyone."

"And Edgar?" Elizabeth asked.

"Edgar had finally come to believe that Brian was the murderer. He went to town to warn Lottie."

"Lottie's family history books were like opening Pandora's Box," Josie said. "All the troubles in the world flew out."

They were still limiting our visitors. Elizabeth stayed, chatted, until a nurse told her it was time to leave.

"Bye, Mom," Elizabeth said shyly. Touched, I squeezed her hand, watched her stride from the room, followed by Keith.

Josie started to laugh. I tried not to. It was killing me.

"You're in, girlfriend," she said. "Part of Elizabeth's sisterhood. I can feel the change in the air. You're going to be her number one guru from now on."

"Stop," I managed to wheeze, but she would not. She finally shut up when the nurses came in to change her dressings.

◇◇◇

Two days later we were sitting on the tiny little patio bordering the hospital courtyard.

"I'm still not sure just how all this started," she said.

I had already told her about Minerva's background and Wilson's disease. It took a while to fill her in on all the rest.

"So Fiona knew Zelda was serious about blackmailing her when she saw the watermark on the paper?"

"Yes, and Minerva panicked when she realized Zelda had copied the letter."

"Everything makes so much sense now," said Josie. "It almost seems logical. Told you your murderer was smart."

"Not smart enough," I said.

Birds rested on the rim of ornate feeder next to a fountain. A finch respectfully waited for a grackle to eat his fill. I felt normal. Aspen leaves gleaming brightly in the morning sun, blew across the courtyard. I turned my face up to the sun, basked in the simple warmth, the return of order.

"Zelda was desperate for money. She couldn't afford a nursing home and Max was showing some of the early symptoms of Alzheimer's. And she never got over the way Fiona treated Judy. Her journals said it all. Her hurt, her bewilderment. Her heartbreak over Fiona's coldness to her precious new baby."

"I don't care how this all came about," Josie said. She unconsciously reached to pet a Tosca who wasn't there.

They had us in wheelchairs. Some kind of hospital rule. The sun went behind the clouds. Chilled, I fumbled to pull the lap robe further up my body. Josie reached for her cardigan. Still stiff, she struggled to pull it over her shoulders. She had asked for medical books containing information on Wilson's Disease. One was face down across her lap.

"Did you read about the fingernails?" I asked. "It's why Minerva wore that weird nail polish. To cover the little rainbows on the cuticles. I always said it wasn't like her to wear nail polish. It seemed inconsistent with her style."

"How are the Hadleys handling this?"

"Keith says none of them are doing well. Edgar won't talk to anyone and Fiona won't leave the house. Minerva burned Zelda's copy of the letter Judy was going to give me, so the family secrets might have stayed hidden. But it was Brian who called a press conference. He said he was withdrawing from politics and exposed his whole history. Then he went into seclusion. He's taking it hard."

"I'm sure he is," Josie said dryly. "There's no formula for taking the news that you were adopted and your real mother was a multiple murderer. Your grandmother, too!"

"Minerva burned the Custer letter along with Zelda's story. Don't know why she would have done that. Custer didn't do anything to her."

"I still have the copy of Zelda's story."

"Yes. I want it for my archives."

"Are you all right, Lottie? With having killed a person?"

"No. I always knew I wouldn't be. Yes, I would do it again. In a heartbeat. And no, I don't want to talk about it."

We sat silently for a few more minutes. "It's getting cold," she said. She reached inside the purse she had tucked into the edge of her cushion and pulled out a tiny leather-bound travel ashtray and snubbed out her cigarette.

"I'm looking forward to tomorrow," she said. "I'll fly straight back to Manhattan."

"Tosca? What about Tosca?"

"The security men who were supposed to have picked you up took her back with them."

I wheeled around and pushed the call light outside the door, and waited for the nurse.

"I have a loose end to tie up when I get home," I said.

She looked up at the sadness in my voice.

Chapter Forty-Nine

I was going to lie, and it did not come easily to me. But it was the right thing to do. My mouth quivered as I walked down the hallway of the Sunny Rest nursing home toward Herman Swenson's room.

Slumped in his wheelchair, restrained by white ties, the broken old man looked up when I walked through the door. He was angry. The aide had left him turned away from the TV set and there was a football game on. Nevertheless, I reached for the remote and clicked off the screen.

"I'll turn it back on when I leave, Herman. There's something I need to tell you, and I need your full concentration."

He sensed something very important was coming, his eyes flickered rapidly.

I knelt beside his wheelchair and looked him fully in the face. My hand trembled as I stroked his cheek.

"Poor darling. This is going to be hard for you. So very hard." My voice shook. "But it's better than not knowing," I whispered gently. "Your life has been ruined by secrets already."

He breathed shallowly for a minute, as if he understood I was preparing him for something of great importance.

"Your baby. The one you never knew. It was a girl."

I was stabbed by the grief, the knowing, in his eyes. "You were right about the baby clothes. Right all along. Someone did take her. That someone was Rebecca Champlin. It was Rebecca." I was crying now. We both were.

"You figured this out, didn't you? After it was too late to make anyone believe you. Too late. Too many changes to your body. You couldn't even talk. Couldn't make them understand."

He closed his eyes.

"And here's the best news of all. Despite being raised by Rebecca she was a wonderful person." *Surely God would forgive me. It was the right thing to say.* "She was an excellent student. Valedictorian of her class. She was tall and strong and beautiful, and you know what was the most wonderful of all? You knew her. You knew her all along. Minerva Lovesey, the woman who reads to you."

If he had had room to faint within his restraints he would have. "Now I have some tragic news. She was accidentally killed last week."

His chest jumped with shock.

"She never knew you were her father, of course," I lied. "She was just naturally drawn to you. Remember how she loved to read to you? All these years. Blood really is thicker than water."

Oh, it was the right thing to say all right. His eyes, his eyes. Full of wonder. Pride. Pride there for the first time in over fifty years.

"I'm so glad I could tell you all this. Sam Abbott knows too. You've been cleared. It won't change your life much now. Being here, I mean."

As I heard myself saying these words, knowing the waste, the injustice, I rose and fled to the bathroom, grabbed a whole wad of toilet paper and sobbed helplessly.

Then I pulled myself together and walked back to his chair. "But people will know. Everyone will know you did not do that terrible thing. You didn't do it. It was Rebecca."

If old rheumy eyes can look triumphant, his did.

◇◇◇

I was back at work. Brought back from Babylon by the powers that be and reinstated in my rightful place in the temple. The pipes clanked. It was bitterly cold outside, stifling in the vault.

Brian Hadley approached silently.

When I turned and saw him, I did not have time to prepare my face. No time to mask my deep grief for this good man who could have made a difference. We looked at one another solemnly. As I waited for him to speak, I was struck by how many of his abilities had come from Minerva. His confident bearing, his keen analytical mind. What a wonder his mother would have been under different circumstances.

"I've come to thank you, Lottie. Thank you for bringing everything out in the open, no matter how painful it is."

"Brian, I'm so sorry. About everything."

He nodded.

"You can try again. You're young. The seat will be open again in another six years."

"I'm finished, Lottie."

"Our last two presidents were elected warts and all. People don't expect perfection. Your disease can be treated."

"Yes, and we have the tabloids and the press circling like a bunch of piranhas. They'll watch for every sign of weakness."

"I know, but…"

"No buts. That's not the real reason I'm quitting. We both know it."

There was a taste of copper in my mouth. The same sour metallic taste Brian had to live with day in, day out.

"I thought I was a Rubidoux, Lottie. Fiona's and Edgar's son. I'm not who I thought I was at all. I don't know who I am, anymore."

"Brian, please. There's a lonely heart-broken old man over there in Sunny Rest. Your grandfather, Brian. Your grandfather. He would just love to meet his only grandchild. He was, and still is a wonderful person. You came from wonderful people. Please believe me. Give him this."

Brian nodded. Then he left.

To receive a free catalog of Poisoned Pen Press titles, please contact us in one of the following ways:

Phone: 1-800-421-3976
Facsimile: 1-480-949-1707
Email: info@poisonedpenpress.com
Website: www.poisonedpenpress.com

Poisoned Pen Press
6962 E. First Ave. Ste. 103
Scottsdale, AZ 85251

CPSIA information can be obtained
at www.ICGtesting.com
Printed in the USA
LVHW02s2316050618
579762LV00001B/61/P

9 781590 588406